# PLUS
# ONE

ADAM LONGDEN

Published by Goldcrest Books International Ltd
www.goldcrestbooks.com
publish@goldcrestbooks.com

ISBN: 978-1-913719-98-2

# CHAPTER 1

Sonny slept the wrong way round.

Not in general, just for one night. To see if it made a difference. To shake things up.

It didn't.

He hadn't been sleeping well, had too much on his mind. A farrago of troublesome thoughts. Negotiating the choppy waters of another restless night, he'd try to find a haven for them – like moving a playing piece to a safe spot on a board game – a sanctuary that wouldn't cause him anxiety or keep him awake. But there didn't seem to be one these days. It was like the latter stages of a game of Monopoly. Money, that was the Mayfair with a hotel – avoid at all costs. His elderly father, Park Lane with four houses. His kids, and not seeing enough of them – Bond Street with a hotel... His lack of a partner. Disinterest in his job. Drinking too much. Spreading himself too thin and achieving nothing...

Only last weekend Sonny had been clearing out his garage, and on finding his petrol can, he had unscrewed the cap and taken a dreamy sniff – just how he had as a teenager. And then he'd continued to sniff it, inhaling deeply, until he was high – just how he had as a teenager; egged on by the other boys. He'd then had to lie down on his bed for the rest of the afternoon, till the high went away, replaced by nausea, then a banging headache; an all-too-vivid throwback to his youth and reminder as to why he and the other boys had stopped; that and a rumour that persistently sniffing petrol gave you brain damage.

But why had he done it that Saturday afternoon as a soon-to-be-forty-year-old man? He couldn't think of any reason, other than because he was bored. The not-so-merry-go-round of life had come lose from its axle, it seemed, and he was drifting.

'Up to anything tonight, Sonny?' asked Jonah, Sonny's work colleague. Sonny was hovering by the front door of the deli where he worked, ready to leave, clutching his holdall of dirty chef's whites.

'Nah, just the usual. See the old man. Game of chess probably. Late dinner for one, bottle of wine, then cry myself to sleep...'

Jonah laughed. 'It's Friday night, man. You should be out enjoying yourself.'

'Tell me about it,' said Sonny.

'No luck on the dating sites then?' This was Michelle, another work colleague. Sonny wasn't a fan. Potty-mouthed and always prying into his love life. Mind you, the same could be said about most of his work colleagues.

'Nah, they're all screwballs,' Sonny said.

'Yeah. Know what you mean, buddy,' said Jonah. 'That or they don't look anything in real life like they do on their profiles.' Sonny laughed and nodded. 'Seriously. I had one the other week – stunner on her profile pic. Turned up – a face like a bulldog licking piss off a nettle! I blame these filters.'

'Listen to you. You men are just as bloody bad!' said Michelle. 'Most of the ones I get look like they've fallen out of the Ugly Tree and bumped their heads on every branch on the way down.' They all laughed.

'Touché,' said Jonah. 'How come you see your dad so regularly anyway? Seems a lot.'

'I'm all he's got,' said Sonny. His father had Parkinson's and was in a local care home, or the 'nuthouse' as Sonny called it.

Sonny's gay boss, Gavin, waltzed in from clearing tables outside. 'Looking buff, Chef. Any hot dates tonight?'

'Nope.'

'Well, there's always tequila and Pornhub. Have a good weekend. See you Monday!'

Sonny took the short walk home, feeling saturnine. As a chef, he'd always craved having evenings and weekends off – and now he did. But what was the point if you were single? He should have that 'Friday Feeling' like Jonah had said. But the thought of his empty rented house left him feeling flat; as if life was elsewhere, passing him by like a train he was meant to be on. The guys at work meant well enough, but their persistent probing into Sonny's social life, especially his love life – one of the main topics of conversation at work – only highlighted his predicament; how life had fallen somewhat short of his expectations and hopes.

Following his usual route, Sonny cut a diagonal across the market square, past the Buttercross, towards the church gates. As he negotiated the cobbled path of the churchyard, he braced himself for the bells, deafening him. And there they were, knelling out the hour. Five o'clock on a biting February day at the arse-end of winter. At least the snowdrops were out, the first herald that spring was round the corner. And it was staying lighter. Everyone kept saying it, 'It's staying lighter, isn't it?' As if it was a surprise, or had never happened before at that time of year. That night, there was the added bonus of a stunning sunset. Orange fading to peach, fading to steely blue.

Sonny passed a couple of schoolkids in uniform, a boy and a girl, both sporting over-sized green blazers. Hand-in-hand, spotty and clearly in love. There were few things sweeter than a couple of young schoolkids in love, Sonny mused. Their whole lives ahead of them. It made him feel wistful. And old.

Heading away from town, Sonny passed the new-build estate, where they were building houses nobody could afford. Swelling the town, shrinking the greenbelt. Behind it, stretching away into the distance, were open fields – what was left of them anyway – punctuated by the black bones of skeleton trees. Then, dominating the horizon, again in inky silhouette against that sci-fi sky, a regiment of wind turbines loomed. Red-eyed behemoths, watching over the town. Somehow dystopian and futuristic. Their blades eerily still that night.

On reaching home, Sonny's cat, Buddy (named after Mr. Holly, not a giant elf) was waiting for him in his usual spot, sitting atop the back yard gate post. He jumped down at Sonny's arrival, a streak of black satin. Waiting to be fed, no doubt. Sonny had a suspicion Buddy was plotting to kill him. He'd become pre-occupied with the notion after reading a book entitled, *How to Tell if Your Cat is Plotting to Kill You*, that he'd spotted in a bookshop window in Whitby. The picture on the cover looked like Buddy. Sleek, jet-black. Slightly mean green eyes. As if he was the devil's cat, or at least had the devil in him. He was constantly zig-zagging in front of Sonny, trying to trip him up. Especially on the stairs in the morning when Sonny was often hungover, bleary-eyed and stumbling to the kitchen to make his much-needed elixir of tea.

The shared back yard smelt of fried bacon and weed as Sonny pushed open the gate. Both smells emanating from the open kitchen window of his neighbours' house. They were gay. One of them transgender. She looked like Tom Petty. He looked like Elton John, but with occasional blue hair. They were always cooking bacon and smoking weed. They had lots of parties.

The second Sonny walked through the door his phone rang. He removed it from his pocket and consulted the cracked screen; he'd had the phone for six years and paid six pounds a month for it. The call was from his father. 'For fuck's sake,' Sonny sighed. He'd just about managed to train his father not to phone him whilst at work, another source of amusement at the deli: '*How can you ignore a call from your own dad? He's got Parkinson's?*'

'*Trust me, it's tough love, he needs to learn,*' Sonny would reply with a smile. Truth was, his father would bombard him with calls every ten minutes if allowed. And on bad days, he still did.

Sonny plonked his holdall down, the cat brushing against him for food, to answer the phone. 'Hi, Dad.' There was the familiar, frantic scrabbling sound from the other end of the phone, as his father tried to put him on speaker. 'Hello, Dad. Can you hear me?' More scrabbling. 'Dad. Can you hear me?'

'Can you hear me?' His father's desperate voice.

'Yes, I can hear you. Can you hear me?'

'Sonny! Can you hear me?!'

'Yes, I can hear you. Can you hear me?'

'Sonny! Can you hear me?!'

'Yes! *Can you hear me?*'

'Ah! There you are. I've got you. Bit of a crisis here...'

'Hi, Dad. What's up?'

'Bit of a crisis, desperate situation.'

'Don't tell me, you're out of rich tea biscuits...'

'Hey? All the underwear's gone missing again. I've got none at all. No jockey shorts, no socks... I'm shuffling around in bare feet. It's inhumane.'

'Well, where are your slippers?'

'Sorry?'

'Your slippers. Where are they?'

'I've no idea. They've gone missing again. Same with my comb. They'll pinch anything. I've been brushing my hair with a toothbrush. Works quite well actually...'

'For Christ's sake, Dad, you're always losing your combs. Have you checked your drawers?'

'Doors? What doors?'

'Drawers. Your chest of drawers. For your underwear.' There was a pause.

'Sorry. You've lost me...'

'Your chest of drawers!'

'What about it?'

'Have you checked your chest of drawers for your underwear? The top drawer! That's where they're kept.'

'Oh. No.'

'Well, check there. If there's nothing in there, they're probably in the laundry.'

'Laundry – they're bloody useless! We need to get our own system in place. Nothing ever comes back from there. And when it does, it's not mine. I saw some bloke wandering about the corridors in one of my shirts the other day. It's not on. They're quality shirts. Viyella. Cost me eighty-odd quid. They never hand wash anything. My jumpers are lamb's wool. Pure lamb's wool. They need handwashing at no more than thirty degrees…'

Sonny held the phone away from his ear and sighed. 'We just need to get you some more name tags, that's all, Dad. I've ordered them, but they haven't arrived yet. But I'll be up in a bit to see you, and I'll see what's gone on. In the meantime, check your drawers.'

'Oh, you're coming up. Well, pick me another comb up on your way. And bring a paring knife, about two inches long.'

'You're not allowed sharp objects, you know that.'

'Just a round-ended one, for cutting up fruit.'

'You're not allowed, Dad'

'Whose side are you on?! Sneak it in. I don't know why you get so worried. There's not a bloody metal detector on the door.'

Sonny sighed again. 'Anything else?'

'A slab of dark chocolate. Minimum seventy five percent cocoa solids. And order some more jockey shorts. M and S. Hundred percent cotton. Organic preferably…'

Sonny finally got off the phone. The cat was sitting next to the food cupboard, giving him the evil eye. 'Alright,' Sonny said. 'I know. Let's get you fed.'

Cat fed, Sonny walked over to his battered dartboard to pluck the darts from it. Playing darts was his way of unwinding. He didn't even play '501'. Just aimed for the frayed, peppered treble twenty over and over again. Or the occasional treble nineteen.

Before commencing his first throw, Sonny decided to send an exploratory message to each of his three kids; he still referred to them as kids, despite his twin teenage girls being seventeen now and his son nineteen. He sent tailored messages to all of them in the hope that at least one would message back. Hedging his bets. He'd just about got used to the hurt of them not replying in a hurry, sometimes not for a day or so. But it had been hard. He still missed them. Missed not living with them and being part of their everyday lives. Them no longer needing him. It could drive him crazy if he let it.

The way he saw it, there were one-hundred and sixty-eight hours in a week, and he currently only saw them once a week for approximately four hours. That wasn't even three percent of their lives, his included. He'd calculated all this during one of his many long nights of lying awake, trying to find a way to sleep. This startling figure didn't seem right. Ate away at him. And then there was the guilt. The persistent guilt that he should be doing more, be involved more. Like an anchor weighing him down. It wasn't for want of trying; it was hard to pin them down to do anything. They were teenagers, young adults, after all. Did he want to spend time with his father as a teenager? Hell, no! It didn't help that they now lived fifty minutes or so apart.

Messages sent, Sonny picked up his darts again and assumed his stance on the oche mat, rolled out on his kitchen floor. One dart in and his phone went off again. Hmm, that was quick for the kids, he thought. He finished his throw – sixty-six, pretty standard; a treble twenty, a stray one and a five – then went to check his phone. It was Gavin, his boss. Sonny dragged the phone screen down to read the message without Gavin knowing he'd read it. '*What are you doing Saturday night?*' followed by the usual barrage of OTT emojis, most of them suggestive. Sonny ignored the message and went back to throwing his darts for a bit. He didn't want to encourage attention from Gavin by replying quickly.

But as Sonny threw his darts, pacing back and forth, his mind kept going back to the message. He couldn't deny his interest was piqued. Gavin wasn't in the habit of asking a question like that. One, he (Gavin) was in a long-term relationship, and two, he knew Sonny was as straight as a lamp post. Immune. *Impenetrable.* Gavin would like that one. Sonny went back to his phone and opened the message. Gavin was still online, as if waiting for a reply, as if he had nothing better to do. He did that a lot. '*Not sure. Why?*' Sonny replied as non-committally as possible. Two blue ticks came up straight away next to the message, signifying it had been read instantly.

Then Gavin typing: '*How would you like to be a plus one?*' Another gaggle of suggestive emojis.

A plus-one? Sonny thought. '*Who for? Where?*' he typed.

'*Sarah, the lady who does our flowers. Good friend of mine. Single. Loaded.*' Half a dozen emojis. Everyone was a 'good friend' of Gavin's, it seemed. Then another message straightaway: '*She's a right dirty bitch. Frustrated.*' Followed by a dozen suggestive emojis. Oh, for fuck's sake, thought Sonny. This was typical Gavin, and all Sonny needed. Some sex-starved middle-aged woman. He was desperate, but not that desperate. How old was she anyway? He typed the question. '*Mid-forties?*' came the reply. Hmm, thought Sonny. Older than he would normally go for. His phone kept pinging with messages, too quick for him to keep up with as his brain tried to mull the prospect over. He'd got nothing better to do, and you never knew... '*Me and Paul will be there, so it will be the four of us,*' Gavin typed. This last message did allay Sonny's fears a little, make him feel a little less vulnerable.

'*Where?*' he asked again.

'*Holme Pierrepont Hall. An awards ceremony. Fancy do*'. '*Is that a 'yes'?*' '*You'd need a tux.*' '*I'll rent you one if you haven't got one.*' '*What are your measurements?*' Another dozen suggestive emojis...

# CHAPTER 2

Sonny started his car. Immediately, the petrol light came on and emitted its irksome, familiar beep at Sonny, letting him know he was nearly out. He always was, only sticking twenty quid in when he made the journey to see his kids. Then back to the orange light again. Fortunately, his father's care home was on the outskirts of town, only a few minutes' drive away.

Sonny pulled up in the car park. He was such a regular there, he ought to have his own parking spot with a placard. He'd stopped at the shops on the way to grab his father's usual supplies, paid for with the old man's card. Fruit, nuts, biscuits, chocolate etc. Sonny got out with the shopping bag.

The home was nestled in a pleasant green and wooded area, surrounded by tall trees and squawking crows, overlooking Bingham's railway line. The location a bit out of keeping with the building itself, which was modern, squat and unremarkable. This made Sonny think of Holme Pierrepont Hall and Saturday night; he'd agreed to go. Surprisingly, he had a little flutter of excitement in his stomach at the prospect. It would be nice to get out, to do something different. Money wouldn't be an issue (it usually was), as Gavin would pay. He was also loaded. The deli was more of a hobby to him, a plaything. Plus, as Sonny had already thought, you never knew... Perhaps he should open up his horizons to a slightly older woman, perhaps that's why the dating sites never yielded anything. It was almost a stubborn 'principle' thing to him. His refusal to consider dating anyone older than himself. He kept in shape, always had, with an athletic build and good head of dark hair. Not a single grey one yet. A source of envy to his male work colleagues, especially Gavin: '*Ooh, you've got such a good head of dark hair, Chef...*'

Shopping bag in hand, Sonny made the short walk to the reception door. Doing so, he recalled the very first day he had brought his father there in the crammed car. His father, terrified, had refused to get out, just sat there on the passenger seat, clutching his prized glass case of pinned butterflies to his chest, as if as a shield. Sonny's father loved butterflies. Some fifteen minutes later, he'd eventually shuffled through the door with it; the case was now hung, slightly skewwhiff, on the wall in his room; an early, half-hearted attempt on the home's part at making him feel at home.

As Sonny neared the building, there was the usual congregation of staff sitting outside, on their phones and smoking. The majority of them seemed to be permanently on breaks. No wonder there was never anyone on hand to let him in, or to help his father when needed. Sonny was too polite to say anything. He didn't like confrontation. 'How we doing, guys?' he said. They said 'hello' back. Sonny knew pretty-much all of their names, and they knew him.

'How's yer season going, bro?' Felix said, unable to suppress his grin. He was a Man City fan. Sonny was Liverpool. They always bantered about the football. But the current gulf in their respective teams' fortunes meant Felix was enjoying their latest exchanges considerably more than Sonny was.

'We still beat you though, didn't we?' Sonny said.

'Not in the cup, you didn't. Knocked you right out.'

'We'll get you back next time at your place – the 'Emptyhad'.

Felix laughed at the expression. 'Not gonna happen, my friend. That leaky defence of yours ain't gonna stop Haaland.'

'We'll see,' said Sonny. They were both smiling as Sonny pushed open the door to the small reception foyer. Thank God he didn't have to do those God-awful Covid tests any more every time he visited, or wear a mask. That had been awful, looking back, such a rigmarole and added stress – and such a scary barrier for his father, all the staff permanently hidden behind PPE gear, as if he'd gone to live on the film set of *E.T.* Sonny pressed the buzzer, then waited as he always did. Betty, one of the residents, or the 'smiling assassin' as Sonny called her, came to stare and talk to him through the glass of the inner door. She never stopped talking – or singing – but had an evil side to her too. Sonny had witnessed it first-hand. Severe dementia, like most of the other residents there. One of her tricks was to sidle up to other residents whilst they were sleeping, pinch them hard, then innocently toddle off.

Sonny pressed the buzzer again – sometimes he had to buzz three or four times before being let in – whilst Betty continued to talk to him. It was as awkward as always. Sonny never knew where to look or whether to smile at her or talk back to her. Sometimes other residents would come and join Betty, to see who she was talking to, to see what all the fuss was about. Or maybe because they were so bored. They would jostle for position, staring through the glass at him, like zombies in slippers and nightwear. The vacancy of their stares troubled Sonny, saddened him, that there was nothing going on behind those faces, nothing that made sense anyway – like RP McMurphy after his lobotomy. Then one of the members of staff from outside would invariably put their cigarette out to come and buzz him in. Tonight was no different. One of the regular women. 'No one coming? I'll let you in, I've finished my break.'

'Thanks,' said Sonny, as she let him in. She reeked of cigarettes. Sonny always imagined what that was like for his father, having that breathed in his face all day. Sonny took the short walk down the corridor to his father's room. There was a stairgate across the doorway, the type you use for toddlers. But in his father's case it was to stop the other residents getting in, rather than him getting out. This had been a constant menace in the early days, a shocking invasion of privacy; twice, other residents had got in his father's bed and gone to sleep. Another time his father had ended up pushing one of them to the floor. This had gone on his 'rap sheet', cited as 'aggressive behaviour'. Something had to give. Hence the stairgate.

The door of his father's room was ajar. Sonny knocked on the door frame and grappled the pain in the arse stairgate open. 'Hi, Dad,' he said, entering the room. The familiar ammonia smell of stale urine immediately clawed at his nostrils, emanating from the adjoining bathroom's toilet bowl that permanently ran, yet nobody ever seemed to flush. Unnoticed, Sonny headed straight towards it. Covering his nose, he flushed the offending sepia-coloured liquid away. Returning to the room, the TV was on too loud as usual. His father, impossibly thin, tall, stooped and doddery, like a drunk heron, was standing at his desk, trying to feed what looked like a piece of cardboard into one of the closed drawers. He was always rifling around in his desk drawers. Rearranging things. Hiding things. He liked to hoard sharp, shiny implements – like a magpie preparing for Armageddon. Peelers, scissors, knives – anything he wasn't allowed – in spectacle cases, drawers and tubs. But at least he was standing. And unaided. His meds must have kicked in. 'Hi Dad,' Sonny said. 'What you up to? I've got your shopping.' The old man still didn't hear or register him. 'Dad. I'm here! What are you up to?' He fought to be heard over the TV.

Sonny's father slowly turned his head on its stooped-swan neck to face him, his sunken-in eyes swivelling in his pale skull. The skin stretched too taut over prominent bone and veins. His condition or the meds or both had prematurely aged him. Sometimes Sonny could almost see the dead man inside him, waiting to get out. Hear him rattling within. A brief look of recognition crossed his father's face, then the familiar scowl. 'What are you doing here? You didn't tell me you were coming.'

'I did. Literally an hour ago. You told me to get you a comb. Here.'

His father huffed, snatched the black comb off Sonny, and ferreted it away in his shirt pocket. 'Close the door. Quick,' he said.

Sonny closed the door. 'What are you do–' But his father cut him off.

'Flip that chair over.'

'What?'

'The chair. The mahogany chair. Flip it over!'

'Why? And can we turn the TV down a bit. It's too loud.'

'Never mind why. You'll see.'

Sonny sighed, plonked the shopping bag down and walked over to the antique chair, the feeling of being instantly controlled by his father depressingly familiar and normal. His father tried to turn to watch as Sonny turned the chair over to look underneath it. 'Hmm. See,' his father said, nodding.

'See what. What am I looking for?'

'Underneath the seat,' his father hissed.

There, carefully embedded in the hessian underbelly of the chair, was a long, sharp-looking pair of scissors. 'For Christ's sake, Dad,' Sonny said. 'Where did you get those from?'

'Hidden in my wash bag from when I was at the hospital. They don't know I've got 'em. Now bring them here. And be quick.'

Sonny sighed and plucked out the scissors. 'Give them to me, I'm trying to get in this drawer. It's stuck.'

'Why is it stuck?'

'I don't know. It's jammed. We've been trying to get in it all day. I've had half the staff in here.' Sonny tried the drawer. It wouldn't budge an inch. He yanked it harder, shaking the whole desk, but to no avail.

'Try the scissors,' his father said. 'Slide them through the gap. Try and dislodge something.'

'They won't fit.'

'Let me try.'

'I'm telling you they won't fit.' His father snatched the scissors off him and tried to feed them into the drawer with his large shaky hands. But couldn't even find the miniscule gap. It was painful and infuriating to watch. A too-loud, ear-splitting applause broke out on some game show on the TV. 'Can we please turn the telly down!'

'What?'

'The bloody telly! It's too loud. Where's the remote?'

His father pointed to the stuck drawer. 'In there, I think.'

# CHAPTER 3

Watching out of his kitchen window, Sonny felt a tug of nerves as Gavin's immaculate, gold Range Rover screeched to a halt out front. It was the night of the plus-one bash. Sarah, Sonny's date for the night, was sitting on the back seat, or at least Sonny assumed it was her; it was hard to make the lady out properly, as she was on the far side of the car. But she appeared to be staring right back at Sonny with a similar expression of nerves and curiosity. Gavin, at the wheel, tooted the horn in an aggressively-musical way, causing Sonny to wince. Talk about making an entrance. Then Gavin said something to 'presumably' Sarah and she threw back her head and laughed. Paul, Gavin's partner, was in the front passenger seat. 'Ooh, hello James Bond – look at you!' Gavin sang, as Sonny climbed in. 'How do you like yours? *Shaken* or *stirred?* Give him a glass, Sarah.' An empty champagne flute was thrust into Sonny's hand by Sarah. She had fancy, expensive-looking nails, rocks on her fingers, and a bottle of fizz clutched between her knees.

'Bloomin' hell, started already, guys?' Sonny said.

'Of course,' said Gavin.

'Not me,' said Paul. 'I'm designated driver. As usual.' He was the total antithesis of Gavin. Quiet. Reserved. Working class.

'Oh, stop moaning,' said Gavin. 'I'm driving on the way there, aren't I? Right. All in? Oo-er, matron – let's go!'

Before Sonny had even had chance to introduce himself – or buckle his seatbelt – Gavin put his foot down and screeched the car away; the Range Rover's powerful engine pinned Sonny and Sarah to their seats. In his haste and showing off, Gavin mounted a kerb momentarily and lost his grip of the steering wheel, causing the car to swerve. Sarah let out a squeal as her drink sloshed about in her glass. 'Careful! I'll spill my drink on my frock!' she said.

'Jesus,' said Sonny, scrambling for a seat belt. Paul silently took it all in his stride. Probably used to it. Or embarrassed.

'Anyway, I'm Sarah.' She laughed nervously.

'Sonny,' said Sonny.

Thankfully back on the actual road now, they settled into the journey. Sonny felt self-conscious in his tux – he was more of a jeans and T-shirt kind of guy – and struggled to think of conversation. The car smelt strongly of Sarah's perfume. She poured Sonny a glass of fizz, L.P. rosé, and as she did, Sonny ran his eyes over her again, taking her in. She was wearing a formal, low-cut dress under a smart jacket. 'Cheers,' she said, clinking his glass.

'Cheers,' said Sonny. He sipped his drink, thankful for the crutch.

'So, you're my *date* for the night,' she said. 'What a lucky girl. Very handsome.'

'He does look handsome, doesn't he?' Gavin butted in. 'Very dashing.'

'Thanks,' said Sonny – to Sarah, not Gavin – blushing. 'You look very nice too.'

'Ooh, listen to you two flirting already!' Gavin piped up again. 'I wonder if they've got rooms at the bash. Ooh, I feel like your pimp, Chef.'

'Oh, give over, you filthy devil!' said Sarah. 'Is he like this at work?'

'Yep,' said Sonny resignedly, and Sarah laughed again. Sonny hoped Gavin wasn't going to keep this up all night, the suggestive remarks. Fat chance...

Fortunately, they reached the grounds of their destination in one piece, and without further embarrassment or any spillages. It was a short journey. Sonny had been trying to surreptitiously steal more glances at his female companion, but it was hard without being too obvious. Her hair was heavily-styled and highlighted. As Gavin had alluded to, she didn't appear to be short of a bob or two. Her clothes, her manner, the adornments. Still struggling for conversation and feeling a little out of his depth, Sonny took in the tree-lined approach to the hall, the grand surroundings, as the salmon-red brick building itself came into view. Its frontage had the appearance of a castle. Sonny had been to the hall once before, to watch an outdoor Shakespeare play. But he had never been inside it properly.

'You been here before?' he asked Sarah.

'Yes. But not to the awards bash. I've never been nominated before.'

'Oh, I didn't realise you were nominated. That's exciting. What for?'

'Retail florist shop of the year.'

'You better not bloody win!' Gavin butted in. 'Charge me a fortune already – you'll be putting your prices up, cheeky bitch.' Flowers were a passion of Gavin's. The deli was always chock-full of fragrant bouquets and sprays.

'I'll always keep special rates for you, my darling,' Sarah said. 'Even when I am an *award-winning* florist.'

They parked up and walked inside, showed their tickets and booked various bits into the cloakroom. The interior of the hall was stunning. Old paintings. Huge, high-ceilinged rooms. A piano was being played. Staff were handing out glasses of fizz on trays to well-dressed folk. Canapes were being offered. The drinks were going down quickly. Paul had a Buck's Fizz, saying, 'that's my lot.' The other three were knocking the fizz back.

Sonny got his first good look at Sarah and decided very quickly that he didn't find her attractive. She wasn't *unattractive*; she just didn't do anything for him. He tried to tell himself it wasn't her age. Gavin had been being kind – or lying – when he'd said 'mid-forties'; Sarah looked fifty if she was a day to Sonny. Her face, although kind, looked as if it had seen too much sun, her mouth slightly too puckered – probably from constant holidaying abroad.

Finally, they were shown to their table. A big round one with four other guests on it. The night went on. It was a good laugh. They got drunk. They ate a three-course meal. Sarah's hand brushed Sonny's leg a few times, and she continued to lean in to him to whisper things. To all the world, they looked like a couple. Excitement and anticipation built as the awards themselves took place.

They waited with baited breath as Sarah's category – and the nominees – were read out. Gavin whooped and cheered, making a right racket. The champagne had been flowing all night. Sadly, Sarah didn't win, and the mood changed a little then. The excitement that had been keeping Sarah buoyant fizzed out. 'Well, that's that then,' she slurred. 'Fuck 'em! Let's have another drink!' But she looked despondent. Sonny felt sorry for her. He gave a consolatory smile.

'That's the spirit!' said Gavin. 'Waiter!'

Sonny groaned inwardly. The last thing he wanted was more booze. He just wanted to go home.

'Do you find me attractive?' Sarah whispered unexpectedly into Sonny's ear. 'I find you attractive. Very attractive. And a man that can cook… Very sexy…' She put her hand on his arm.

'Erm…' Sonny cleared his throat, not knowing how to react or what to say. He was too polite. It always got him into trouble.

'Come back to my place. For a nightcap – or a coffee. See where it leads to.' She moved her hand to his leg. 'It's just one night. You only live once…' Sonny gulped. He looked over at Gavin, hoping to be rescued, but he was still trying to get hold of a waiter.

Shit, thought Sonny. He felt trapped. And drunk all of a sudden. 'I need to go to the loo,' he said.

Post-pee, Sonny studied himself in the toilet mirror and adjusted his hair. He did look good in a tux, if a little older. Another drunken thought then occurred to him. You can keep the same suit hanging up in your wardrobe and, with a bit of luck, wear it for ten years or more – and the suit won't change. But your face does.

A bit like *The Picture of Dorian Gray*, but in reverse. 'What to do, what to do,' he said to himself. 'Fuck it.'

Sonny returned to the table.

'Well?' Sarah said.

'OK,' Sonny said. 'Just a coffee.' He really was too polite.

'Gavin! Cancel the fizz, we're going,' said Sarah.

Paul dropped them off at Sarah's house, a huge detached job in Upper Saxondale no less. Whilst a swaying Sarah struggled to get her key in the lock of the front door, Sonny's phone went off in his pocket. Sarah dropped her keys. 'Shit,' she said, giggling. As she bent to pick them up, Sonny checked his phone. It was Gavin: '*Dirty dog. Hope you've got some condoms!*' followed by the usual assault of emojis. Twat, thought Sonny, annoyed, stuffing his phone back in his pocket. The message made him feel dirty. Made him question again what he was doing there. Why hadn't he just gone home? That feeling of drifting washed over him again, of life just happening to him without his input or stewardship. Like a crewless boat that had veered off course. Just a coffee, he thought, as Sarah finally let them in.

Sonny found himself in a large, echoey hallway with impressive wooden flooring. It was uncomfortably warm after being outdoors. He looked for somewhere to put his jacket. 'Here, hang it on the banister,' Sarah said, as if reading his mind. She removed her coat and showed him. Sonny followed suit, removing his jacket and hanging it on top of hers. He also undid his bowtie and loosened his collar. He could feel Sarah watching him as he did so, whilst at the same time removing her shoes. 'That's better,' she said. 'I can get a good look at you now.' She toddled over to him, considerably smaller without her heels. Quite petite, in fact. Girlish, with a good figure. 'You're in good shape,' she said. 'Do you work out?' She touched his arm again.

'A little, just to keep in shape,' Sonny said, embarrassed.

'A little goes a long way...' Sarah said, seemingly admiring him again and sighing. She looked into his eyes, clearly drunk. Sonny looked away.

'You're shy, aren't you?' She put her hand on his face and turned it towards her again. 'It's sweet.' Sonny felt awkward, as if he was being seduced against his will, Mrs Robinson style. But the touch of her hand also felt surprisingly sensitive, good. This shocked Sonny. Must be the booze. 'Let's get you another drink. Come on.' She took his hand and pulled him down the hall.

Sonny was led into another impressive room, exuding wealth. Oil paintings on butternut squash-coloured walls. Ornate white plaster cornicing. 'Now you just sit yourself down here, and I'll fix us some nightcaps.'

'No, a coffee's fine, really,' said Sonny, sinking into a plush sofa that seemed to receive him a little too gratefully, a bit like a Venus flytrap.

'A special coffee then,' said Sarah, letting her hand linger on his shoulder. 'Sugar?'

'No. Thank you.'

'Sweet enough, eh?' She sashayed off.

Whilst she was gone, Sonny again questioned what he was doing there. He yawned and surveyed the room further, taking it in. Lampstands with huge patterned lamp shades, bordered with decorative string. A marble fireplace where family photos were conspicuous by their absence.

Sarah returned with a steaming mug and a heavy-set glass tumbler with what looked like whiskey in it. She passed him the mug. Sonny wafted it under his nose. It reeked of whiskey. Great, he thought. He took a small sip, winced, then placed it on the coffee table in front of him. Then there was an awkward silence. Two strangers, through circumstance, thrust together. 'So, here we are then...' said Sarah, voicing it. She took a good glug of whiskey, big eyes staring at Sonny over the rim of the glass. Mascara slightly smudged. Sonny didn't know what to say. Again. More silence followed.

Sarah, too, placed her tumbler on a coaster on the glass table. Then, totally without warning, she threw herself at Sonny, straddling him with one satin tight-clad thigh and pressing her lips to his as her dress rode up. Her lips were hot, wet and alcoholic, her tongue a probing snake in his mouth. A very unwelcome invasion of privacy.

Sonny recoiled and pushed her away, but not roughly or unkindly – more of a natural reaction. 'Sarah stop!' He held his palms up. 'I'm sorry, but I don't want this.'

Sarah immediately burst into tears. It was a shock and Sonny felt awful. She had her head in her hands, her shoulders shaking with sobs. Sonny put his hand on her shoulder, to comfort her; he wanted to make her feel better. 'I'm sorry,' he said again.

To his surprise, Sarah grabbed his hand and clutched it, as if desperate for the human touch. 'I'm sorry,' she said.

'No, it's fine,' he stopped her.

'No, it's not. Do you find me unattractive?' A similar question to that which she had asked earlier. 'Am I that repulsive?' She looked at him through her tears, her mascara making a dash for her cheeks now.

'God, no. Don't be silly. You're attractive, you're very attractive.' He stopped himself from saying 'for your age'.

'Really?' she said.

'Yes, really. It's just–'

'Don't say it!' It was her turn to hold a hand up, as she let Sonny's go. 'My age, I know. I'm past my prime and no one wants to know. No one decent anyway…' Sonny didn't know what to say. 'I get so lonely,' she sniffed and broke down again. 'I just want a man in my bed for one night. One night to love and to hold someone. Is that too much to ask? To make me feel good and wanted. To make me feel like a woman. Or in my house even would be a start! I know you're here now' – she reached for his hand again – 'But I miss having a man around the place permanently. The silly things – like the sound of a man having a wee. It's different to a woman – more, well, *manly*.' She laughed at herself. 'Does that sound weird?'

Kind of, thought Sonny. But he knew where she was coming from; he missed certain things too. Female things. The smell of perfume. Cosmetics on a chest of drawers. Knickers on the bedroom floor. 'You will find someone,' he said. 'It will happen. A woman like you… Have you tried the dating sites?' He felt a hypocrite for saying it, knowing the luck he'd had with them.

'Huh!' she said. 'A load of old saddos.' Then she laughed. 'Listen to me. I'm as bad.' She sniffed again. Sonny spotted a box of tissues on the table, plucked one out, and handed it to her. She received it gratefully and dabbed at her eyes. Then she looked at Sonny again, studying him, as if considering something. She reached for her whiskey again, took another glug, then cradled the glass. Then she looked at him again. 'You're kind,' she said. 'A kind, good man. I can tell...' Sonny blushed. He didn't feel like a good man half the time, the way he lost his temper with his father, the frustration with him. But it went both ways. Their relationship was like an active volcano. Simmering, volatile, only a matter of time till it erupted spectacularly again. 'Would you?' she said. Sonny was drawn back to the conversation by the question, aware he was being asked something; he had been drifting again, his thoughts elsewhere.

'I'm sorry?' he said.

'Would you consider sleeping with me?' *What the hell!* thought Sonny. He was shocked at her forthrightness, and reddened further.

'Sarah, I don't think that would be appropr–'

'Just for one night. Just once. For me. No strings attached. No one needs to know. I won't tell Gavin – or anyone – I promise.' She reached for his hand and squeezed it. Sonny was torn again. A victim of his own niceness, his inability to say no and to hurt people. And for a brief moment he considered it. Actually considered it. What was it they called it? A pity-fuck? But then he thought of the mechanics of it. The reality of it – actually 'doing it'. And he couldn't. He pulled his hand away.

'Sarah, really, I couldn't. Thank you. I'm flattered, but really I couldn't.'

But his indecision, his patent consideration was enough to spur Sarah on; and she said something that totally floored him: 'I have money. Lots of it. I could pay you. Five hundred pounds. A grand. Whatever... money means nothing to me.'

'What?! God, no. Don't be silly. That's a horrible idea!' Sonny stood up. 'Look, this is getting out of hand. I'm going to go.'

'OK. I'm sorry. I've offended you.' She had her head bowed, as if in shame. As if she was going to cry again.

'No, not at all. I just think... I just think we'll both be a little embarrassed by this in the morning...'

# CHAPTER 4

The next morning Sonny was awakened, not by his usual work alarm that he forgot without fail to turn off at the weekends, but by a message coming through on his phone. He groaned. What time was it? He felt rough. Nothing new there. Mornings were usually a struggle for Sonny, mainly down to alcohol consumption the night before. Blindly, he scrabbled around for his phone amongst the familiar chaos of his bedside table. Empty wine glass and bottle, glasses of undrunk squash, crisp packets, TV remote, crossword book, pens... 'Shit!' He knocked the phone onto the floor. 'Fuck's sake,' he said, reaching for it and groaning again.

Through bleary eyes, Sonny consulted his phone. It was seven-thirty and the message that had just come through was from Gavin. There were other unread messages too from his kids. Typical, thought Sonny, they either reply in the middle of the night, or when he can't message back. He was seeing them later that day. Tried to every Sunday without fail. He couldn't bear the thought of becoming a peripheral figure in their lives.

Someone of little significance. He was already starting to feel like it.

Sonny opened Gavin's message up first. 'Well?' it said. '*Did you do the dirty?*' The events of last night came flooding back to him. Especially the culmination of it. What was that all about? As predicted, he felt embarrassed for Sarah; she had actually offered him money for sex. A lot of money. It didn't seem real to Sonny. Like a dream, or something from a film. She must have been absolutely plastered, he thought. Or unstable. Or desperate. Maybe all three. Thank God he hadn't gone through with it.

Sonny didn't reply to Gavin, he could wait. He didn't want to give him the satisfaction of an answer, the dirty git. Plus, it was him that had put Sonny in that awkward situation in the first place. Did he know she was going to do that? Did she make a habit of it? Did *he* make a habit of it, procuring men for her like lambs to the slaughter? Should he even bring it up with him? He said he was really good friends with her. It would embarrass her further if she knew he knew – if he didn't already that was...

He turned his attention to the kids' messages instead, praying they weren't cancelling. It was both the girls, his twins, that had replied on the separate group chat he had with them. One of them, Charlotte, had sent an attachment or photo. It was of a car, a second-hand one. '*I've found a car!*' with smiley faces. The other twin, Bea, had just put: '*Me too! I think!*' Oh, bloomin' hell, was Sonny's first thought. And typical again. They only message when they need or want something. Usually money! Both the girls were having driving lessons.

Sonny had managed to talk the old man into paying for a block for each of them for their birthdays, and Sonny had always promised them that when they'd found cars he would help them out financially with them, or at least go halves with their mum. And then there was the insurance too – about a grand each... That was the thing with twins. Always twice the cost at the same time. Sonny was pleased for them, it was all part of life's journey, those rites of passage, but he had also been dreading this day coming. He just didn't have the money. Struggled to make ends meet as it was. You always think that when an expected financial hit is well in advance, something will come up by then. Or your circumstances will change. But they rarely do.

Sonny bought a lottery ticket religiously every Saturday morning when he bought the paper for the crossword – in the hope of changing his and his kids' lives, so they didn't have to go through what he had gone through, a life of bad decisions and too much work for too little gain. He'd love to be able to ring them up and say, 'Guess what?!' or 'Choose a car. Any car!' He didn't do the EuroMillions – the big money – just the standard Lotto. The tickets were cheaper. Plus, he wasn't greedy. A few million would be enough. That wasn't too much to ask, was it? A few million? But he never had any luck. Not even a tenner. Just a drawer of folded-up pink slips. He kept them for some reason, maybe hoping to see a pattern or a formula in them. Yet despite the sometimes too crushing disappointment of another failed week, and him vowing 'never again', once Saturday rolled round, he just couldn't help himself. It had got to be worth it, hadn't it? Just on the off-chance? What was two quid a week? There was always that niggling hope. That maybe... just maybe... Out of desperation, he'd even tried sports-betting once, another attempt to change his life; he'd spent hours obsessing over data, head to heads, tables and form guides. All to no avail in the end, other than a mild addiction and the conclusion that he was the unluckiest man on the planet; betting really was the proverbial 'mug's game'.

So, the cars were a dilemma. '*Yay*' he messaged back. '*How many miles?*' Then he rolled back onto his back in bed, staring at the ceiling. His mouth was dry, and his head was beginning to pound. He needed to sober up and sort himself out. He needed to sort his life out. He needed his morning cup of tea... Why couldn't the stupid cat make tea? He'd probably poison it with something if he could...

Talking of the cat, as if on cue, there was a familiar scratching at the bedroom door. Or more a ripping of the carpet, as Buddy sharpened his claws, vying for some attention and food. Sonny banged on the wall for him to stop. It was a rented carpet. Maybe he'd been scratching for ages, but Sonny had been too zonked out to register it. The cat was locked out of the bedroom at night, for fear of Sonny having his face scratched to pieces. 'Alright! I'm coming.'

Mid-morning, cat fed and dirty chef whites put on to wash, Sonny was finishing his breakfast with a cup of coffee and the crossword. The big one with both cryptic and quick clues. He always tried to get it finished by the end of the weekend. Rarely did. The fact that it was the highlight of his weekend, though, spoke volumes. His phone went off again, surprising him. It reminded him he hadn't replied to Gavin. It was probably him again.

To Sonny's surprise, it wasn't. It was from an unfamiliar number, accompanied by another photo. He clicked on the message. Again, much to his surprise, the photo was of his tuxedo jacket hanging up on a banister post. Shit, he thought. His dinner jacket. He'd left it at Sarah's. He'd left a little flustered after what had happened. Or *not* happened. The accompanying message said: *'Thanks for last night. You are a true gentleman – and there aren't many of them about these days. Did you leave your jacket on purpose?'* followed by thinking and monkey face emojis. Hmm... clearly not embarrassed then. And how did she get his number? He thought for a second, trying to recall last night – all a bit of a blur in the end. Had he given her his number? He was sure he hadn't. Gavin, he thought. I bet she got it off Gavin, using the left jacket as an excuse. Sonny was still pondering this when his phone went off, making him jump again. It was Sarah again. She would have known he'd read the message. *'Oh. And the offer still stands...'* followed, this time, by a kiss emoji. What the hell? thought Sonny.

Sonny cooked lunch for his kids. It was far cheaper than eating out – despite this, it still impacted his weekly finances. He hated having to worry about it. They discussed the cars again, the insurance, it was all becoming very real, very 'imminent' and unavoidable; they were planning on getting interim, provisional insurance once they had got wheels, to speed up the learning process and increase their chances of passing first time. Sonny was quiet, pensive, as he chewed his dinner. At times like these, he always felt he had failed them. A man of his age, in this day and age, earning a little over twenty grand. He'd been earning more at the turn of the millennium – twenty-odd years or so ago – than he was today; the price he paid for being a chef who chose not to work evenings and weekends; he'd already done enough of those to last a lifetime. Not to mention all the Christmases and New Years, the special occasions...

He paid his maintenance still, but what precious little that was left once his bills were paid didn't go anywhere. And his paltry savings from selling the house were all but depleted. He had a grand left, a grand he had been fiercely clinging on to. Which still wasn't enough to significantly help with two cars and two sets of insurance. He hated letting his kids down.

Post-lunch, the twins offered some momentary light relief for Sonny, via a snippet of overheard conversation whilst, pre-occupied, he washed up. 'I should have killed you whilst we were inside,' the marginally elder twin, Bea, said to her sister, Charlotte.

'You tried, but guess what? I survived...' replied Charlotte.

Sonny's identical twin girls had suffered from 'twin to twin transfusion syndrome' – a prenatal condition where one, more dominant twin, is taking too much of the blood supply from the placenta they shared, resulting in one twin, in-effect, starving, whilst the other grows more quickly – they'd had to be taken out early as a result. The girls' typically dark-humoured, teenage take on it made Sonny smile as he looked out of the window. They were very close, and he loved them deeply.

That evening and overnight, the car-money dilemma became Sonny's number one preoccupation. It stuck to him like a stray wet hair he couldn't rid himself of. He wanted to be able to help his kids out. The frustration of it was killing him. A loan wasn't the answer – even if he could get one, he wouldn't be able to afford the repayments. And he couldn't ask his father again; he was haemorrhaging money as it was – the care home cost twelve-hundred a week. It was crazy. Hence, Sonny being long-resigned to any potential inheritance down the line going up in smoke. Story of his life...

Of course, none of this helped with Sonny trying to sleep. Insomnia, that merciless nocturnal beast, had him firmly gripped in its talons. Master and puppet. Tossing him. Toying with him. It had gotten so Sonny dreaded going to bed. Brushing his teeth, knowing it was waiting for him. Some nights Sonny thought he could see that ever-elusive sleep, always tantalisingly out of reach. Sometimes in the form of floating flowers – kaleidoscopic, drifting, shifting flowers. Sometimes it was like the morphing shapes of a Rorschach test. Other times it was like clouds of magic dust in a galaxy, like the dusty, miniscule stars of the Milky Way, as his intrusive thoughts perpetually orbited. And when sleep did finally take him, it was usually morning and the strangled-yeti-cries of the nearby, passing trains would then keep him awake.

But the more Sonny pondered the specific dilemma of the cars, the more a desperate, potential solution kept prodding away at him – Sarah's offer. As outrageous and despicable as it was, it could get him out of a bind – if she was serious that was; maybe she'd still been drunk the next morning when she'd reiterated her offer? He hadn't replied to it, nor had he said a word to Gavin about the whole thing. But how could he find out if she'd meant it? And could he really go through with it if she had? The jacket…

'Well, hello handsome, I didn't expect to see you again so soon. Couldn't keep away?' Although expecting him, Sarah seemed genuinely pleased to see Sonny, as she greeted him on her doorstep. 'Come in.' She was casually dressed, albeit with a full face of makeup, in peach velour loungewear with a hooded top (designer by the looks of it), that made her look more youthful to Sonny.

'Thanks,' said Sonny. He stepped inside, acutely aware of the fresh tang of his aftershave once the door was closed. Had he overdone it? He felt guilty as to why he was wearing it. He'd also showered. Meticulously so. It all seemed so calculated, as if he was a date-rapist or something. But he also felt nervous, with no idea how this was going to play out, if at all.

'Drink?' Sarah said, as they returned to the lounge, the scene of Saturday night's 'incident'. There were the remnants of a half-eaten meal in a bowl and magazines spreadeagled on the coffee table. An empty wine glass too, stained with red wine. 'Sorry, I've been slobbing it all day, the shop's closed on a Monday,' she said, before he could answer. 'Cup of tea or anything, or are you in a dash to get off?' There still didn't appear to be any embarrassment on her part from the other night.

This was it then, thought Sonny. He gulped. 'Erm,

I'll have a quick glass of wine actually.' He was going to need it.

'Ohh!' Sarah said, clearly pleased again. 'Hair of the dog. I'll join you. Red OK?'

Three glasses later, they were still sitting on that squishy sofa, talking, or rather slurring in Sarah's case, her legs tucked up next to her. The wine had gone to Sonny's head too. As if buoyed by this and taking advantage of a lull in conversation, Sarah said: 'You're still here then?' She gave him one of those looks from the previous night. Drunk. Flirty. Suggestive. Sonny smiled awkwardly, not knowing where to look, his heart starting to thump a little. Then, in what was becoming typical forthright style: 'I know what you're here for, mister, and it's not that jacket... It's written all over your face, bless you.' Sonny reddened, so blatantly caught out. He could never fake or hide anything. 'I knew it the moment you came in, reeking of aftershave, you naughty man' – she prodded his leg teasingly – 'And what's more – it's OK.' She took another glug of wine. 'Maybe you're hard up, or maybe you're just wondering what it's like to be with an older woman. Either way, I really don't care – I'm a woman of the world – and as I've already said, the offer still stands...'

Sonny gulped again, tongue-tied, unable to speak. He felt so ashamed. So guilty, confused even, as he stared intently into his glass.

'Come on,' Sarah said, taking his hand. 'Take me to bed, or lose me forever!'

Sonny downed the last of his wine, a good third of a glass, then followed Sarah's velour-clad derriere upstairs. There were embossed letters on it. PLAY. Once in the bedroom, he still couldn't speak. Nor could he look at the bed or the room. Or at Sarah. 'Can we turn the light out?' he said.

Afterwards, Sarah lay with her head on Sonny's chest as it quickly rose and fell. She sighed. Sonny stared at the ceiling, his heart still thumping hard. He was thinking, how did he get out of there? He wanted to go home and shower. He was also thinking about the fact that they hadn't used anything. It hadn't come up; it had all happened so quickly. Should he be worried? She didn't seem to be. But he'd got through it. Just. In the dark, he'd been able to somehow detach himself from the situation. To think of something else. Random fantasies. This had worked up to a point. Enough for him to be able to function. The wine had helped massively too. But he hadn't been able to finish. Sarah had – eventually – and that had been the worse bit. Getting her 'over the line', which had seemed to go on forever. He started thinking about the money; he wanted to 'finish the job', to give her her money's worth, so to speak. Which was a ridiculous and bizarre notion – and situation to be in. And that's when reality kept creeping in. The physicality of what was happening. The mechanics. The physical feel of her underneath him. Around him. But he'd done it – which was remarkable and somewhat shocking to him. He'd surprised himself. He'd always been a relationship-sex kind of guy, never a one-night stand man; he had to feel comfortable and loved by a partner in order to enjoy sex. And he'd invariably hated the first time with a new partner – not that there had been many.

But he still felt so ashamed. 'I feel like I should light a cigarette,' said Sarah. 'Like in the movies. But I haven't smoked in years. Thank you.'

Back home, post shower, Sonny was still reeling from what had happened. He was towel-drying his hair when his phone went off on the bedside table. It was a bank notification: 'MONEY IN | £1000 TRANSACTION. SARAH DEVILL...' That shock-cited tingling sensation immediately flooded his chest and stomach. He clicked on the notification, opening up his bank app. A deposit of one thousand pounds had been credited to his account. It made him feel strange. Very strange. And guilty. Mainly for accepting the money at that juncture, rather than what it was for. He'd clumsily tried to tell Sarah not to pay him before leaving, and that it had all been a big mistake. A momentary lapse of reason on his part. On both their parts. But she wouldn't hear a word of it. She had just made a joke about cash changing hands seeming seedy, and a bank transaction being a much more 'tasteful, modern payment for prostitution'. She seemed to find the whole thing amusing and entertaining, liking the quirky wildness of it, rather than feeling any sense of shame; as she'd alluded to – 'a woman of the world'. But there it was nevertheless. £1000 credited to his account. She had simply written 'THANK YOU' as the reference for the transaction.

Before he could change his mind, and as if wanting quickly rid of the money, Sonny transferred his last grand out of his savings into his current account, then transferred a grand to each of his daughter's. A contribution towards their cars, and also to hopefully help with their insurance too. This made him instantly feel better. That he had achieved something and contributed in a significant way towards his childrens' lives. Relatively speaking anyway. His payment reference for them was always the silly 'DADDY PAYMENT'. A distant part of his brain mocked him that 'SEX MONEY' would have been far more truthful. God, if only they knew. Knew what their father had been up to. He quickly banished this thought. Didn't want to think about the two things in the same breath, letting those two worlds collide. The money was sent, and his bank account was pitiful again. Worse than before without the back-up grand in his savings account. In one hand and out the other as they say. Back to being broke again...

# CHAPTER 5

Monday morning, and the first two poached eggs Sonny dished up were like a pair of perfectly-formed little ghosts, the cartoon, bedsheet-draped kind. This normally augured well for the day, a little superstition of Sonny's. But by mid-morning, he was feeling more out of sorts than normal. The lack of motivation. The tedium. That 'treading water' feeling. The routine of putting deliveries away, the writing of endless 'use by' dates on sticky labels to stick on tubs; Sonny spent the majority of his working day writing use-by dates, it seemed – the scourge of the modern chef – and it was a real drag. People watched these cooking shows on TV, *MasterChef* and the like, and saw some glamorous, creative lifestyle, all about the cooking and presenting of fancy ingredients, but the reality was very different. It was scouring sticky, caramel-like grease off an extraction canopy. The chemicals and grease dripping down your arm and into your eyes. Endless washing up and cleaning. Flattening cardboard boxes. Recording daily, multiple fridge and freezer temperatures. Temperature-probing food and recording the findings. Check sheets. Paperwork. All in aid of providing 'due diligence' to the dreaded EHO and keeping them off your back.

By midweek, this feeling of ennui had grown. Sonny wanted to change his life, both financially and day to day; and a nagging suspicion that the previous weekend's exploits had only exacerbated this. Firstly, the going to the do, the bash. The getting dressed up and anticipation of meeting Sarah, getting to know a new person, a stranger. And then, to his shame, the culmination of the weekend – albeit, that part being an experience he wasn't in a hurry to repeat. But the rest of it, he could certainly handle again – the plus-one bit – and the getting paid. He couldn't deny it had been a buzz. Something out of the ordinary. Something different. Not to mention being able to help the kids out with their cars. The girls had been chuffed to bits with the money he had sent to them and couldn't wait to view their respective motors. Sonny had loved this.

To make matters worse, Wednesdays at the deli for Sonny meant the return of working alongside his second-in-command, a lad in his early-twenties called Rick. Always a trial in itself. Rick meant well-enough, and the arrangement worked well – he covered the weekends when Sonny was off – but boy was he hard work. With more than a passing resemblance to Adolf Hitler and a grumpy, aggressive demeanour – worse when Sonny wasn't there apparently – he'd been secretly nicknamed the 'Fuhrer' by the front of house staff. He shouted rather than spoke, and was never wrong. Nothing was ever his fault. Burning another in a long line of teacakes under the grill for example, he would say, 'Well, I didn't *make* the teacakes, did I? Clearly the bakery puts too much sugar in the mix!'. Accidentally setting fire to things was his trademark – tea towels, pans, food items, even himself. He had singe-marks all over his chef's jackets. You would think he did it on purpose. The amount of times Sonny would hear a yelp from behind and turn to see Rick batting out another fire, shrouded in a cloud of pungent smoke. It shouldn't be funny, but was, and often had Sonny and the other staff in stitches.

Rick also saw himself as an ever-spouting font of knowledge for pretty much any subject that was brought up. A self-confessed 'pedant', labelling himself 'Rickipedia'. Everything was 'Well,' this and 'Technically,' that: 'Well, *technically*, a tomato is not a vegetable, it's a fruit!' or, 'Well, *technically*, 'Stop the Cavalry' isn't a Christmas song, it's an anti-war protest song!' It was exhausting. Not to mention the body odour... Someone had once bought him a deodorant set as a Secret Santa present as a hint.

Post lunchtime rush, glad for some 'Rick-spite' and much-needed fresh air, Sonny headed out the back of the deli for his fifteen-minute break and snap. He always sat on the stairs to the flats above the deli, for the shelter and privacy. There was a launderette next door, and the air was often filled with the intense, baby-soft aroma of a particularly-pleasing combination of washing powder and softener. The fragrance seemed to get trapped in the stairwell. Today was no different. Sonny drank it in; it was somehow comforting and homely.

Taking a bite out of a sandwich, Sonny got his phone out and started to research 'plus-ones', and if there was a commercial call for them. Turned out there was. A huge one. He went down a bit of a rabbit hole with it that ended up in the unfamiliar and murky world of male escorting, which, to Sonny's shock, pretty much meant 'male prostitute' – a man who got paid for entertaining women – or men – invariably incorporating sex. He was adamant he wasn't going to go down that route; last weekend had been enough. Is that what he had inadvertently ended up being for Sarah, a male escort?

According to an online *Cosmopolitan* article, a combination of a relax in morals and taboos, the privacy and anonymity of the internet, along with smartphones and easy bank transfers, had exploded the market. Some agencies even had their own apps for customers. Apps for male escorts! A bit like *Uber*, the dating sites, or *Just Eat*. What did people do, scroll through a menu and choose?! Maybe he should set up his own – '*Just Greet*' or '*Sonny Side Up*'. Again, according to the *Cosmopolitan* article, the escort being interviewed was earning up to three and a half grand a week. *Three and a half grand a week!* The financial possibilities began popping in Sonny's head like popcorn kernels. He was then disturbed by the sound of the kitchen back door opening and Jonah's fat head appearing. Sonny blushed and fumbled his phone content closed. You didn't get a minute's peace, it seemed. 'Sorry mate, you nearly done?' Jonah said. 'Had a bit of a rush, the Fuhrer's getting a bit swamped…'

Just then there was an almighty and shocking bang from the kitchen, almost like a gunshot going off. Sonny and Jonah dashed inside. Gavin and the rest of the front of house staff had already piled into the kitchen. 'What the hell was that?!' said Gavin. Rick was standing by the gas burners of the stove, his face red and slightly blackened. The smell of melted plastic filled the air. He'd left the gas lighter they used to light the gas rings by a naked flame and it had exploded. '*Well! It's not my fault we don't use matches, is it?!*' he said.

# CHAPTER 6

A seed had been sown by Sonny's online foray into the world of 'plus-ones', a seed well-watered by his desire to change his life financially. And that night, with the trials and drama of the working day behind him, he continued his research. After some deeper delving and a couple of bottles of beer, he came across a discreet, locally-based, online agency actually called *Plus One*. Better still, they promoted themselves as a 'strictly companionship' agency. Also, at the signing-up stage, the escorts could choose whether they entertained male or female clients – or both. Thank God for that, Sonny thought. Imagine going on a date with a man? Could he do it? He didn't think he could. Imagine getting someone like Gavin? Imagine *getting* Gavin! Cheating on Paul. Who knew what went on with that guy?

It felt very uncomfortable for Sonny, checking out the agency's website, skimming over the profiles of the escorts, a few of the men posing shirtless, but only a very few thankfully. Still... So much for 'strictly companionship', Sonny thought. The escorts appeared to range from early twenties to white-haired gents in their sixties, covering all bases it seemed. Sonny couldn't help but wonder what their stories, their motives, were. How many of them did it full-time, for example? Some of them looked like fairly normal guys to Sonny looks-wise, not overly-handsome. Some were annoyingly handsome. Others just looked corny. But what did he know?

Sonny was onto the wine now, and he poured himself a second glass. 'Fuck it,' he said. And before he could chicken out, figuring he had nothing to lose, he began to fill in the online application form. It asked for his particulars – height, weight etc. – and a recent full-length photograph. It all felt a bit superficial. As with the dating sites, it made him feel like a commodity, a piece of meat to be examined, picked over and prodded, then chosen or rejected. What if they didn't want him? Did his brittle self-confidence and ego need that hit? He also had to provide proof of identity (passport), a clean driving licence and, if he were to be taken on, a clear DBS check – paid for by himself. Great, all he needed. It all seemed a bit draconian, but the agency's fastidiousness and thoroughness were also reassuring in a way to Sonny. Clearly, they didn't take any Tom, Dick or Harry on. Probably couldn't afford to take the risk in this day and age. They didn't want to be responsible for introducing rapists and murderers to women. They might get sued and prosecuted. Not holding out much hope, Sonny pressed send.

After another restless night, Sonny came round the next morning feeling fuzzy. It hit him almost straightaway, what he had done. Applying for a male escort job. His stomach sank. What had he been thinking? Carried away by alcohol as usual. He briefly wondered if there was any way of cancelling or retracting his application. Probably not. It had been sent and that was that. He groaned and rolled over in bed.

At work that day, he couldn't stop thinking about it. It felt how he imagined it would feel if you applied for a TV game show after a few drinks, like *Who Wants to be a Millionaire?*, as it seemed a good idea at the time and you probably wouldn't get chosen anyway. Then the reality hits – shit, what if I do?

Then, mid-morning, to his utter surprise, Sonny got a reply – an invitation to an initial interview that coming Thursday in Nottingham city centre. At first, he was in shock. Oops, now you've torn it, he thought. But as the news sunk in and the nerves settled, he started to feel better about it. Going about his work, preparing and cooking food, he even felt a little thrill inside. That he had a secret, an exciting reason to exist, and hopefully, ultimately, a chance to ameliorate his financial situation. Imagine getting paid, just for being someone's company for the evening?

In another fortuitous stroke of luck, the interview was scheduled for five-thirty pm (an unusual time by normal standards), which was after he had finished at the deli; he could make it into the city centre for five-thirty, no problem. This would save him the difficult task of having to book time off for it. They were so nosey at the deli, and heaven forbid, he drew any attention to his new plan. Gavin and the guys at work would have a field day. He also briefly wondered if it said anything in his current contract about 'moonlighting'.

In preparation for the interview, Sonny had a much-needed hair trim at the Turkish barber's on the corner. He'd been putting it off due to the cost, but saw this as an investment, a way of improving his chances at the interview. Since when had a haircut become an investment? He turned down the offer of a beard trim, having been duped into that before at an extra cost, opting to do it himself, along with his unruly nostril and ear hairs and eyebrows. He got dressed up for the interview in a shirt and tie and put on aftershave. He felt nervous again. Who was he trying to kid that he would be attractive or appealing to someone? Suit or no suit.

# CHAPTER 7

The Plus One premises were down a side alley off the market square. Unless you were looking for them, you never would have found them – just a small, gold, embossed plaque, announcing the businesses name, next to a nondescript door. That was the idea, no doubt, Sonny thought. Discretion being the order of the day. But it wasn't lost on him that the business must be doing OK to have a designated office. Surely all this stuff could be done online these days?

He stepped inside and found himself in a small, dark foyer or waiting area, with a cushioned bench, a few magazines, a standard lamp and a *Chat Noir* poster. To his left, was another door with an intercom next to it. Feeling nervous, he cleared his throat, then pressed the buzzer. A female voice: 'Stacey, can I help?' Sonny recognised the name from the lady he had been emailing.

'Hi. It's Sonny. Sonny Garfunkel. I'm here for the interview.'

'Hi Sonny. Come in.' She sounded friendly, which was comforting. The door clicked, signifying it was unlocked. Sonny pushed it open.

He found himself in a surprisingly modern, but small office that smelt of lilies, brighter than the comparative gloom of the foyer. Behind a desk was Stacey. She stood to greet him, holding out her hand, whilst quite blatantly looking him up and down. 'Pleased to meet you, Sonny, thanks for coming,' she said as they shook hands, her scrutiny finally resting on his face, his eyes. She had a Claudia Winkleman-style fringe and a nice smile, Sonny registered. He had no idea what she was thinking.

'No, thanks for having me,' he said, trying to sound cool and collected; he felt anything but.

'Sit down, please.'

Turned out Stacey *was* the agency. A one-woman band. This surprised Sonny. She gave him an opening spiel about how being female gave her a unique insight into the market, and what women wanted. 'Five years and counting, speaks for itself!' she said. But she was professional. And convincing. Hard-headed when it came to the business side of things, with a very modern, customer-based approach. There was so much more – a jaw-dropping amount – to escorting than met the eye. Different levels of service and rates. Pre-chosen locations, bespoke plans, special requests... most of which were agreed before the date. 'It's all about matching the right client to the most suitable escort,' Stacey explained, 'and that's where I come in. It all starts with me, the personal touch. Sometimes I can spend hours on the phone with a top-end client, getting to know them, their likes and dislikes, their background, discussing concerns – just *listening* basically. And that's the most important thing I look for in a potential escort. Are they a good listener? Because that is what you will spend most of your time doing. Listening. Unlike some agencies, our service is not about *sex* (she whispered it)' – Sonny breathed a mental sigh of relief – 'They all say they're not – they have to – but most of them are, trust me. Plus One is about companionship. Providing emotional support. Emotional pleasure... Someone the client can talk to – that isn't family, a partner or work colleague – someone that will make them feel good, feel better about themselves, flattered and indulged even. Give them a release. Maybe they're going through a divorce? Maybe they're looking to get back on the dating scene after a long time out? Maybe they just like a good-looking guy on their arm? Whatever the reason, our escorts are not there to judge. Or to cure or pity clients, merely to provide pleasure.' It all sounded well-rehearsed. Stacey paused for a moment. 'So. Are you a good listener, Sonny?' She sat back for the first time, with her hands folded in her lap.

Sonny felt put on the spot. His natural instinct was to say something witty – like, 'Sorry, did you say something?'; an attempt to try and endear with charm and humour. Instead, he opted for the much less risky: 'I would like to think so, yes. My dad has Parkinson's–'

'*Really?*' Stacey cut in. 'I'm sorry to hear that, bless him. So did my mum – she's passed now sadly. How advanced is he?'

'Oh, I'm sorry to hear that too,' Sonny said, but was glad he had inadvertently stumbled onto a connection. He gave a grave and sympathetic smile. 'Eighteen years and counting.'

'Gosh, that is quite advanced.'

'Yeah, guess so. It's the movement – or lack of – that's

the main problem, the flat spots. He gets frozen, seizes up... as full well you would know.'

'Yep, unfortunately I do. And the shakes.'

'Ah, my dad isn't really a shaker as such. Save for a little in his hands. Never has been fortunately. A *shuffler*, but not a shaker. He's always been pro-active with his meds–'

'I think they're all shufflers, aren't they?' she laughed. 'And don't start me on the meds! Slaves to them, aren't they? You're not his main carer, are you?' A faint trace of concern crossed Stacey's face as she said it.

'No,' said Sonny quickly. 'He's in a home. A care home. I'm his next of kin, I do a lot for him – errands and that – but I don't 'care' for him as such, you know, the day to day...' Stacey leant forward to scribble some notes for the first time, again concerning Sonny. 'I'm a chef,' he added. As if to make a point.

'Ah, yes, a chef – I remember from your application. You don't work weekends?'

'No,' Sonny said again quickly. 'Nor evenings. Strictly nine to five – well, eight-thirty till five, to be precise.'

'A chef that doesn't work evenings and weekends, now there's a rare thing.'

'I know. I'm lucky,' said Sonny. 'It's a deli, you see, daytimes only, and I've got a good second-in-command. Plus, I've been there, got the T-shirt with the long, unsociable hours...' He didn't want to come across as lazy. Meanwhile, Stacey made some more notes, that fringe of hers practically covering her whole eyes, as she bent her head. She looked up again, brushing it aside with her pen.

'So, back to why you're here. We've digressed... Why *are* you here? Tell me a bit more about yourself.'

'Why am I here? Now there's a question... Same as anyone, I guess... ultimately, to earn some extra money, then, who knows? See where it goes... I'm free most evenings and weekends, have no kids living with me... sick of being skint! I went on a date the other night, you see, a blind date – as a plus-one – I'd never done it before, as a favour for a friend – my boss, actually. It was with an older lady, not old, old, just older than myself – ten years or so – and, well...' Sonny paused, realising he'd started a story he didn't want to finish; or that might make him look bad – rinsing lonely, single ladies for money by sleeping with them. 'I kind of enjoyed the experience, it went well – I think! She said she enjoyed it anyway, asked to see me again, in fact.'

'And did you?'

'No,' he lied. 'Well, only to collect my dinner jacket – I left it at her house.'

'Her house?'

Shit, thought Sonny, blushing. 'We had a coffee afterwards – just a coffee!'

'It's alright,' Stacey, said, laughing again, genuinely amused at Sonny's uncomfortableness and eagerness to please. 'What you get up to in your spare time is your business – within reason! You're not even on our books yet... talking of which, let's get down to some brass tacks. I'm sure you want to know what's involved, financially and otherwise, what our cut is, for example...'

'Sure, said Sonny. He could feel his heart start to thump harder in his chest. It seemed to have crawled up his windpipe, closer to his throat.

'So, as an agency, we hire out our escorts at different rates for peak hours and off-peak hours. Peak being your weekends, off-peak being your daytimes – no good to you currently – weekday nights etc. For peak social companionship, our maximum charge per hour is £200, for peak intimacy, we charge £350.'

'Peak intimacy?' asked Sonny, still trying to get his head round those jaw-dropping figures.

'Physical intimacy. Contact. Holding hands, touching, kissing, cuddling, massages...'

'I thought you said–'

'I only said massages' – she held up her palms – 'Ladies love a massage...' Sonny blushed again, suddenly looking unsure. 'Are you finding this conversation uncomfortable?' Stacey said.

'No,' he lied again.

Stacey looked at him from under that fringe for a while before continuing. Shit, thought Sonny. *Don't blow it! Don't blow it!* 'Off-peak you're looking at £150 social companionship, and around £275 for intimacy. Payment is made directly from client to escort via bank transfer, in advance, at the time of booking – so it is out of the way and everyone knows where they're at; gone are the days of escorts turning up for a booking and clients handing over a dubious envelope of cash that then needs to be counted prior to the evenings' proceedings beginning. All too stressful and, quite frankly, in bad taste. Sets completely the wrong tone. Once you've been paid, we, the agency, collect our booking fee from you. That's how it works. Oh, forgot to say, should have said so earlier, you'll need to register as self-employed of course, in case that's a problem, all our escorts are... we don't employ anyone ourselves and it saves you getting done by the tax man – providing you pay your taxes, of course! You keeping up?' Sonny had gone quiet, scribbling mental notes. There was just so much to think about, so much involved. Would it affect his other job, for example, registering as self-employed? He'd never considered this, or done it before.

'Yep. Just!' he laughed.

'Good. I know it's a lot to take in. Where was I? Oh, yes...booking fees... As for our cut, we take 30%, which you will find is a pretty good deal, considering the groundwork we – I – put in. Advertising, marketing, getting you a profile set up – you have seen our website, haven't you?'

'Yes.'

'Good, so you've seen the profiles. All very simple. Just a first name – you can use a false one if you want – some of the guys do, some don't, figuring, 'my pics on there anyway, if you know me, you know me!' A client will see your surname when it comes to payment time anyway – unless you set up a designated business bank account.' This was another thing Sonny hadn't quite thought about in detail. Worrying. 'One nice pic. Basic info. Height, weight etc. No fake bullshit – 'Simon likes swimming, pub quizzes, has three children and is partial to a 'cheeky Nandos'. From experience, the less *personal* info our clients know about their chosen escorts, especially to start off with, the better. Makes it easier for them – they don't want to think they might end up canoodling with someone's husband, or if it's a younger guy, someone's son for example – who's then going to return home to his cosy family afterwards. They want to think that that guy is *their* guy for the night or weekend, and no one else's. Make sense?'

Sonny nodded. It was all so much to take in. 'Once a booking has been made, the escort is then provided with an overview of the woman – or man – they are going to be entertaining. How in-depth this is depends on the level of the booking. But every little helps. We also encourage our escorts to keep abreast of topical stuff, read, watch stuff, anything relevant etc., especially in the case of top-end clients, *especially* if you are going to be spending a whole weekend with them. I mean, to put things in perspective, we can – and do – negotiate up to two and a half grand, plus travel, for twenty-four hours. You could do just one of these a month and earn a decent living! How you go about that side of things, your availability, the duration of your services, weekdays, weekends, is up to you. The escorts dictate this themselves. We just promote you and book you out, handle the admin stuff. So, back to the point, we don't think a little light reading, a little bit of advance 'homework', is too much to ask! Other than that, your job is just to turn up, look presentable – impeccable personal hygiene a must! Smell nice and, well, *be* nice!' Sonny laughed. 'Now, being totally up front – I always am, you'll find that with me – these figures I have mentioned are for our top-end earners – seasoned guys that have been with us for a while, guys with a string of great reviews under their belts – we actively encourage these, anonymously of course, they give the clients' confidence in choosing, and help the guys to earn more dosh.' Gosh, imagine being rated and reviewed, thought Sonny. What would they say? Great arse, but breath smelt and conversation was somewhat disappointing? 'Guys the clients have specifically chosen, or are used to,' Stacey continued. 'Having said that, we don't allow a client to make more than six bookings with the same escort – this is to discourage feelings or attachments developing. Anyway, back to the figures... a potential newbie, such as yourself, *should* you be successful, would be starting on around two thirds of that. So, let's say peak social companionship, you're not up for the intimacy at this juncture – they all say that to start off with by the way–'

'No, I'm really not,' said Sonny. 'Honestly.'

'They all say that, too. Till they see the potential earnings and bookings they're missing out on.' It was almost as if she was pushing it, the more he earned, the more she earned, Sonny figured. But still, he wasn't ready for that, not at any level, not yet anyway, once had been enough – he hoped it wouldn't scupper his chances. 'Peak social companionship would be charged at around the £135 an hour mark, minus our cut' – she tapped into a large calculator on her desk with her pen – 'So, around ninety-five quid an hour to you, rounded up. How does that sound?' She looked up from under that fringe, straight at Sonny.

'That sounds amazing!' he said, smiling broadly, unable to help himself. 'When can I start?'

'Thought you might say that. Slow down mister, I want to do a little role play with you first, all part of the interview process – don't worry, strictly verbal, you don't have to massage me or dress up as a Nazi and spank me!'

By the time they had finished, Sonny's head was reeling from all the information he had been given. The stuff to digest and think about. The interview had been intense. Like a crash course, a behind-the-scenes insight into a whole, new world, a whole, new industry.

Stacey watched Sonny leave, carefully and consideringly again, as he left her office and re-entered the real world of pavement, city and traffic outside.

# CHAPTER 8

The following day, Friday, Sonny spent all day on tenterhooks. Stacey had concluded the interview by enquiring when Sonny could potentially be available from, then informing him she would let him know if he had been successful by the close of play on Friday. This had left Sonny somewhat in turmoil. What was 'close of play' to an escort agency? Midnight? Did they ever close? Why hadn't he asked? There was so much riding on it financially for him. Almost unprecedented. It would be like a low-key winning of the lottery, a life-changing event, for him. He'd nearly called Stacey on his lunchbreak to put himself out of his misery, but somehow managed to refrain, figuring he could blow any chances by appearing pushy and, well... desperate.

As the day dragged on, Sonny kept checking his phone at increasingly shorter intervals. At one point, it rang, making him jump. He grabbed it, but it was his father. 'For fuck's sake!' Sonny said, pissed off at him, especially for ringing at work. He ignored it. About five minutes later his phone pinged with a message; again, he grabbed it – the agency? No, a notification telling him he had a new voicemail. It would be from his father; this is what he did, leave rambling voicemails, sometimes ten or fifteen minutes long, forgetting he was on the phone, just talking. Sonny sighed in exasperation.

Shift finally finished, Sonny headed towards the downstairs cellar behind the bar to get changed. It was clear-down out front. Gavin was sweeping the restaurant floor, his balding pate shiny with sweat. Jonah was behind the bar, polishing glasses. Michelle was on barista. 'Anyway, this one guy,' she was saying, 'can't even remember his name – Tony, Terry?' She paused dramatically, cloth in hand, from cleaning the coffee machine, whilst making a big deal of trying to remember. 'Anyway... he'd get blind drunk, clamber on without so much as a by your leave, then fuck me like an animal.' Sonny cringed inside and quickened his pace, scooting past her.

'Gosh, that sounds hot!' said Gavin, stopping sweeping the floor to lean on his brush and listen 'Tell me more!'

'God, no' – Michelle pulled a face – 'It was gross. Sometimes I'd be asleep, and then I'd wake up and he'd be at it. Rutting away.'

'Technically, I think that's called 'rape', Michelle...,' said Jonah, deadpan as ever. 'Who was this guy, Ted Bundy?'

'Who cares?' said Gavin. 'You still got his number?' He let out his trademark, ear-splitting, Charles Hawtrey laugh, like the gurgle of a plughole.

Now at the cellar steps, Sonny shook his head and scurried downstairs to the sanctuary and silence of the locker room.

Sonny walked home from work, that familiar, depressing Friday night feeling – a lack of another social weekend stretching ahead – dragging him down. But worse than ever, as he hadn't yet heard from the agency. What had made him think he was going to? He shouldn't have let himself hope. Hope that things were going to change. Duty-bound, he reluctantly listened to the voicemail his father had left. The old man wanted to go out on the 'buggy' tomorrow; this is what he called his mobility scooter. Sonny kept it in his garage, along with his weight bench and weights. And also could Sonny print him some bank statements off and get him some photo paper for his printer... so on and so forth...

Sonny hung up and trudged on, carrying his holdall. Was this it? he thought. Was this going to be his life? Work, and being at the beck and call of his father? He tried to gee himself up, telling himself there was still time left in the day yet to hear from Stacey. He also tried to remind himself that he ought to count himself lucky that he didn't have to work evenings anymore. He could be counting those dead afternoon hours down till he had to go back to work that night. To sweat his arse off in a kitchen, cooking for people out enjoying themselves. Really living. He shuddered at the memory of it. He needed a drink. Sonny always needed a drink – just for different reasons. Sometimes it felt as if life was just one, long list of excuses to drink. Because he was stressed. Because he was bored. Because he was happy. Because he was down. To reminisce. To forget. Because he was watching a film. Because a certain song came on. To get him through the week. Because it was the weekend. Because he deserved it. Just... because...

He'd lost count of the times he'd tried to stop, or at least to cut back, especially at the turn of the year, the perennial, 'New Year's resolution', but he could never make it beyond a week – and even that was a struggle. Addictions were like weeds. You rip them out, try to get rid of them, but they just come back. And as sure as bread leaves breadcrumbs, before too long, Sonny would need a drink again.

Sonny was on the way to the care home, riding his father's mobility scooter; the last thing he wanted to do on a Saturday morning. Having not heard from Stacey the previous night, he had resigned himself to the fact he had been rejected and dealt with it the only way he knew how – by drowning his sorrows. As usual, he'd got a little carried away, stayed up too late, and was feeling hungover. Why did he do it to himself?

Embarrassingly, he could even vaguely remember shouting a defiant 'fuck you!' meant for Stacey, to the empty house, scaring Buddy, who'd hissed in response and then skedaddled. Probably retiring somewhere to plot his revenge.

Being spotted riding the scooter around town was a regular occurrence that Sonny had got used to. Even some of the customers from the deli bantered with him about it: '*I saw you the other day!*' or '*Can I jump on the back next time?*' In all honesty, Sonny normally found it amusing in an anarchic way – the looks he got from passing cars, or the tuts of disapproval from pedestrians – but not this morning. And what he *really* didn't find amusing was the prospect of chasing his father around town on the thing. Again, a regular sight, and a source of torment and entertainment for his father. He would go rogue on Sonny, choosing his own route – normally the totally wrong one – then pretend he couldn't hear Sonny calling him to stop. Once he'd even cranked the speed up to maximum, shouted, 'Ten! Seeya!' at Sonny over his shoulder, then razzed off – at a sedate 8 miles per hour... He'd better not get up to his tricks this morning, Sonny thought. I just might let him drive off into the distance until he is truly lost. Then let's see how he fares.

At least it was a fine, warm morning, the first real one there had been that year. Spring had finally showed her petals. It was as if everything had suddenly woken up, including the sun. The day felt different. Smelt different. Breeze in his hair, Sonny checked his reflection in one of the wing mirrors of the scooter. In the harsh, unforgiving reflection of broad daylight, he could see too many fine red veins on his face and nose, the tell-tale signs of too many years of drinking. Sonny hated them. He was ashamed of them.

Then, as a not-so-welcome diversion, the sudden appearance of a police car appeared in the same mirror behind Sonny. That was a first whilst he was out on the scooter. He gulped, automatically feeling as if he had done something wrong, which he did every time he saw the police. But he wasn't breaking a law, was he? The car passed him by slowly. Very slowly. As hard as Sonny tried not to look – continuing to stare straight ahead as the scooter trundled along the pavement – he couldn't help himself. The police car was exactly level with him, two officers, a man and a woman in the front seat, leaning to gawp at him. Shit, he wasn't technically 'drink driving' was he? Not knowing what else to do, he gave them a friendly wave and nod. The officers shook their heads, then, thankfully, continued on their way. Sonny breathed a huge sigh of relief.

Happy to see the departing bobby car, Sonny arrived at the care home and swung into the carpark for the second time that morning. His father had chosen the linear walk, a disused railway cutting on the outskirts of town, as their chosen destination that day. This meant Sonny had already had to transport his push bike to the home in his car to ride on. The whole thing was a rigmarole, a total pain in the arse for Sonny, but being a haven for butterflies and wildflowers, the linear walk was his father's favourite local haunt. The old man had become obsessed with spotting the elusive and much-fabled 'grizzled skipper', a rare butterfly that apparently had been spotted down there at some point or other. Probably *never*, thought Sonny. It might more aptly have been named the 'Scarlet Pimpernel'.

On Sonny entering his father's room, as had become familiar, his father was in the bathroom, using the toilet. He seemed to spend most of his life in there. In his defence, he was probably trying to empty his bladder before the outing – sometimes, most frustratingly, he wouldn't even think of it till Sonny got there. But what his father forgot was how long it took him to go for a pee from start to finish. Sometimes up to half an hour on bad days. And then he wouldn't be able to do his trousers or belt up afterwards and Sonny would have to do it.

Sonny could see him through the partially open door, only the back of him, thankfully. He would be peeing into one of the plastic urine bottles he used. Otherwise, it got messy. 'Dad, I'm here!' Sonny shouted through the door, then went to sit on the bed and wait, hoping he wouldn't be too bloody long.

A few minutes later, Sonny heard his father humph, then matter-of-factly state: 'Half a pint,' before the collected urine was sloshed into the toilet. Sonny grimaced. His father was obsessed with measurements and capacities, proud of his supposed ability to gauge them, then state his approximations out loud. He could often be seen clutching his tape measure, another thing he ferreted away lest it got stolen, muttering, 'four inches' or 'sixty mill,' having just measured something. Sometimes he would even measure things with his feet, a sofa he was passing in the care home corridors for example, tottering unsteadily, placing one foot in front of the other. 'Six feet,' he would say. 'My feet are a foot long.' He meant his shoes. Sonny had often wondered if his father was autistic, increasingly so of late. Old age and the Parkinson's seemed to have brought out what had already existed in him.

Sonny heard the toilet flush – that was something at least – then another five minutes or so of groaning and taps being turned on and off. He shouted through the door again to ask if his father needed any help. No answer. Another five minutes later and the old man finally shuffled out of the bathroom with his frame. 'Oh, you're here,' he said bad-temperedly, spotting Sonny. 'Why didn't you say?'

'I did. And I asked if you needed any help.'

'What?'

'I said 'I did,' and asked if you needed any help.'

'My belt? I've done it already. No thanks to you.'

Leading his father across town on the scooter, him on his push bike, was as stressful as always for Sonny. There was so much to negotiate. Too-much traffic, with everyone in a rush. Too many pedestrians. Half a dozen pedestrian crossings. And then there were the adverse cambers of the pavements, the dips and slopes – all hazardous, potentially fatal, to an elderly mobility scooter rider; they'd had some close calls in the early days. Then there were the obstacles, the bins, the dogs, the cycle barriers, the narrow pavements with their dreaded stretches where the dips in the kerb for crossing disappeared for what seemed like forever; miss one and you could end up going miles out of your way. Sonny had never noticed or considered these things until he'd experienced them through the eyes of a mobility scooter rider. Over time, he'd learnt the best path across town, navigating and leading his father with vocal directions and arm gestures. Keeping the traffic at bay like a lollipop man whilst they crossed the many side road openings. Sonny wouldn't have trusted anyone else with it, nor would he have wished it on anyone else. All in a day's work for him...

It was always a relief to finally reach the entrance to the linear walk without major incident (even though, the longest part of their ride out hadn't yet begun). And on doing so that day, Sonny took the opportunity to stop and check his phone. Again. Still no word from Stacey. He sighed.

Cycling slowly next to his father, they soon hit the sheltered, natural tunnel and open banks of the railway cutting. The slices of intermittent sunshine, the flitting birds. The sweet pot pourri of surrounding flora, a myriad of heady scents. Such a welcome contrast to the noise and stresses of the town. His father was in his element there. He came alive, taking it all in. Stopping annoyingly too often to point out and name every plant and butterfly. But there were more people than butterflies that day. It was still early in the season. The trail was surprisingly busy, though. The sun bringing everyone out. Young couples. Dog walkers. A nerdy-type fellow with a satchel with an audio version of what sounded like *Robot Wars* coming out of it. A gaggle of sweaty D of E kids crowding past them with rucksacks strapped to their backs. Most of them respectful of the old man and his scooter. Along with the wonderful smells, the kids reminded Sonny of his own childhood, where he'd always been outdoors and everything had seemed magical. Well, most things...

Sitting astride his bike, waiting for his father who had stopped again, it set Sonny's still drink-fuzzy mind to pondering. How at some point the magic had gone out of the world. The wonder. An innocence and belief that there was more. As a kid it had been so simple, the magic was everywhere. Constant. Waking up in the morning with no more immediate concerns on your mind than trying to decipher what the wood pigeons were hooting about. Nothing but another day of wonder and adventure ahead. Treasure maps. Making perfume from rose petals for girls at school. *Top of The Pops. Super Mario* and Nirvana. Cartoons and after-school TV. The smell of sweet shops and chlorine from the swimming pool that seemed to cling to you for days. Roald Dahl books from the library. Long, hot summers and proper winters made for sledging. Cosseted in the woolly blanket of an 80s and 90s world... Even his father's rages and beatings had been a form of comfort in their regularity and familiarity. You got used to them, just 'padded up' when it looked like one was brewing. He figured everyone got them.

Being the long-awaited firstborn, Sonny had been named after Santino 'Sonny' Corleone, Vito Corleone's eldest from *The Godfather*. It was Sonny's father's favourite film. The man had been obsessed with it. Maybe he'd wanted his own version of a mafia family, with a brood of tough guy sons ready to carry on the tradition of keeping things and people in line by meting out physical punishment. In that respect, Sonny felt he had always disappointed his father, failed to live up to his namesake. And being a very rural, white, East Midlands upbringing, rather than his name being something to instil fear in the schoolyard, it had been more of a source of ridicule. It didn't help that the family surname was Garfunkel. Cleverly but cruelly changed by some kids to Sonny Carbuncle. That or the, '*hey, Sonny, where's Cher?*' or, '*hey, Garfunkel, where's Simon?*'. The stillborn birth of Sonny's brother a year or so after he, himself, was born put paid to any ideas of a big family anyway. Sonny's parents never tried again after that. Sonny's mother, now long-passed, had never really gotten over it.

Sonny's phone pinged, disturbing him from his reverie. Stacey? No, a bank notification telling him his account was overdrawn and that charges would apply. It cranked up the financial pressure. 'For fuck's sake,' Sonny said under his breath. Up ahead, a couple had stopped with binoculars to stare at a bank. The old man, now slightly in front of Sonny, pulled up next to them, figuring they'd spotted something significant. He scoured the bank where they were looking, craning his neck. 'Grizzled skipper?' Sonny said, pulling up too.

The couple turned round to look at them both. 'Hello. No, more's the pity,' the man said. 'Probably a bit early for it.' Just then the butterfly they'd been scrutinising took flight and headed further down the bank.

'Comma,' the old man said in his barely audible voice.

'I think you're right,' the man said.

'I know I'm right.'

'You know your butterflies then?' the lady said. The old man looked pleased. He proceeded to tell them about the ledger he kept – a huge tome documenting decades' worth of butterfly habits and numbers. He only ever really spoke to people about butterflies, or else just didn't bother. As usual with his father, conversation was difficult – they struggled to hear him, and he them. Often Sonny would end up translating for him. But today Sonny couldn't be arsed and left him to it. The job rejection had really knocked him for six. Left him flat. A familiar empty ache inside that this was it, all life had to offer.

Sonny's phone quickly pinged again with another notification. This time an email and his heart jolted. He pulled his phone screen down, not daring to hope. But hoping anyway. To his absolute amazement, it was from the Plus One Agency – or Stacey to be precise. The subject line read: CONGRATULATIONS. And then visible below: *Dear Sonny, apologies for not getting this over to you last night – long story! Anyway… congratulations!*

*Subject to a DBS check, your application to join Plus One was successful (smiley face). Please read our terms and conditions, and if happy sign the contract (both attached) and return asap...'* What the hell? Sonny's face lit up and he nearly toppled off his bike. He couldn't believe it. Greedily, despite his environs, he opened up both attachments to read them. His father and the couple were still talking – his father could talk for hours about butterflies.

Scanning the contract, there appeared to be quite a surprising number of stipulations and company policies in it, things to adhere to – you couldn't express extreme views on anything whilst entertaining a client for example, racism, immigration, sexism etc. There was also a 'three strikes and you were out' policy, whereby if you turned down three consecutive jobs that were within your remit – preferred hours, sexual preference etc. – your contract would be terminated. This was something to bear in mind. Also, you couldn't have, or be in, a relationship with any client. Again, if this was not adhered to, your contract would be terminated. Despite the numerous stipulations the contract contained – none of which at first glance Sonny had a problem with – it was all written in a personable way that Sonny liked. It was very 'Stacey'. He could practically hear her voice. And the whole thing was all professionally done and presented, amazing again to Sonny that it was the work of one woman. But should he have been surprised, given Stacey's professionalism at the interview? She signed off with a reminder about the DBS check. Nothing would happen until she received that. Then she would be in touch again to organise getting a designated profile pic. done.

Both attachments read, a sudden surge of emotion welled up in Sonny, taking him by surprise. He took in a shaky breath, as tears smarted his eyes. He very well might just have got his wish – his life changing dramatically for the better, and for good – just like that – and he had instigated it. Made it happen. Him. No one else. It was too long a time since something good had happened to him. The agency's acceptance of him had also made him feel wanted. Normal.

Sonny and his father said goodbye to the couple and carried on along the trail, Sonny in a much brighter state of mind, bordering on euphoric. Unlike the sky that was starting to darken, worrying considering he hadn't brought his father's coat with them. Sonny mentioned this as they stopped to take his father's meds, swilled down with some orange juice. It was his father's turn to look glum. No sunshine normally meant no butterflies. 'But we haven't reached the graffiti bridge yet,' he said. This was their normal turning point. After that, the terrain got too bumpy for the scooter, causing his father to look as though he was riding a 'boneshaker' rather than a mobility scooter. 'There!' he said. He'd spotted something and was pointing with a bony, hooked finger to the nearest bank. Or maybe he was just stalling. Sonny followed his finger, but couldn't see anything.

Handing back the bottle of juice, the old man clambered down off the scooter, stooped and unsteady on his feet. Holding his back, he vultured and shuffled over to the bank. A lurching duffel bag of angles. Sonny sighed, watching, but hoping for his father's sake that it was the elusive grizzled skipper. 'Humph,' his father said. 'Just a bumble bee.' His poor eyesight playing tricks on him.

'Come on, Dad, let's head back, you'll miss the tea trolley at the home.' Really, Sonny was keen to get his father dropped off so he could get back to his own home and sign that contract – and to get that DBS check done. How did you even do a DBS check?

This had to wait a little longer than Sonny liked; to his exasperation, once back at the care home, his father insisted on them having a game of chess before he left. 'You're always in some desperate rush to get off!' he said. 'It would kill you to stick around for a bit.'

'Oh, don't be so dramatic, Dad. I spend half my bloody life here.'

There was a knock at the door and a member of staff appeared. He was a relatively new one, a cheerful, young Chinese chap called Wai (pronounced 'why') whose main job appeared to be the dispensing of the tea and cake. A job he took great pride in, Sonny noticed. 'Hello, Mr. John,' Wai said to Sonny's father. 'Would you like some tea?' He gestured to his trolley.

'Sorry?'

'Would you like some tea?'

'Tea? I've not had my lunch yet. Why would I want tea already?'

Wai looked at Sonny, confused. 'A cup of tea, Dad. To drink. Not *food* tea. Do you want a cup of tea?' Sonny said.

'Oh. Yes. Go on then. But no cake. They're always trying to stuff you full of cake to shut you up. As if it's the answer to everything!' Wai looked at Sonny confused again.

'Yes, he'll have a cup of tea, please. Sorry.'

Wai nodded and smiled, clearly pleased he could prepare a cup of tea. 'You want sugar, Mr. John?' he said.

'Why does he keep calling me Mr. John? It's *John!* Not Mr. John.'

'Ah, sorry, Mist–, John. My apologise.'

'It's like me calling you Mr. Sun or whatever your name is. What *is* your name?'

'Sorry?' Wai looked at Sonny.

'He wants to know what your name is. Sorry,' said Sonny.

'Ah, Wai.' He gave the old man a big smile.

'Why? Cause I want to bloody know, that's why. You know my name.'

'Yes, Wai.' He smiled again, pleased.

'Why what? Stop bloody grinning at me. Is this guy a comedian?'

'His name's Wai, Dad. *Wai.*'

The old man looked at Sonny gone-out. 'Are the both of you stark raving mad?!'

Tea dispensed, Sonny and his father commenced a game of chess. Butterflies aside, chess was Sonny's father's other main passion. He had numerous chess boards and sets, some intricately hand-carved by the old man himself in his former life as a joiner. The board they were playing on that day, also hand-made by his father, was made from purple heart wood. He pointed it out every time.

Sonny had an interesting relationship with chess. As a child, forced by his father, he had been taught the rudimentaries of the game and then been enrolled in chess club at school. He'd soon lost interest, preferring more physical pastimes. But, again, due to his father, the game had been a constant in his life ever since. Sonny had flirted with it over the years, taught his kids it, and had a game with his father now and again, but, unsurprisingly, had never beaten him. Ever. Not even come close. This was perhaps one of the reasons Sonny had never enjoyed the game and shied away from it. His father had always been ruthless in his thrashing of him, not giving an inch or any form of concession.

But since his father had been 'infirmed', with nothing else to do, they had been playing regularly and Sonny had been increasingly enjoying the game. Probably, because their games were becoming a lot less one-sided. He even looked forward to playing. Chess had become an oasis of calm, where his roving mind and thoughts would leave him alone for a bit, and he could just concentrate on the game. His next move. It also passed the time with his father and shut him up for a bit. Nothing but them, the board and the pieces.

As a result, Sonny's game had been vastly improving. Which, in turn, made him want to do better, play better. Of late, he had even started giving his father a run for his money. The games were lasting longer, sometimes up to forty-five minutes. And instead of merely staving off the inevitable defeat, Sonny was actually applying a bit of pressure and getting his father in trouble a few times. Sonny was unsure yet as to whether his faring better was due to a decline in his father's game, or due to the improvement in his own. He liked to think the latter. However, he had noticed that the longer he kept concentrating himself, not slipping up, his father would invariably do so, and that's where an opening would appear. A chance to pounce. It was a war of attrition.

Sonny didn't know any of the formal, opening sequences of play or anything, but he had started to develop his own tactics. His own strategies. One of them being to protect every one of his pieces, sometimes with up to three other pieces. Another was to attack to defend. Instead of getting bogged down with what his father was doing and trying to stop it, he would plan his own attacks. His father would then have to give up what he was doing to defend.

That day was no different, but even more so, and Sonny sensed something starting to build. Despite having to sacrifice the majority of his own major pieces in the process, he'd kept the upper hand and picked off his father's one by one. Usually, his father would find a way to turn the tide, a tactic to turn the game around, but not that day. He'd got his father on the ropes with nothing but his king left. Sonny only had his king and a pawn left himself, but he mercilessly advanced, move by move, his heart walloping in his chest. *This is it!* he thought. *I've finally got the old bastard!* His father was pinned into a corner with no move left. Nowhere to go that wouldn't put him in check. 'I've got you!' Sonny cried. 'I've finally got you! After all these years... You've nowhere to go... I've won! It's checkmate.' It was his lucky week.

'No, it's not,' his father said.

'It is. You've nowhere to go!'

'I know, but it's not checkmate. It's a draw.'

'A draw! How can it be a draw?' He felt cheated.

'Because I'm not currently in check, but have no legal move left. It's a stalemate. Ergo, a draw.'

'Don't 'ergo a draw' me, you cheating old git!' Sonny said, incensed. 'Why didn't you tell me this? Did you know this was going to happen?' His father laughed. 'You did! That's why you ran for the corner! How am I meant to win if I don't know all the proper rules? You kept them from me.'

'Well, you know 'em now.'

Sonny left in a huff.

# CHAPTER 9

Sending his bank account plummeting a further twenty-five pounds into the red – don't think about it; it's another investment, he told himself – Sonny applied for a basic, online DBS check. It took forty-eight hours for the certificate to come back. Wasting no time, Sonny immediately forwarded it to Stacey.

It took another trip into the city, back to Plus One's fragrant, lily-scented 'HQ' to get his profile photo done. Again, to his surprise, this was something that Stacey did entirely herself, setting a sort of mini photo shoot up in the office, with some basic, but nevertheless surprising, kit. Lights, tripod, screen etc.; she really was a 'one-woman band', with a seemingly never-ending set of skills at her disposal, Sonny thought. Prior to the shoot, she had also given Sonny some specific instructions as to what to wear, also some further grooming advice. She seemed to have strong visions and ideas for every aspect of the process, an attention to detail. Sonny liked this, it took any indecision or rather *decision-making* out of his hands. He certainly wasn't used to thinking so much about what he looked like, or what he wore. It was alien to him. Nor was he used to so much attention; and he found the shoot itself, being scrutinised and photographed whilst posing, very embarrassing and awkward.

Stacey, meanwhile, seemed to enjoy the whole thing and find it amusing. Her idea or 'vision' for him was of a simple, black and white, top-half shot in a white shirt and dinner jacket, with some neatly trimmed 'salt and pepper' stubble. 'Some guys can still look a million dollars in any old T-shirt and scruffy jeans,' she said. 'I see you more as a rough diamond that scrubs up rather well. But approachable. Trustworthy. The helpful guy next door...' Sonny didn't know whether to take this as a compliment or insult.

Either way, the photos that came back were nothing short of a revelation. And, again, embarrassed Sonny. He'd never seen himself look like that. He didn't even *look* like that! Whether it was the soft lighting she had used, some sort of filter, or Photoshop, he didn't know. But he looked younger, less creased and wrinkled, any of the blemishes he hated so much erased. Surely this was only setting a client up for disappointment? He decided to use his real name for his escort profile. Simply, 'Sonny'. As Stacey had said, if someone he knew spotted him, they would know it was him anyway (despite the misleading photo). Plus, Sonny couldn't imagine being called something else during a date – David or Mark for example. It would make him feel like even more of a fraud and confuse things. What if he didn't even register they were addressing him?

And then it was the waiting game for Sonny. Waiting for his first booking to come in. He tried to keep busy, keep healthy. Drinking less, working out more, more than he had in a long time. Getting the job at the agency had inadvertently done wonders for his motivation in that respect – he had something to strive and work for; as opposed to him thinking, why am I bothering? Who's going to see me anyway? Also, for his state of mind. A much-needed fillip. He was even sleeping a little better. Not dreading going to bed so much, for the feral terrors night times brought.

Heeding Stacey's advice, he kept himself well-groomed, ensuring all visible hair departments remained neatly trimmed and in check. He had a lot to live up to – that photo for a start. But along with his recent haircut, all of this new-found attention to his personal appearance didn't go unnoticed at work. They were used to Sonny rolling in a little pink-eyed most mornings with his overlong hair slightly askew. So, he got several new uncomfortable ribbings and enquiries as to if he'd got a date or a secret girlfriend. Attention he didn't need. Especially from Gavin. Sonny had tried to keep a low profile with him since the awards bash. Still feeling ashamed about the whole thing, the 'transaction', Sonny couldn't help wondering if Gavin knew. How close he and Sarah actually were, and if she had spilled the beans. If she had, Gavin certainly wasn't letting on, which would suggest he didn't. He was the 'king' of gossiping, rumour-mongering and backbiting. Or should that be queen?

Another change that didn't go unnoticed at work – they noticed everything, it was like working in a fishbowl – was how Sonny had started listening to the radio in the kitchen, as opposed to listening to his own music. Again, he'd been heeding Stacey's advice, trying to keep abreast of the news and current affairs more; he'd also been putting the TV news channel on at home in the background when pottering about. He was taking this whole escort thing seriously. He had to. He needed the money. It was exciting though, having a secret, he just wished he had someone to share it with.

And then it happened. The email came through, whilst he was at work. His first booking enquiry. Marked 'CONFIDENTIAL'. He felt like a secret agent, like 007, getting a mission. He hadn't got round to reading it properly yet – it was mid-service and he had checks on – when his phone rang. An unknown number, so he ignored it. A few minutes later his phone pinged with a notification, telling him he had a new voicemail message. It had to be connected to the email, surely? he thought. What if it was Stacey? He'd never stored her as a contact; she mainly communicated through email, as it was more discreet. He was itching to find out, and to read that email. His first assignment!

The second Sonny got a break from the checks, he let Rikipedia know he was nipping to the loo and took his phone with him. Sitting on the loo with the lid down, Sonny listened to the message. It was Stacey: *'Hi Sonny, Stacey here! Sorry to call, I know you're probably at work, and I wouldn't usually, but wanted you to know I have just sent you an email with your first booking enquiry. Exciting!'* she sang. Sonny smiled. *'Didn't want it ending up in spam or something. Anyway… Have a look at it when you get chance, the details and date and that, and if you're happy, send me a confirmation via the form and we'll get it booked in. She's a regular of ours, nice lady – bit eccentric! Middle-aged, ease you in gently! Spotted your pic and thought she'd try you out, seeing as you're a newbie, I've been bigging you up. Lol* (she actually said, 'lol'). *So, yeah… let me know. Oh, and if you've got any questions or want to give me a call, I'm here till late. Usually am. That's it, I think. Yep. Ciao for now. Biy-ee!'*

Sonny's heart was pounding as he hung up the phone. He suddenly felt very nervous and under pressure. She'd been 'bigging him up', she said. Why? Who was he? Who was he that knew anything about entertaining a woman for the night? A deli-chef currently hiding in a toilet. Especially a woman who had money – which she must have to be spending it on male escorts. Regularly. A regular, she said. And the thought of her checking him out… It made him squirm. He wasn't that type of guy, didn't have the confidence. What was he letting himself in for? *What had he been thinking?* His hands were shaking a little as he checked out the email on his phone.

The booking was for that coming Saturday night. He was free, which was a relief. Who was he kidding? He was always free, save for when he was seeing the kids or his father. A Ms. Susan Emerson. 46. He was booked in for four hours, for 'dinner and companionship'. Ah, sounds straightforward enough. Sonny felt suddenly relieved and calmed down a little. He was just starting to work out what he would earn when the toilet door handle rattled. Sonny nearly dropped his phone in fright. It was always happening, people trying to get into the toilet when you were in there – there was only one toilet and no 'engaged' sign on it. He quickly got up to wash his hands and put the dryer on.

Abdicating the loo, an old lady was waiting outside. She looked surprised to see him. A chef in full gear. 'Sorry,' said Sonny. He always felt uncomfortable exiting the toilet with someone waiting. Grubby. Preparing food and toilets were an unpleasant combination to think about. At least he hadn't actually been.

'Oh, no problem,' the lady said. 'Sorry myself,' then, *'They really ought to invest in another loo,'* she whispered.

Back in the kitchen, hoping he hadn't been too long and feeling guilty at what he'd been doing, Sonny realised he needed the loo.

# CHAPTER 10

Shortly after his first booking was confirmed, Sonny received his very first payment and earnings as a male escort. A milestone moment. And one that a couple of months ago could never have been fathomed or foreseen. The amount was five-hundred and forty pounds. A ridiculous sum of money, and hard to be believed. Way more than he earned in a week at the deli. And he hadn't even done anything yet! The graft and hours he would have had to put in to earn that cheffing...

He then had to remind himself that this was nowhere near the real figure he was going to earn for this one job. Stacey's cut was yet to come out – thirty-percent – and then there was the taxman's cut of what was left, around another thirty-percent, taking national insurance into consideration (he'd been doing some research). Bloody taxman! After doing some calculations on his phone, his actual take-home pay was going to be around two-hundred and sixty-odd quid – less than half the original amount. This was somewhat sobering for Sonny. And disappointing. He then gave himself a reality check –

that was still two-hundred and sixty quid for four hours work. He mustn't forget that. Tax was tax and there was nothing you could do about it.

As he had promised himself he would religiously do, once the booking fee had come out of his bank, he transferred thirty percent of what was left to his linked 'everyday saver' account. This he was going to use to pay his taxes; he'd read it online that this was the best way to do it, so as to avoid getting into trouble further down the line. Whilst he was doing so, he couldn't help but notice the original payment that had been made to him by the client, S EMERSON. It struck him as bizarre that this lady, Ms Susan Emerson, was paying money into his account when she didn't even know him, or had never met him. It was very trusting, and she must trust the agency. She must also have a crazy amount of disposable income. What did she do for a living? How often did she do this? Sonny thought. Stacey had said she spent a 'shedload of money' with them. A CEO or something. No pressure then... He consulted the info. on her Stacey had sent.

There wasn't a great deal to go on really. It was only four hours at the end of the day, Sonny supposed, they weren't going to be spending the weekend together. Susan was into the theatre, the arts, movies... She liked 50's music, flowers and Italian food. Well, some of them he could talk about. He liked watching movies and was a huge Buddy Holly fan – it didn't get more 50s than him – and Johnny Cash, especially the early Sun Records stuff. This gave Sonny an idea...

It was Date Night. Sonny was standing outside a fancy Italian restaurant on West Bridgford high street with huge, fragrant hanging baskets outside it and an awning with its name on it. *Cortile*. He'd googled the place, the menu and prices, and was glad he wasn't paying. He was a good ten minutes early, as he didn't want to be late, or to keep his client waiting. Despite it being a warm evening, he was wearing a smart-casual, sky-blue shirt and navy suit, with tan-brown brogues. But no tie; he felt that would be going too far. With the money he had received upfront, he had invested in some new clothes specifically for his escort work. He simply couldn't have turned up in his old, well-worn gear that he'd had for years. He rarely bought clothes, and when he did, they were usually from Primark – or *Primarni* as he jokingly called it. His latest items, he had up-scaled to Next for.

He wanted to look the part – the role or 'persona' that Stacey had created with her profile picture of him. He took pride in his work, whatever it may be, and felt the client deserved it. His first one – and a loaded CEO, no less. He was genuinely concerned that she might be disappointed at the difference between the real-life him and his profile photo. He couldn't wait, however, to get inside and get the jacket off. The last thing he wanted to do was to start sweating, with glaring dark blue patches under his arms, a worryingly likely scenario given how full of nervous energy and anticipation he felt. A walking cocktail of chemicals, hormones and pheromones. This was such a bizarre scenario for him. A galaxy out of his comfort zone.

In his slightly clammy hands, he was clutching a bunch of flowers that he had bought for Susan, at his own expense. He had no idea if this was the done thing, or how the gesture would go down. But he had taken a gamble on it; it had felt natural to him and he had wanted to do it, especially given how Susan supposedly loved flowers. Annoyingly, he'd had to go out of town for them, given the local flower shop was owned and ran by a lady he'd been paid a thousand pounds to have sex with; it was a crazy thought that that incident had pretty much directly led to this new, secret life for him.

Talking of which, he was also clutching a pay as you go phone that Stacey had given to him during a first-date pep talk and preamble the previous day. In a scene reminiscent from *Breaking Bad* or *Better Call Saul*, Stacey had pulled the phone out of a drawer of many – and random chargers – in her desk, rummaging amongst them first like Saul Goodman himself from the shows. 'You're gonna need this,' she said to him. 'It's yours to keep now, for communicating with clients. Never give 'em your own number. We won't either. It's for organising meet-up times, locations, or if you or the client are running late for example...' She pulled a few chargers out, trying them to see if they fit the phone whilst she spoke. 'Ah, there you go. That one fits, you can have that too. Just see if it's got any life in it...' She pressed the phone on, flicking her fringe aside, whilst she waited. The phone emitted a start-up melody. 'Aah, it's got some juice left. And credit. Good.' She then flicked through the phone for a minute, concentrating, with an increasingly puzzled and distasteful expression on her face, whilst Sonny watched and waited. Then she shook her head and fringe in what looked like surprise or disbelief.

'Everything OK?' Sonny said, intrigued as much as anything.

'Yeah, no, yeah... makes sense now. Burt had this phone last – an ex-escort of ours. He was a piece of work... I'm just gonna delete these...' Sonny presumed she meant messages. Or what if she meant pictures? His mind boggled. After a further few minutes of pressing various buttons and more head shaking, without volunteering any more information, Stacey then pulled some sanitary tissues out of a pack on her desk. She proceeded to clean the phone with one, whilst pulling a bit of an icky face, and then her hands with a fresh wipe. Sonny watched her in fascination. He found her increasingly interesting. What was her home life like? Did she have a partner or husband? He couldn't imagine her being anywhere but behind that desk in her office. Sitting at home on a sofa, eating pizza and watching *Coronation Street*, for example.

'Right, clean,' she said, passing him both the phone and charger and smiling. Yeah, in more ways than one by the sounds of it, Sonny thought, taking them from her. What had Burt been up to? 'It's your responsibility to keep it topped up now – we don't pay for everything! So, it's in your interest to keep your usage to a minimum – and obviously stick the costs down as expenses on your tax returns. Tax deductible, you see...'

Leaving the office and walking back to his car, Sonny had once again felt a little like James Bond; this time having just been given a new bit of tech or gadgetry for his mission. Maybe the phone had secret powers? Infra-red or white-hot lasers? Maybe it self-destructed once the mission was completed?

He consulted the same phone, a very basic outdated Samsung, that was now in his hands as he stood outside the restaurant. Five minutes to seven, it said. He scrolled through his messages. There were a few already from Susan. Introducing herself, where to meet and when etc. Stacey had said this would happen, it was normal, exactly what the phone was for. It helped the clients feel more at ease in the run-up to a date, to communicate directly and build up a bit of a rapport. Susan put kisses after all her messages, Sonny noticed. He had kept his replies professional and short, *sans* kisses. He didn't want to give a wrong impression from the outset. This booking was strictly social companionship as far as he was concerned.

There were a couple of messages from Stacey on the phone too. She'd surprised him with a good luck text, prior to him leaving the house. She really must live these dates herself, Sonny had thought. Or was it just because he was a 'newbie', as she called it, he was getting special treatment? Sonny had replied *'thanks'*. To which she had then replied, *'just checking you've got the phone and that it's working'* Did she ever switch off? Sonny had put a 'thumbs-up' in return.

He put the phone in his pocket, set to vibrate, just in case. Two phones on his person, that was a first; he felt like a drug dealer. 'Come on,' he said quietly to himself, looking both ways up and down the high street, a busy thoroughfare bursting with eating and drinking establishments, some of them with chairs and tables outside, especially on the opposite side in the sun. He so wanted to get the meeting part over and done with. He was also dying for a drink. To quell the nerves.

He was driving, so it had been torture not necking a beer or two before he'd come out. Plus, he couldn't turn up with booze on his breath. That would be highly unprofessional. And off-putting.

Maybe one or two with the meal early doors wouldn't hurt? This was the demon on his shoulder. Again, he didn't know what the etiquette with this was, presuming Susan was a drinker herself. Did clients prefer you to have a drink, to join in? Or was it frowned upon? He wished he'd asked Stacey – or googled it. There was so much information out there on the net, forums and advice for escorts, it was crazy.

Susan hadn't said how she was arriving, on foot or in a car. She certainly wouldn't be on a bus! Sonny thought. He'd parked in a nearby carpark, which he'd had to pay a couple of hours for; it was free after eight. More expense. But it was another thing he could put down as business expenses. Must keep the ticket, he reminded himself. Ooh, that's a point, he could put the flowers down as expenses too. He was glad he had kept the receipt.

Just then, a very new, shiny black jag with private reg plates pulled up at the kerb not far from him. It had blacked-out windows. Quite intimidating and impressive. This is it then, Sonny thought. Got to be her... He half-expected a be-capped chauffeur in white gloves and proper regalia to step out and walk round the car, as if letting some dignitary out. Instead, the nearside rear door opened and a lady in large sunglasses stepped out.

Sonny hadn't quite known what to expect physically with Susan. Possibly, subconsciously, someone similar to Sarah. This lady was plump, short, and had what looked at first glance like dyed black hair. It was done in the style of classic Elizabeth Taylor. In fact, what with the sunglasses, expensive-looking clothes and handbag, you could say her whole image was modelled on Elizabeth Taylor. 'Thank you, Ian. See you later. I'll buzz you what time!' she said to the driver. Her voice was quite shrill, older-sounding than she looked. Then she closed the door. 'Right!' She headed towards the restaurant, clutching her bag and phone.

Sonny tensed, smiling, waiting to be spotted, the flowers clutched behind his back as a surprise. But as the lady approached, prodding at her super-sized phone, she all but walked past him, head down, straight towards the restaurant door. How had she not spotted him when she pulled up? It was a bit shady under the awning, he supposed. 'Excuse me. Susan?' Sonny said, putting his hand on her arm.

'Oh, goodness!' she said, turning to him and clutching her phone to her chest. 'I didn't see you there. Miles away. Bloody phones! Sonny, I presume? My *date* for the evening?' she said theatrically. A first glimpse of her mentioned 'eccentricity'.

'Yes, I'm Sonny. Pleased to meet you. And these are for you.' He produced the bouquet of flowers from behind his back.

'Oh my. How sweet of you! Thank you! I can't remember the last time I got given flowers on a date. *Some of them are animals, you know,*' she whispered. Then she went to kiss him on both cheeks. Nearly crushing the flowers in the process. It was a little awkward and unexpected and Sonny blushed. 'Mmm, you smell divine,' she said, pulling away. 'I was just messaging you actually to say I was here. But we did say to meet outside, didn't we, come to think of it?' She talked quickly, almost nervously, Sonny thought. 'And here you are...' She looked him up and down with eyes hidden behind those impenetrable shades. 'Hmm... you looked taller on your photo... handsome though...' Sonny felt uncomfortable being commented on physically, and grimaced a smile. 'Shall we?' She gestured towards the door.

'Allow me,' said Sonny, rushing to open it for her. Where had that come from? he thought. He wouldn't usually be so formal.

'Aah, a gentleman,' she said.

They walked inside, Susan leading the way. Immediately, they were greeted by a smartly-dressed maître d – what was the Italian for maître d? – in a white shirt, black waistcoat and pinny. 'Susan!' he greeted her enthusiastically. A camp, Italian Richard. E. Grant. 'Ciao Bella.' They kissed on both cheeks.

'Vincent! How is my favourite waiter?' Gay waiter, thought Sonny. Vincent almost definitely was.

'All the better for seeing you. And, *oh my gosh!* Are those flowers for me!' He held his hands to his chest in feigned surprise.

'No, these are from my date for the evening. This is Sonny,' Susan said, turning to him. 'Isn't he gorgeous?'

'He most certainly is!' said Vincent. 'Delighted to meet you, Sonny.' He nodded in Sonny's direction.

'And you,' said Sonny, wondering just how many different men Susan had come here with. It all seemed so routine. So cosy and familiar.

'Now. Can I show you gorgeous people to your table?' said Vincent, plucking a couple of giant menu cards off a stand.

'You most certainly can,' said Susan. 'But first, would you be a dear and put these in water for me? I would hate for them to wilt.'

'Of course. *Anna!*' Vincent called to a nearby waitress. Then he gave her some instructions in Italian in a markedly less obsequious manner than the one he used with Susan. The girl took the flowers from Susan, beamed silently, then scurried away.

The restaurant was busy as they walked through it. Sonny felt slightly uneasy, as if they were being watched. As if everyone knew what their game was. What *he* was. It was a strange feeling. He felt a trickle of sweat drip down the side of his torso, underneath his shirt. Shit, don't do that, he thought. To his surprise, they were led straight through the restaurant and out the back to a pretty, spacious courtyard with more hanging baskets and outside seating. Some of it under cover. Sonny had no idea it existed. Kind of explained why there was no seating out front. 'Alright here?' Vincent said, showing them to a table.

'Perfect,' said Susan. Sonny didn't get a say, although he was glad of the tables tucked-away location (not that anyone knew him in West Bridgford). He also didn't get chance to pull Susan's seat out for her, as he had intended to. Vincent was upstaging him. He waited for Sonny to sit down, then dished out the menus, Susan first. 'Signora. And for you, Signor.'

'Thank you,' said Sonny.

'Now, can I get you lovely people something to drink whilst you peruse the menu?'

'You know me, Vincent. And what I like. I'll have the usual, please – with two glasses.' She leant across the table. 'Please tell me you are going to share a bottle of fizz with me, not like some of those other dreadful bores.'

Sonny laughed uncomfortably. How was he supposed to say no to that? Even if he'd wanted to. 'Well, I am driving…' he said; he wanted to come across as responsible. 'But one glass won't hurt, I guess.'

'Bravo!' said Susan, sounding relieved, and Vincent laughed. 'You'll have to get an Uber next time, though, you silly sausage. Life's too short.' 'Next time?' thought Sonny. Bit presumptuous. But he figured he must have made a good first impression. Early days, though. Time to fuck it up yet. 'Could we also get some of those delightful olives whilst we wait, please? The mixed ones.'

'Of course,' said Vincent.

'Oh, and a bottle of sparkling water for the table, please.'

'Perfetto.' Vincent bowed and minced off. Bet she tips a fortune, Sonny thought.

They perused the menu. The prices were eyewatering. Sonny was always interested in other establishment's menus. For ideas, but mainly just to scorn them. A chilled drinks stand was placed next to them by Anna. Prosecco was poured with ceremony. Another waiter provided the water and olives; all very attentive, but Sonny wasn't a fan. He liked to be left to it. He didn't like someone else meting out his alcohol share for a start, or deciding when he drank it. 'Are we ready to order yet?' the waiter said, hands clasped behind his back.

'Not yet dear, give us five minutes,' said Susan.

'Of course.' The waiter nodded his head and disappeared. Sonny couldn't help but note again how Susan was happy to take the lead, to make the decisions for them. This was clearly her date. She was paying for it after all. Although this was a new scenario for Sonny, he was happy to let her do it. 'Mmm, a cold glass of fizz and olives are my weakness,' she purred, spearing a plump, glistening khaki-green one with a cocktail stick, popping it into her mouth.

'Me too,' said Sonny. 'I love olives.'

'Well, there's a good start,' said Susan, 'Something we have in common.'

They sipped their fizz whilst continuing to peruse the menu. Sonny was reading the words, the dishes on offer, but not really registering them or coming close to making a decision. He was too distracted, somehow too aware that he was there to do a job, to provide his *own* service – entertaining and providing companionship for his client. Come on, he said to himself. Earn your money. Speak. 'This courtyard's lovely,' he said, taking a break from the menu and sitting back. 'I never even knew it was here.'

'*Cortile*,' Susan said.

'I'm sorry.'

'*Cortile*.' She removed her sunglasses and gestured around her with them. 'It means courtyard in Italian, hence the name of the restaurant.'

'Ah. Well, I never knew that.' Sonny felt foolish. And uneducated. Must do better, he scolded himself, taking another gulp of fizz. He studied Susan for a second as she continued to read the menu. It was strange seeing her without her huge sunglasses, seeing her whole face for the first time, as if a mask or disguise had been removed. She had small eyes, a little too close together and squashed by plump, dimpled cheeks. Sonny was glad he didn't find her attractive. It made his job easier, took away any element of sexual tension on his part, any awkwardness in trying to impress. 'Do you speak Italian then?' he tried.

'A little. Mainly restaurant stuff!' she laughed.

The waiter returned and hovered hesitantly. 'Are we ready to order now?' Sonny looked at Susan, waiting for her lead. Meanwhile, the waiter took it upon himself to pour them both a glass of sparkling water. Sonny accepted it silently without protest, although he'd never *got* sparkling water. It had always felt too harsh on the throat to him, painful even. His ex used to drink gallons of the stuff.

'I think so,' Susan said. 'I'll have the...' A mild panic set in for Sonny whilst Susan ordered, the pressure of not having decided yet, and he consulted the menu again. For all the world he wanted to order the pepperoni pizza, another weakness of his and his 'go-to' in an Italian restaurant. But he didn't want to appear any more uneducated, anymore heathen than he already had, especially considering he was a chef. To make matters worse, Susan had opted for a starter too, more decisions...

'And for signor?' Shit, out of time, thought Sonny.

'Erm... I'll have the bru*schetta* to start,' he said, emphasising the correct punctuation of it, the *sk* sound – he heard Susan make a purr of approval in the background – 'followed by the pollo pesto.' He resisted the urge to negotiate adapting the dish with the waiter to his own taste, as was his chef's wont. It was hard not to for chefs, knowing how easily something could be added to or left out of a dish when something is freshly prepared to order. But chefs were the first ones to moan and kick up a fuss when they were on the receiving end of it, easily taking precious offence at their dishes being altered.

'Of course, grazie.' The waiter took the menus from both of them. 'And will we be wanting any wine with the meal?'

'Ooh,' Susan narrowed her already slitty eyes further and looked at Sonny, as if weighing the situation up. It was a torturous question for Sonny. Of course he would be wanting wine – he could demolish a bottle in no time – but he couldn't bloody have any! This was going to be a new thing for him going forwards, it went with the new territory. 'You're driving, aren't you?' She said it almost as a leading question, as if testing the water, to see if he had changed his mind already. Sonny nodded soberly. 'Better not,' Susan sighed, 'Don't think I could tackle a bottle of wine on my own as well. Could get messy. Let's see how long this fizz lasts, we can always have another glass or two if we run short.' Sonny felt a mixture of relief and disappointment. He was so pathetic, so easily led when it came to alcohol. Hence, he rarely put himself in situations where he couldn't drink. The waiter topped up both their glasses of fizz – probably in order to get them to purchase more alcohol. Then he disappeared with the wine menus.

The pair of them left alone again, Sonny tried a swallow of fizzy water to combat the urge of immediately reaching for his prosecco. As expected, the innocent-looking liquid was like fire on his throat. He winced, then hiccupped.

'I know it's awful, but I hate that you know,' Susan leant forward again and whispered.

'What, sparkling water?' said Sonny, confused.

'No, silly! The mispronunciation of bruschetta. And other food items. It's one of my bug bears.'

'Oh, right! Sorry,' Sonny laughed. 'Yeah, me too.' And he really did. 'Niçoise, that's another one, you get it all the time at the deli, all manner of weird pronunciations – nickoisy, nickaswayze...'

'Oh God, yeah I bet.'

'Ciabatta, that's another one – siyabatta!' They both laughed. 'Jalapenos and fajitas, both with a 'J'...'

'Oh my!' said Susan, genuinely tickled. 'And not forgetting the wines. Rioja with a 'j'... Chianti and Chab*lis*, both with a 'ch'...' They both laughed. 'Well, that's another thing we have in common then. Here's to the correct pronunciation of food and drink items. Cheers!' She held her glass out to be clinked.

'Cheers!' said Sonny, clinking her glass, then taking another gulp. The prosecco tasted good. Too good. Cold and dry. He speared another salty olive, still smiling, and whilst doing so he realised he was having a good time. Hmm... Who'd have thunk it? And he was getting paid for it. Crazy.

'So, you're a chef I hear,' Susan said, out of the blue, rubbing her sunglasses then donning them again. 'How marvellous. Tell me all about it. Where do you work?' This was unexpected. So much for being anonymous, Sonny thought. How did she know? Stacey, no doubt.

'Oh, it's nothing exciting, I'm afraid,' he said, playing it down. 'Just a deli in town, better hours you see.' He tactfully avoided saying where. Or which town. The last thing he needed was the risk of Susan turning up at his work. They would have a field day. And it would potentially blow his cover.

'Yes, that's the downside to cheffing I suppose, the hours. You still get to cook fresh food, I hope?'

'Oh yes, it's all freshly prepared.' This was a boring subject for Sonny, but he had to remind himself of his role and what Stacey had said. About entertaining. About listening. This probably *wasn't* boring for Susan. An insight into an industry. So he continued: 'So many of them don't, you know – prepare everything fresh – especially the chains. Even the Jamie Oliver ones.'

'No!'

'Yes, seriously. I know a guy who worked in one, a decent chef. Said all you had to do was snip open bags of pre-prepared sauce and reheat them, Bolognese and that, that came from a central factory kitchen. Soul-destroying. He could only hack it a month...'

'Well I never,' Susan said, genuinely taken aback. 'Well, I certainly won't ever be eating in one of them again!'

'Oh, I wouldn't worry. You can't anyway. They're all closed down now. Went bust.'

'Really? Well, good riddance, I say. No wonder! Ah, here's our starters. *Freshly prepared* starters. Marvellous! No bag-snipping here I hope, Luca?'

'Sorry?' the waiter said. 'The ancini for Signora and bruschetta for Signor.' He placed the dainty, pretty-looking dishes in front of them. They smelt divine, exuding mellow garlic and the tang of balsamic vinegar.

'No bag-snipping. Like Jamie Oliver.' Susan acted out a lively demonstration with scissor-fingers.

Luca laughed. 'No, no snipping here. Only our bags of fresh Arabica coffee beans!' And they all laughed.

'Oh, they do make a divine coffee here.' Susan groaned and rolled her eyes.

The evening went on. Sonny gave her a brief resume of his long cheffing career, touching on his past awards and stints in Michelin-recognised establishments. Susan was impressed. Clearly, a real foodie. Sonny made sure he asked about her career too, showing an interest, and letting her talk. She, likewise, considered her own profession a dull subject. Boring board room meetings and trying to hit unrealistic targets mainly. The main courses came and went, and so did the bottle of Prosecco. Sonny had been desperately trying to make his last to the end of the meal, but it was nigh-on impossible. Despite his best efforts, he'd still managed to put away two-and-a-half glasses – more than he'd intended to – to Susan's three-and-a-half. And they still had dessert – which Susan had insisted upon, as the tiramisu was also 'divine' apparently – and another two and a half hours of the date to go yet.

Sonny was now in a dilemma. He was still at the stage where he, albeit foolishly, considered himself OK to drive. Yet, he'd had enough alcohol to get a taste for it and to crave more – exacerbated by the fact that Susan was ordering herself another glass of fizz to have with their desserts. Two-and-a-half hours without alcohol, watching her drink, thought Sonny's already-affected brain. The alcoholic voice in his head: You'll be alright for one more… Every hour that passes, some of it leaves your system… And then that old classic: Have a strong coffee before you leave, that'll negate the effects… 'I really shouldn't, but go on then, I'll have one more glass with you,' he said.

'Ohh, bravo!' said Susan again. Clearly unbothered or too tipsy to care that Sonny would now definitely be drink-driving.

Their prosecco arrived whilst they were waiting for their desserts, brought to them by Vincent himself no less. 'And how are we doing? Everything to our satisfaction, I hope?' he said.

'Simply wonderful, my dear!' said Susan. 'The crab ravioli was to die for, melt in the mouth. Send my compliments to the chef – not this one.' She put her hand on Sonny's arm familiarly, giggling. Sonny blushed.

'Ah, we have a chef amongst us!' Vincent said. 'And does Chef also approve?'

'The food was lovely,' said Sonny. 'Really good, thanks.'

'Fabulous,' said Vincent. 'Enjoy your desserts.' He minced off.

'Cheers!' said Susan again, picking up her fresh glass. She appeared to be enjoying the evening.

Buoyed by the fillip of a fresh, cold glass in his hand and remembering Susan's interests, Sonny steered the conversation round to the subject of music, specifically 50's music. Susan really came alive at this point, more animated, her face flushed. Shiny and more youthful. The veneer of a CEO dropping to reveal a young girl inside. Conversation was easy. Enjoyable. They waxed lyrical about various artists and recordings, including the Buddy Holly biopic and what a fab job Gary Busey did, how he should have won an Oscar for it. Their desserts arrived, and were equally as scrumptious as the rest of the food. Sonny was impressed. He had the cheesecake and Susan the tiramisu. They tried each other's desserts, like a couple already at ease with each other.

'Mmm... tiramisu – Italian for 'pick-me-up',' Sonny said, spooning some of the creamy trifle into his mouth.

'Ooh, well I didn't know that!' Susan said, impressed. 'Makes sense, though, all that coffee and alcohol.'

'Looks like that's one apiece then.' And Susan laughed.

By the time their desserts had been cleared, their glasses were two-thirds drained and they were both three-thirds full. Sonny was also now bordering on tipsy. 'Coffee?' Susan said.

'I don't think I could,' Sonny said. 'I'm stuffed.' Although he'd planned to, to help with the drinking, as with sparkling water, he'd never really got that 'drinking coffee with a meal' thing. Something from another generation, it seemed to him. The only thing you should drink with a meal was wine. Unless it was a curry of course, then cold lager was the order of the day. Preferably Indian.

'Me too. Hmm...' Susan consulted her watch. 'We've still got a couple of hours to go yet. I've still *got* you for a couple of hours.' It was the first time she'd alluded to it out loud. Drawn attention to the fact. That she had 'hired' him. A paid-for date. Almost a commodity. He wasn't going anywhere yet. 'You can't drink anymore...' She let it hang, as she had before. As if testing the waters again, to see how far Sonny would go. Sonny looked at what was left in his glass. A mouthful. Shit, two hours, he thought. 'We could always go for a bit of a walk if you fancied it? A bit of fresh air. It's a fine evening and there's a nice park nearby.' There was. Sonny knew it. And it was a nice park. Although filled with a kid's play area, and he didn't really fancy a two-hour walk. 'Or we could always head back to mine for a bit...' Again, she let it linger. Was she suggesting something? Sonny thought. It was hard to read her behind those huge sunglasses. Did she normally do this with her dates? Get them drunk, weakened, vulnerable, then lure them back?

But Sonny was neither weak nor vulnerable. Nor was he *that* drunk yet. Yet the alcohol was still *in* him. In his blood. Swirling round his system. Agitating and stimulating him. And he wanted more. Selfishly, he wanted more. That was his overriding priority. He swallowed what was left in his glass in one gulp. He had to make a decision. He was at a Rubicon; once crossed, he wouldn't be able to turn back. Part of him also wanted to please, to pull out all the stops on his first date. To get a five-star review. He checked his inside jacket pocket, feeling his 'trump card' there. The DVD he had been saving. He'd wanted to see how the night had panned out first.

'Do you live nearby?' he said.

'Oooh.' Susan made a surprised, pleased noise. 'Not far. The Park. A ten-minute drive across town, depending on traffic. What were you thinking?'

The Park, that figured, thought Sonny. The most exclusive postcode in Nottingham. A gated community. 'Do you have a DVD player?' he said.

'A DVD player?' She sounded even more surprised. 'Never use it, don't even know where the control is, but, yes, I do own a DVD player. Now you've got me intrigued...'

Sonny cleared his throat. Suddenly feeling a little foolish. 'I've brought us a movie to watch, just in case. I mean, we don't have to, it was just a thought...'

'Oh my, it sounds like a wonderful idea.' She put

her hand on his. 'You have no idea. No idea just how wonderful.' Her voice wobbled then, and a surprise sob came out, shocking Sonny. Instantly sobering him. Where had that come from? Up until now it had mainly been laughter and jokes. Banter and confidence. Susan sniffed and put a pudgy finger under one of her dark lenses, presumably to wipe away a tear. Sonny watched her, feeling sorry for her. It reminded him of Sarah somehow. 'I'm sorry,' she said, sniffing again and reaching into her giant bag for a tissue.

'No, don't be silly,' Sonny said. He put his hand on hers. It happened naturally. He wanted to comfort her, to make her feel better. Not just because it was his job to that night. But it was as Stacey had said, he was quickly coming to realise this – these women, despite all their money, their trappings, were lonely. Emotionally vulnerable. It sounded bad, but desperate even. They must be. Why else would you pay money – a lot of money – for company, for companionship? For sex? It made him feel responsible. More mindful. Not because of the money, but because of Susan's wellbeing. And he didn't know how the weight of this new responsibility sat with him. Like how the offer of watching a movie together had so affected her. How he had been so responsible for someone else's mood and happiness. He wasn't used to that, especially not of late, being single. 'I mean, you don't even know what film it is yet,' he said; an attempt at lightening the mood.

And it worked, for Susan laughed. 'Not a horror, I hope. I can't watch horrors. Not living on my own as I do. They give me the jitters and I can't sleep. Think someone's in the house and is going to stab me in my sleep.' She shuddered.

'Don't worry, it's not a horror,' Sonny said, relaxing a little again. 'I think you'll like it. We just have one problem. My car. I've probably had too much to drink already to drive (bit of an understatement). I'll probably be OK in a couple of hours to get home. And I do need to get home, I've got an early start tomorrow.' He lied, wanting to get that in there before she got any ideas.

'Say no more.' She put her hand up, suddenly becoming animated again, as if snapping out of the sudden funk she had slipped into. 'Ian will sort it.'

'Ian?'

'My driver. He can pick us up, and then he can also drive you back home later in *your* car. Sorted. That way you can have another tipple whilst we are watching the movie – I can see that you're dying for one. Another thing we have in common. Takes one to know one...' She nodded, presumably winking behind those shades.

'Oh, no. I couldn't possibly expect him to do that, to go to that trouble. It'll be late. And how would he get home himself afterwards?'

'Darling, it's his job. He's used to it. And a *cab* of course – don't worry, I'm paying for it! I won't hear another word about it.' It really was another world, thought Sonny. 'Luca! Sorry, Luca!' Susan waved her hand. 'Can we get the bill please?!'

Susan's house was even grander than Sarah's. On another level. Sonny had never actually entered The Park before. Not many had. It was strange driving through the gates, so exclusive, exciting even. And, again, a different world from Sonny's two-bedroom rented house in Bingham with its shared yard of fake, plastic grass and stink of fried bacon. Ian dropped them off without any fuss, then disappeared. Clearly used to this sort of thing. God knows where he was going to in the interim, Sonny thought. What did he do, just sit on a street somewhere? Go home? Where did he live himself?

They settled down to watch the film with large glasses of quality red wine. Not the Aldi merlot Sonny was used to. It was ages since he'd had a decent glass of red. To Sonny's pleasant surprise, Susan had a cat. A long-haired one called Spag-Bol – it was the first proper meal the cat had tucked into apparently. 'Ooh, she likes you!' Susan remarked, as the cat made a beeline for Sonny's lap and sat there contentedly, purring and being fussed. Unlike Buddy, who was still mistrustful of Sonny, never mind strangers; anyone would think he beat him.

The film, *Walk the Line*, the Johnny Cash biopic, was a sensation as always – Sonny must have watched it a dozen times. The relationship between Cash and his father reminded him of his and his own father's. How Cash could never please him, never earn his respect, yet always wanted to. How it ate away at him. How he felt like 'nothing' in his father's eyes and turned to pills as a release. And the scene where he hits rock bottom and June Carter says to him, 'You are not nothin'. You are a *good* man,' – every man needs to hear that now and again – always got to Sonny and brought a lump to his throat. But not that night. It was Susan's turn to turn on the waterworks (again). The film – sad, joyous and romantic in equal measure – had her crying on numerous occasions. She put her head on Sonny's shoulder at one point and Sonny let her. Having never watched it before, it was a revelation to her. 'Couldn't have been more perfect,' she said. And 'Could she borrow it to watch again?' Despite them polishing off the bottle of red between them, Sonny wasn't so drunk that he didn't wonder if this was an excuse for them to see each other again (she could just watch the film online). But he couldn't think that far ahead at that juncture. She could keep the DVD for all he cared, the disc had no sentimental value. He too could watch it online any time he liked.

'Gosh. We've ran over by an hour,' Susan said as they were waiting for Ian to arrive (the film was two hours-plus and a surprise round of cheese and biscuits hadn't helped).

'I'm sorry?' Sonny said, a little woozy and done-in after the effort of the evening. Too many sleepless nights.

'The time. I only booked you for four hours. I'll have to transfer you some more money.'

Sonny looked at his phone. They had. It was gone midnight. He had lost track of time, and the fact that he was there doing a job. Bloody booze. Interesting it had happened, though... Was she being serious about the money?

'Don't be silly. You can have that one on me,' he said. 'Let's just keep it between ourselves – Stacey'll want her cut otherwise!'

This tickled Susan and she laughed out loud. 'She would as well! You are a true gentleman. The very cherry of charm. Thank you.' Some lights flashed through the hallway window. 'Oops, that'll be Ian. 'And then she looked serious. A little sad. A distinct change, so quickly. Like earlier. She leant up and kissed Sonny on the cheek. 'Seriously. Thank you,' she said. 'For tonight. For everything. You have made a lonely lady very happy. Even if just for a short while... Goodnight Sonny.'

Sonny said goodnight and left. Remembering his jacket. And both his phones.

# CHAPTER 11

Sonny was awakened by the familiar scratching at his bedroom door. Bloody cat. What time was it? As he fumbled for his phone, he depressingly became aware he had a hangover. Not just the usual woolly head, but something a little more serious. His thumb was shaking again too, a slight, but persistent, tremor that had worryingly crept in lately. What if it was the onset of Parkinson's? Hopefully just the alcohol, which still wasn't ideal. Why did he do it to himself? He'd got home last night, kindly dropped off by Ian – of which was a bit of a fuzzy memory, and he hoped he hadn't made a fool of himself – and instead of going to bed like any normal human being, he'd proceeded to stay up and drink. Celebrating the evening's success. His first job. Understandable in a way, he dimly justified to himself. But still... Twat! At least he'd zonked out and pretty-much slept straight through for once.

Consulting his phone (his real one) through bleary eyes, Sonny was surprised to see he had a message from Stacey. Bit early. And on a Saturday. It was a Saturday, wasn't it? A brief panic gripped him that he'd slept in on a work day. No, it was a Saturday. And it was nine-thirty. Not that early either then. He was also surprised to see the message was through WhatsApp, rather than the usual email. It said: '*Sounds like last night went well! Well done (smiley face). Client is more than happy and wants to book you in again! What did you do? (a thinking and surprised, open-mouthed face emoji)*'.

Was that a rhetorical question? Sonny thought. Or did she actually want him to reveal all his secrets and tricks for making a woman happy? He lay back on the bed, pleased with himself and his exploits. It somehow meant a lot to him that he had impressed Stacey and that she was pleased with him, somehow more than Susan herself. She was his boss after all. He then picked up his phone again, realising he hadn't replied. As he went to do so, he noticed Stacey's little round profile picture for the first time and clicked on it to make it bigger. To look at it. It was a smiling, head shot of Stacey. A nice pic. He realised he was smiling himself. '*Now that would be telling...*' he replied with a winky face emoji and pressed send. Then instantly regretted it. Shit, shit, shit. Had that sounded flirty? Too familiar? Bloody booze. He was still pissed. And horny. First time he'd felt like that in a while. Almost involuntarily, lazily, he slipped his hand down his pyjamas bottoms and considered masturbating.

Just then his phone rang, making him jump. It was his father calling. 'For fuck's sake,' Sonny said. He couldn't talk to him now, not feeling like this and having just woken up. Just the sight of his name and the ringing was making his head pound in time to it. Talk about a passion killer. He winced, waiting for it to stop. Finally it did, and Sonny lay there, knowing his father would be leaving another rambling voice mail right now; it was only a matter of time till his phone pinged with the notification of it.

This reminded Sonny of something from last night. He had professionally and respectfully kept his phone on silent in his jacket pocket throughout the duration of the date. Checking it on the way back in the car, Ian driving, he'd discovered his father had tried to call him four times during the meal *and* left a voicemail. He had listened to the voicemail last night, but couldn't for the life of him remember what it had been about. His chest rose and fell and his head pounded some more whilst he tried to recall. Ping! And there was the voicemail. And there was the cat scratching again. 'For fuck's sake,' Sonny said again, throwing the covers back. He was going to have to get up.

On opening the bedroom door, Buddy burst in mewling as if there was a fire out there in the corridor. 'Alright, alright,' Sonny said. The cat jumped up on the bed and gave it a longer than usual sniff. Then, realising Sonny was heading downstairs, followed him out, zipping past him at speed and trying to trip him up on the stairs. The usual scenario. 'Bloody cat!' Sonny was always grumpy with him first thing. He was so over the top, dramatic and anxious. Why couldn't he be chilled and relaxed like Susan's cat? Wanting some fuss. Maybe he could smell her on him?

Cup of tea made and cat fed, Sonny listened to the voicemail from his father; talk about OTT, dramatic and anxious... 'What are you up to?' was how it started. Straight in there, Sonny thought. 'Why aren't you answering your phone?' He sounded angry. And paranoid. Nothing new there. Sonny put the phone on the side on speaker and plucked his darts from the board. 'You're up to something,' his father continued. 'I can tell. You're as bad as this lot in here.' Sonny immediately felt like a child again. 'The toilet's blocked here and going to overflow. They're not doing a damn thing about it. I've tried clearing it with my shoe horn, but it's not budging.' Sonny groaned in disgust. His father's shoe horn was royal blue, plastic and about a foot and a half long. He could just picture him prodding and poking a toilet full of his own shit with it. What an image. He'd seen the stuff first-hand with his own eyes, and if he didn't want to be reminded of it, his father was going to anyway. 'It's these damn tablets. They harden everything up. Nothing for about a week, and then when it comes it's the size of a brick. Rips you open. One of the carers said it was like I'd given birth to a black baby!'

'Oh for fuck's sake!' Sonny said, throwing his last dart angrily into the dartboard. Why him? He'd heard enough and jabbed at his phone to end the call.

During the course of that day, Sonny and Stacey exchanged a couple more messages. Clearly, she was at work on a Saturday. Or at least Sonny presumed she was. She hadn't responded to his first reply for some time and Sonny had found himself checking his phone often. Anxious that he had been unprofessional, or stepped over the mark. Or so he told himself. He needn't have worried, though. Stacey eventually replied with a trio of sideways laughing faces, which had made Sonny smile again. But that was it. He felt somehow disappointed and didn't know whether he should reply again. What would he say? He realised he was thinking about it too much. Bored on a Saturday, on his days off, as usual. Restless, longing for some company. Female company. He considered going on the dating sites again, seeing what was out there. But just the thought of it depressed him. You invariably saw the same faces, the same profiles, even across multiple sites. The same poor souls that would disappear for a while – probably thinking that they'd found 'the one', giving a relationship a chance – then washing back up again, like driftwood, flotsam and jetsam, on a singleton-shore. Is that what people thought of him on there? A perennial failure in love? Not that he came and went. He'd never struck up a serious-enough relationship since his ex to take himself off the dating sites.

The second time Stacey got in touch that day, around three pm, was via email. Again, Sonny was pleasantly surprised to receive it. The email read: *Hi Sonny, thought I'd touch base about a couple of exciting bits before signing off for the weekend. Firstly, congrats again about your first gig. A great start! Not only has Susan left you a 5-star review (have you seen it? If not, click on the link), but she has also requested – wait for it – a cultural city-break overnighter the weekend after next! Big bucks! Go you! Secondly, you have also got a brand-new booking request! I'm not surprised, weekends are prime browsing time and your profile is getting plenty of traction. #Mr. Popular! It's a midweek one next week,*

*Wednesday. Have a look at your diary, see if you're free, if so, just quickly confirm and I will book that one in today – will send you all the proper details, form etc. on Monday. Re: the Susan one, appreciate this might need a bit more thought – you might already have plans and it's a big commitment. Especially so soon. Susan also mentioned about you cooking a meal for her at some point! Think you've got a big fan there (palm-face emoji) and a good string of guaranteed bookings ahead. FYI, don't want to blow smoke up your arse, but Susan is normally a strictly once a month booker, sometimes even two months. So, good for us and good for you. Well done. It's another string to your bow though, the cooking thing, social companion and personal chef! Not all escorts can boast that. Anyway, hit me back about the midweek one if poss. Ciao for now. Enjoy the rest of your weekend.Stacey (smiley face emoji).*

'Yeah, you too,' Sonny said out loud, closing his phone down. Wonder what she's doing with it? It still seemed totally bizarre to Sonny, being called an escort. His mind was reeling. Mainly about the overnight request and opportunity. Susan was a lovely lady, they had fun, but a whole day or two with her? The thought of it filled him with fear and trepidation. What would they talk about the whole time? Would he be constantly on edge, feeling he had to perform and entertain? The prospect of it seemed exhausting. And what about the sleeping arrangements? It went without saying that it would have to be a social companionship date. Separate rooms. What if she got ideas or tried it on? Plus, he normally saw the kids on a Sunday…

These worries aside, the email as a whole was great

news. Especially the other new gig. And of course he would be free. He clicked on the link to his profile Stacey had attached, feeling a bit vain to be doing so. As always, seeing his picture made him cringe and feel like a fake. No change there. He still couldn't believe this was happening. That he was out there in the world as a commodity. And being chosen. Something to be hired for money. For everyone to see – including his work colleagues. Shit! And his kids! Heaven forbid they should ever stray across it. But why would they? He felt bad keeping such a secret from them, though. Under his profile were the words *1 review*, accompanied by 5 pleasing stars. He clicked on the review. '*Utterly charming. Fantastic company. A true gent. Would highly recommend!*' Ms. E.

Bless her, Sonny thought. It could be the first step to him earning some really decent dosh. He replied to Stacey, thanking her for the email and confirming he could do the midweek gig. He felt excited about that one, something to look forward to, what it would entail and bring. Not to mention the money. Being midweek, it would be at the lower rate of course, but still... Add that to the potential earnings the big weekend one would bring and he would already have earnt a month's salary – more than a month's salary – for a few days' work.

# CHAPTER 12

Sonny was buzzing for days about how the date had gone and at the new booking requests. Going about his working day, it was all he could do to stop himself from smiling. It was as if he was carrying around a big secret that none of his work colleagues knew about. He liked that. And every time his phone went off, he hoped it was Stacey with some further news or another booking request. It had become a bit of an addiction, an itch for the next high. He kept having to pinch himself that it was happening.

Sonny hadn't had to think too long about the overnighter with Susan. Despite his trepidation, it was a no-brainer really, and he had accepted. He couldn't turn that money down. It was what he had signed up for. He was also aware he would most likely ruin any further potential bookings, and therefore earnings, with Susan if he declined. There were worse people in the world to spend a night away with anyway – and get paid for it – he figured. She was a nice, interesting person. Thus far anyway. He just had to think what he was going to say to his kids...

Sonny was as regular as clockwork with his Sunday meetups with his kids and rarely missed one. Even when he'd had a rare Saturday date or night out in the past it wouldn't affect the Sunday, he'd just be hungover. A source of amusement to his offspring. The girls had both managed to get their cars. They'd sent pictures of themselves, sitting in them, smiling. Bless them, Sonny thought. He was thrilled for them. But, how had that happened? His girls behind the wheel of a car, old enough to drive? Where had that time gone? It made him feel sad in a way; he missed them being little. Scared him, too. The thought of them shortly being on the roads, driving. At the mercy of all the other idiots out there. *'Fab. Be careful!'* he had messaged back.

Wednesday night's date could not have been more different from Sonny's first gig. And it was a wakeup call, a bit of a shattering of the escort-life glitter ball for the inexperienced Sonny. Firstly, he was only booked for two hours, the minimum the agency allowed, and a short date in anyone's book. Secondly, instead of being asked to meet at a restaurant or public place, Sonny was to go to an address. Also, tellingly in hindsight, the address was changed at the last minute by the client via the company mobile: *'Sorry! Put wrong address in by mistake. Nitwit (palm-face emoji.) It's 6a, not 6. See you at 7. X'.* Sonny had replied: *'Ah, no Problem. See you then. Sonny (smiley face)'.*

The address turned out to be a flat. A fairly decent, maisonette flat in a small block, but still, a far cry from the homes of the two ladies (Sarah included) that he had previously visited. He had to climb a short set of concrete steps with a black handrail to get to it. Reaching the top, he thought he could smell weed. Another tell-tale augury, looking back. The white PVC door said 6a on it. Sonny knocked, then waited, adjusting his hair, his shirt and trousers and clearing his throat. Putting his game-face on. He became aware that his heart was beating fast again, like last time. The adrenaline and anticipation of the unknown.

The woman that answered the door was younger than Sonny was expecting. Late twenties, early thirties at a push. She said hello, but didn't open the door fully, then asked Sonny to come in. Probably shy, he thought.

'Hi. I'm Sonny, pleased to meet you,' he said and stepped inside.

It wasn't until he was inside that he noticed exactly what the lady was wearing, a satiny, flimsy dressing gown and similar shorts and T-shirt pyjama set. How odd? Perhaps she wasn't ready yet? And then, physically taking Sonny aback, he noticed a man of similar age to himself, sitting on a sofa, rolling what was probably a joint – the apartment reeked of weed – on a glass coffee table in front of him. The man was wearing a buttoned-up navy polo shirt, along with a gold chain. He had one of those *Peaky Blinders* haircuts that the younger lads sported and tattooed letters on his fingers. It was impossible not to judge, and alarm bells began to ring in Sonny's head. 'Erm, sorry, have I got the wrong address?' he said, addressing both of them, stopping short of saying, 'Did someone order an escort?'

'Nah, this is the right address, you the escort, right?' The man said, licking the length of the spliff to stick and seal it.

'Yes, but–'

'Then you've got the right address then.' He put a lighter to the end of the spliff, lit it and took a few long drags to get it going. Then he blew on the end of it. The flat filled with a pungent, invasive smoke-plume of weed.

'Erm, bit confused,' said Sonny, turning to the lady. 'Are we going out? Shall I wait outside?'

'Nope, we're all stayin' in,' said the man before the lady could answer. 'And you're going to fuck her.' He slouched back on the sofa, spreading his legs.

'For fuck's sake, Dave!' said the woman.

'Erm, no I'm not,' said Sonny, reddening. 'We're not that sort of agency.'He started to head for the door.

'Yer an escort, aren't yer?' the man said, sitting up.

'Yes, but not that sort of escort!' Sonny reached for the door handle, an angry head of steam building.

'Wait! Mate, wait!' the man said, getting up. 'Don't go. Have a smoke first. Loosen up, I didn't mean to spook you.'

'Stay back!' Sonny said angrily. He opened the door and blessed fresh air washed over him. Then he slammed the door shut behind him.

'For *Fuck's sake, Dave!*' the woman shouted again, so loud Sonny could hear it as he bolted down the stairs. 'You didn't even give him fuckin' chance! That's four 'undred fuckin' quid blown!'

'It's my fuckin' dosh innit. You didn't do anything to help, did yer!'

'It was your fuckin' idea, I didn't want to do it in the first place!'

And then Sonny was at the car park and their voices

were gone. He was breathing hard, his heart was pounding and his face was flushed with anger and embarrassment. He felt seedy. Dirty. He couldn't ever recall being in a more awkward situation. And he'd felt vulnerable, trapped; it had been a horrible feeling. God only knew what someone like that deranged twat was capable of. Stabbing someone more than likely. Sonny opened his car door, plonked himself down, and then slammed the door shut. Then he locked it for good measure. He let out a huge breath. As he did so, his anger became directed at Stacey. At the end of the day, she had put him in that situation. Shouldn't these people be vetted? Shouldn't there be safe-systems in place? Who knew who was lurking behind a closed door? What weirdo? Luring someone to an address? And he was a man – imagine what it was like for a woman? A female escort?

He started the car and sped off. The stereo came on loudly, startling him. Buddy belting out 'Rave On'. He'd been singing to it on arrival; how buoyant and expectant his mood had been then compared to now. He quickly turned it down. On the way home, a thirty-minute drive and waste of petrol, Sonny thought about phoning Stacey, having it out with her. What time was it? Seven-fifteen on a Wednesday night. She would have finished work. He couldn't bother her now, not with a phone call. Message her instead. How could he explain all that on a message, though? Email her. When he got back. Keep it professional. She would want to know. And he wanted to know if he was still getting paid.

The first thing Sonny did when he got home was crack open a bottle of beer, necking half of it in one go. He needed it as a stress-calmer. Then he got undressed in the kitchen, pulling off his shirt and trousers, as they reeked of smoke. Dressed in just his boxers, Sonny plonked himself down on the sofa with his laptop to compile that email. The cat paced backwards and forwards along the back of the sofa behind Sonny, sniffing him and tickling his neck. 'Pack it in, Buddy!' Sonny said. Buddy let out a low growl in return, then turned to stretching his body out, splaying his paws and sinking his claws into the sofa instead. Sonny did his best to ignore him and concentrate.

In the email, he described what had happened as best he could and expressed his concerns about safety going forwards. He also asked if the client's payment was non-refundable; he had turned up at the end of the day and made himself available as per the booking; it wasn't his fault the client(s) had some wacko ideas about what 'social companionship' meant. Signing off, he was glad he'd had time to cool down before contacting Stacey. Sonny padded back to the kitchen, scratching his backside on the way, to get another beer. That one had barely touched the sides. Buddy followed, mewling and zig-zagging, trying to trip him up. 'Alright, alright,' Sonny said. He shook some dry biscuits into the cat's bowl, then pulled another beer out of the fridge.

Returning to the sofa, movement outside and a bright flash of colour on the yard caught his attention. It was Tom Petty with her peroxide blonde hair, hanging some of her dresses out on the line. He thought she was called a she anyway, her actual name was Lesley-Anne; Sonny knew this because he had seen it on Amazon parcels that sometimes got delivered to him by mistake. But she looked for all the world like a man, with a man's body, save for when she had her make up on. Then she looked like a man in drag. These things confused Sonny. Like sometimes on hot days she walked around bare-chested in leather trousers. Wasn't that the same as going topless for a female? Thinking this made Sonny suddenly realise that he, himself, was wandering around in only his boxer shorts. He quickly closed the blind in case she saw him and got excited.

Just then his phone rang, surprising him. 'If that's that twat…' Sonny said, anticipating his father. He wasn't in the mood. Sonny looked at his phone. It was Stacey! He immediately felt bad that he had emailed that night, rather than the morning, probably stressing her out. The poor woman deserved some break at the end of the day at least. 'Hello!' Sonny said, trapping his phone in the crook of his neck as he grappled his frothing beer open.

'Sonny!' said Stacey, somewhat breathlessly. 'I've just seen your email. You OK?' She sounded genuinely concerned.

'Yeah, yeah. Fine,' Sonny said. 'Look. I'm sorry for emailing tonight, I just wanted–'

'No, no. Not at all. *I'm* sorry. Sorry you had to go through that. Sounded awful.'

'Yeah, it wasn't the best. To say it was something I'm not used to would be the understatement of the year!'

'God. Yes, of course…'

'And so unexpected. Especially after last time. I mean, does stuff like that happen often?'

'No, no it doesn't. Not like that anyway. Not how you described it.'

'But it does happen then.'

Stacey went quiet for a moment, as if choosing her

words carefully. 'Very rarely... And like I say, not like that. So blatant. If something like that ever happens it is normally when someone has booked social companionship with intimacy and then got carried away or something – you, know, crossed a line, or had misconceptions in the first place as to what it entails. Or, again, very occasionally a client might book social companionship, then, after a few drinks, take a shine to their escort and try it on with them. But yours... it was as if they'd planned it from the outset or something. You know, booked the cheaper rate with the intention of trying their luck in the worst way possible when you got there.'

'Yeah, well that's what worries me,' Sonny said. 'The planning bit. I mean, what's to stop any weirdo booking an escort and luring them back to an address?'

'Well, we do try and vet people as best we can, get background information and that, addresses, phone numbers, bank card details etc. *and* they have to pay up front as you know – which hopefully answers your question; no, they won't be getting a refund! You turned up, made yourself available, and they tried to instigate something they hadn't paid for.'

'Good,' said Sonny. 'That's a relief.'

'Yeah. But maybe we can tighten up our booking process... More rigorous identity checks and that. Could put any potential weirdos off. But I'm not going to lie, there is always going to be an element of risk in this game. Whether it's at the start of the night or the end of a night, you know, going back to a private abode and that. That's why most female escorts don't do it, or if they do, they have a 'safe person' nearby at the end of a phone. You don't want to be going down that route.'

'No, I can look after myself for a start.'

'I'm sure you can. Look, maybe you don't do home visits – or at least not with a new client, always public, then it's up to you after that. Your choice. A lot of the guys do that. Just might limit some of your booking potential that's all... That reminds me actually, whilst I've got you – and I'm not changing the subject, I promise – you still adamant about not going down the intimacy route? I've had four email enquiries so far asking if you will.'

'Really?'

'Yeah.'

'Why? I mean, how come?'

'I dunno. Maybe people are finding your picture irresistible!' She laughed. 'Sorry, I shouldn't joke.'

'Hmm,' Sonny said. He found the whole thing embarrassing.

'So, is that a 'no' then?'

'Yeah, it's still a 'no". What had happened that night had only highlighted how he didn't want to get involved physically with anyone. Strangers. Once – Sarah – had been enough.

'OK, fair enough. I won't ask you again. And for what it's worth, I respect your decision. Your stance on it. It's refreshing.'

'Thank you,' said Sonny.

'You're welcome.'

'Anyway, we've got side-tracked – you said you weren't trying to do that.'

'I wasn't!' Stacey laughed again.

'Hmm,' Sonny said again, smiling. He was enjoying talking to her. He always did. 'So, back to what we were talking about... What *were* we talking about?'

'People luring you back to their houses for untoward purposes.'

'Ah, yes...' Why couldn't he stop smiling? His indignance so quickly dissipated. 'God, it was just so messed up! What's wrong with people?'

'I know. Tell me about it. You don't know the half of it, though, trust me.' Yeah. I bet she'd seen a thing or two in her time, Sonny thought. There was a pause in conversation, and he thought he heard her take a sip of something.

'Are you drinking?'

'Yeah. Glass of wine.'

'Me too. A beer. I needed it after that!'

'Me too. The day I've had.' Sonny wanted to ask her about it, but felt it was too familiar. Didn't know if she wanted him to. So, there was another pause instead. 'So, are we good then?' she said. 'We're not going to lose you? I'm sorry again that it happened. Genuinely. Especially so early on in our journey together.'

'Yeah. No. We're good.'

# CHAPTER 13

Sonny's next gig, on paper at least, looked a much more normal, professional affair – if there was such a thing in the world of escorting. A pleasant surprise and a huge bonus; a last-minute plus-one as a wedding guest. Not only was it on a Saturday, which garnered the higher rate, but the booking required his services for more than eight hours, around ten to be precise, which was classed and charged as a whole day. Therefore, Sonny was set to net around the six hundred quid mark. He simply couldn't believe his luck, or that people had that kind of money to spend.

His mission this time involved travelling by car, the client's car, to Sudbury in Suffolk – about a two-hour journey away. According to the brief, the client, a lady in her mid-forties called Julie (but everyone calls me Jules), had been invited to a wedding – ceremony, sit-down meal, evening do, the whole shebang – of some old uni friends and didn't want to come across as a lonely singleton, or old spinster. Basically, she needed a pretend boyfriend for the day. The old, classic scenario.

She said the journey down would give them time to get to know each other – and their story/false background straight. It was straight out of a rom-com movie and, again, Sonny couldn't believe people actually did this stuff in real life. To give him a head start, he was also given some general background info on the lady to gen up on.

This Sonny relished and set about with gusto. It gave him something to do. He was quickly realising how varied his bookings as an escort could be, and kind of enjoying that aspect of it. And, to some extent, getting to know new people too – providing they weren't weirdo swingers of course...

Julie, or 'Jules', was, how could Sonny put it... 'trying'. And he could see, pretty quickly upon meeting her, why she was single. This was a shame, because, physically, she was fairly attractive to Sonny – possibly, the first one of his clients or dates he could have fancied. The emphasis being on 'could have'... It was funny how a person's personality could render them unattractive, despite their physical appeal. Almost in the same way looks could ruin a cracking personality. Either way, this was all new and interesting stuff for Sonny to ponder on.

Jules reminded Sonny of Amanda – one of the main characters off the BBC sitcom, *Motherland*. She was vacuous, vain, materialistic, loved the sound of her own voice and to namedrop. Privileged. She worked in 'the city' – Sonny presumed she meant London. Drove an Audi. She loved to talk, but not to listen, asking Sonny very little about himself, or showing much interest in him – and the rare occasion she did ask, when Sonny tried to answer, she would immediately interrupt, or talk over him about herself again. Surely this was going to be a problem later on? Sonny thought. How is she going to know anything about him – his likes and dislikes etc. – if people ask?

What she *was* interested in was their 'story', or *supposed* story. How they met etc. Apparently, this was at the gym. Jules said she'd got a couple of possible scenarios planned out, but on meeting him, she quickly decided the gym would work. 'I'm addicted to the gym! Can you tell?' she said. She'd also got a fake career for him planned out – 'he couldn't be an escort!' – until he pointed out he was a chef in 'real life'. 'Ah, amazeballs!' she said. 'That solves that then. Was worried you were going to have to pretend to be an estate agent or something all day. Could get ropey if we end up with a genuine estate agent on our table! Hold on, what kind of chef?' Sonny told her. 'Ah... OK... well, can you be an executive chef or something? Don't they get paid more? Yeah, let's say you're an executive chef at some fancy restaurant.' It was going to be a long day...

And it was. By the time they got there, a relieved Sonny practically sprung out of the car. The whole journey had been a 'let's talk about Jules snooze fest' for him. Most of it spent with her 'testing' him. Asking him questions about herself (her favourite subject), as if she was a celebrity, or worthy of a quiz round being dedicated to her and her life. Where she was born, where she went to school and uni, what her favourite food and colour were... He was to call her 'darling' for the day, and she would refer to him as 'hun'. 'You know, short for honey,' she said. Talking of food, Jules was vegan and lactose and gluten intolerant. Apparently. She'd had to request a special meal at the wedding.

The only good thing about the journey for Sonny, the latter part anyway, had been hitting the rural, Suffolk countryside. Seeing the numerous, pink and timbered buildings. Utterly charming and so unique to the area. The wedding venue was no different. The nuptials themselves, and subsequent celebration of, were to take place in a purposely-converted pale pig-pink 16th century barn with a thatched roof, oozing character and redolent in the spring sunshine of days gone by, rural-living and horse and carts. Adding to its chocolate-box appeal were a skirt of multi-coloured tulips in wooden planters at the base of its walls. They looked like sugar candy, good enough to eat. The barn was set in the grounds of a grand hall that also boasted a pretty lake, a tree-lined avenue and wild flower meadow, all perfect for wedding photo opportunities no doubt.

The interior of the barn was even more impressive. The walls and roof constructed out of a network of exposed timbers. One half set up as a mini-chapel with an aisle and seats. The other decked out for the wedding breakfast with linen-clad round tables. Subdued lighting, flowers and candles everywhere. 'Wow!' Jules said on seeing it. It echoed Sonny's thoughts. About the only thing they had agreed on so far. Seeing it all made Sonny feel wistful. He'd love to get married again. To the right person of course.

Bit by bit, Jules bumped into and sought out people she knew, including the groom. 'Moi, Moi,' She kissed him on both cheeks, exclaiming how dashing he looked. Sonny, the dutiful boyfriend, was introduced and tasked with handing over the wedding gifts, expensive looking bags from designer outlets with dangling gift tags cynically embossed with '*Love and Congrats from Jules and Sonny. xx.*' It was breathtakingly manufactured to Sonny – the lie and pretence – and didn't sit right with him at all; he was not sure how she could do it. To Sonny's mind, the groom to be didn't seem particularly bowled over at seeing Jules or that she had made it. No genuine closeness or warmth emanating from him. Perhaps he wasn't a fan? He seemed quite keen to make his excuses and 'do the rounds', in fact. 'We'll all catch up properly later!' he said.

Sonny's suspicions that Jules was maybe a somewhat token, peripheral, guest there went further still when Jules consulted the table plan for the wedding breakfast. 'I don't know any of these people we're sitting with!' she said, put out. A glass of buck's fizz in hand, and expensive handbag, swinging from her wrist. 'Where's Trish and Michael? Where's Rob and Marie, where's any of the old gang?' She continued to peruse the table plan. 'Ah, typical, top table. Trish'll be Maid of Honour no doubt – bitch.' Charming, Sonny thought. 'And Rob'll be best man, thick as thieves that pair... Bloody hell, even Kaz and Vicky are on a table together, for fuck's sake, they never even liked each other, always bitchin' about each other.' She looked genuinely hurt. Her mood darkened. Old memories flooding back – the exclusive cliques and hurtful shuns of the playground – like delayed echoes returning to haunt her. Sonny stood there, feeling a bit of a spare part, and a bit sorry for Jules for the first time. Not knowing any of these people, he didn't know what to say to placate her. 'Oh, well,' she said. 'Come on, let's make the most of it – just hope we're not stuck with a table full of boring twats!'

Marriage ceremony over, Sonny and Jules were settled at their designated table. As the wine was being poured, the day then took a dramatic, downward turn for Sonny. And, as quite often in his life, the somewhat defining moment involved alcohol. 'Red or white, Madam?' an earnest waiter said to Jules.

'Oh, erm. White for me. Not too much. Actually, you know what, hun?' she said, leaning into him, 'Are you alright driving? I fancy a drink now.'

Such a simple, innocent question. But one that sent Sonny's mind and day into turmoil. As if a blaring klaxon had just sounded, 'whoop, whoop, whoop!'. Sitting there, smiling patiently through the whole marriage service, he'd been looking forward to this bit. The free meal and more importantly alcohol. Having met Jules, it was going to be his reward, the thing to get him through the rest of the day. He had been watching the waiter do the rounds of the table, again waiting patiently for his turn, salivating almost in anticipation. 'Yep, white for me – to start off with anyway!' he would have joked, anticipating the laugh and guffaw of his fellow dinner guests. 'Just leave the bottle there!' That's what weddings were for after all, wasn't it? Getting pissed? Sonny loved a wedding for that reason, all the free booze; he would famously hoover up anything on the table. Any drink. Anyone's drink...

Having said all that, he had still intended on taking it fairly steady that day. To pace himself. He couldn't go getting pissed at every gig he had. It wouldn't go down well. He'd get a reputation for it, bad reviews: '*Escort was a pisshead! Avoid!*' He had to remain professional, remember he was doing a job. But he *had* intended on having a good few drinks to get him through. Why did she have to say that? And so casually? It hadn't been discussed. It should have been put in the brief if he was driving. He turned to her, grimacing a smile. It seemed as if everyone was listening, waiting for his answer, including the waiter.

'But I'm not insured on the Audi, *darling* – we never got round to it, remember?' he said, thinking, *yes, yes, yes,* and mentally patting himself on the back for his quick-thinking and ingenuity.

'Oh, yes. Of course. Well, if you're fully comp you can drive anyone's car. You're fully comp, aren't you?'

'Yes, darling, you know I am, but–' Why did he say 'yes'! It just came out! 'I've never heard of that being a thing.'

'It's true,' some twat, a guy, then piped up on the table opposite them. 'She's right. If you're fully comp, you're technically insured on anyone's car, providing they're fully comp too. It'll be in your policy somewhere. Have a look.' Thanks a lot, mate, Sonny thought, privately seething. Wanting to stab him with his starter fork.

'Well, I don't have my policy on me, don't even know how to find it. It'll be on an email somewhere, and then I'd have to log in...'

'Ahem.' The waiter cleared his throat, still waiting.

'Please, hun, I really fancy it. I always drive.'

'Go on, let her have a drink,' twat said. What had it got to do with him?! He didn't know them from Adam.

'OK. Sure. No problem,' Sonny said, whilst dying inside.

'Aaw, thanks, hun. You're an angel!' She suddenly grabbed hold of him and kissed him on the lips. 'Fill her up!' she said to the waiter.

'Yay!' said twat. Clearly, he fancied her.

Sonny's mind was reeling from what had just happened. He felt he had been ambushed, setup. And he also wasn't too pleased at being kissed on the lips; that wasn't in the remit. Strayed into the realms of 'intimacy' in his book. Not to mention the torturous sound of cold white wine currently being generously sloshed into Jules's glass.

The next seven hours or so were up there with the longest of Sonny's life; and that was saying something, considering the mind-numbing, leg-aching long shifts he'd put in over his cheffing career. Sitting through a three-course meal, whilst engaging in pointless chit-chat with people he would never see again. Ditto with listening to the interminable wedding speeches with their saccharine, gushing eulogies and 'in-jokes' – these people meant nothing to him. Then there was Jules...

There were few things more annoying in life than a drunk person when you're sober, Sonny thought. But a drunk Jules was one of them. She spent most of the evening on the dance floor, forgetting he was even there half the time by all accounts. And when she did return, she would drunkenly try in vain to drag him back up to the dance floor with her, branding him a 'bore' and a 'spoilsport' when he refused. Sonny wasn't a dancer. *Really* wasn't a dancer. No rhythm, two-left feet. He had to be absolutely plastered to dance, and then it had to be to the right song. So, he palmed Jules off, saying, 'Maybe if there's a slow one,' or by flattering her: 'Nah, you go ahead, I'm happy to watch. You're a great dancer!' But the awkwardness of the situation did highlight that learning a few basic dance moves might not be a bad idea going forwards; being a plus-one, it could crop up over and over again.

Sonny soon regretted telling Jules she was a great dancer, as it only seemed to spur her on. She started dancing with other people, men mostly, drunkenly. More outlandishly, provocatively. Perhaps the booze had made her forget she had a partner – supposedly – if she wasn't careful, she would blow their cover. Seemed she had totally lost track of time too; it was approaching leaving time and she showed no signs of slowing down. Sonny hadn't, and kept consulting his phone. They had that two-hour journey home yet.

Eventually, he had no choice but to go up there, jostle his way through the dance floor, and tell her it was time to go. She squealed when she saw him. 'Dance with me first! Just one! Pleeasse. It's a slow one! You said you'd dance to a slow one!' In order to avoid a scene, Sonny felt he had no choice. So, he succumbed to an uncomfortable, clinching slow dance with Jules to 'True' by Spandau Ballet. A song he actually liked; he was just on a dance floor with the wrong woman that was all. Arms around her waist. Hers around his neck. Inhaling her sickly perfume that he didn't like. Her hairspray. The booze on her breath. He felt detached. Wooden. Unrelaxed.

His disinterest must have showed. 'Cheer up, you're getting paid for this aren't you?' she said, a little too loudly over the music for Sonny's liking. Then she sunk her head onto his shoulder, almost as if she'd fallen asleep. It was a good point though and he gave himself a mental kick up the arse. You're here to provide a service. Be professional and accommodating. Think of the money. And the potential review. The last thing he needed was Jules giving him a bad one.

When it was over, he practically had to carry her out of the place, she was that plastered. Propping her up, staggering, with his arm around her. Thankfully – for her sake more than his – no one really paid attention to them leaving. And then the fresh air hit her. 'I think I'm going to be sick,' she groaned.

'Oh, for fuck's sake,' Sonny muttered under his breath. This was all he needed. He was no good with other people being sick. Even with his own children, it was a trial. 'Just hold on,' he said. 'I'll go and grab the car, just wait here. Where are the keys?'

'Huh?'

'The keys. Where are your car keys?'

'Don't know.' She could barely speak, her eyes glazed.

'Think. Are they in your bag? Hold on, where is your bag? Jules, where's your bag?'

'Don't know,' she said again. She began patting her dress, her hips, as if it should have been hanging there. 'Must have left it inside.'

'Oh, for fuck's sake,' Sonny said again. He would have to go back in and get it. If he could find it. It could be any-bloody-where. 'Wait there,' he said.

'S'got my phone it,' Jules slurred. 'Sonny, it's got my phone in it. I need my phone.'

Back inside, the music was still thumping away. Drunk people everywhere. Sonny made a beeline for the table they'd been sitting at. The bag wasn't on it. Shit. He rooted around in the dark under the table cloth for the seat she'd been sitting at. No joy again. Fuck. He put his phone torch on and shone it round the table. There!

Bingo! He spotted the white strap of the bag, hanging on the back of a seat. Must have been searching on the wrong seat – unless, she'd hung it on the wrong seat at some point. More than likely. He grabbed the bag and beat a hasty exit.

Reaching the exit door and opening it, the first thing he noticed was a retching sound. Oh no, please no! he thought. And then he heard a voice. A stranger's voice. A Scottish female one. 'Aaw, bless you darling. Let it all out. We've all ben there.' Another retch and splutter. The unmistakable sound of someone vomiting. Bracing himself, Sonny stepped outside. Jules was bent double, chucking up all over the poor, beautiful tulips. She could have done it somewhere else. Poor owners of the venue too. That was going to be a mess tomorrow – and right by the entrance. He couldn't believe this was happening. Did things like this always happen with escorting? Or had he just had bad luck? His last two gigs had made his first one seem like a one-off.

A lady had her hand on Jules's back. 'Hi,' Sonny said. 'Sorry about this.'

'Ah, nae bother. We've all ben there! I just came out for a fag and saw her, poor theng.'

'You OK, darling?' Sonny said to Jules. It grated on him to call her darling.

'Huh. Who's that?' Jules said.

'It's me, Sonny. Your *boyfriend*.' He rolled his eyes in a light-hearted way to the Scots girl. She laughed.

'Do you want a glass of water?' the girl said.

'No, I want to go home... I want a tissue... In my bag. *Did you get my bag?*'

'Yes, I got your bag. Hold on.' He unzipped Jules'

bag and routed around in it, feeling a bit weird to be doing so. Thankfully, her phone was in there, along with lots of makeup clattering about, and then some tissues. 'Here.' He handed her one. She wiped her mouth. 'You Ok? You done?' He really wasn't very good at this, but having the girl there probably helped. Forced him to be more sympathetic. He tried not to look at the mess. But he could smell it.

'I think so, I want to go home.'

'We'll be OK now. Thanks,' he said to the girl.

'Nae bother,' the girl said.

Back in the car, Sonny strapped Jules in. She was still out of it, her head lolling. Sonny prayed she wasn't going to be sick again. Especially in the car, or all over herself. He wasn't sure how he would deal with it. He buckled his own seat belt and fumbled through Jules' keys for the car one. The key didn't look like his, it was just the plastic bit. 'Jules, where's the blade on this key? How do I start the car?'

'Huh?'

'How do I start the car? There's no key blade.'

'It's a starter button, dimwit.' She pointed to the dash, without opening her eyes, her head resting on the back of her seat.

Aah, feeling a little better? he thought. He located the starter button where she was pointing. Never having used one before, he pushed it, but nothing happened.

'Clutch,' she slurred.

'Ah,' he said, putting his foot down on it and trying the button again. The Audi purred quietly to life. So different to his own car. 'Let's go.' About to set off, something then occurred to him. He didn't even know where Jules lived, where they were going. And then another thing... How was he going to get home when they got there? She'd picked him up.

'Jules.' He tapped her leg. No response. 'Jules!'

'What?' she slurred.

'Don't go to sleep, not yet. I need to know where you live.'

'Why, you coming back to mine?' she said dozily, then snorted laughter.

'No. Yes. But only to drop you off.' He'd have to get an Uber back. There was no way he was staying the night at hers. He wanted his own bed for a start. And for this night to be over.

'Shame. You're a good-looking guy. Not tall enough, but not bad looking. I prefer tall guys...' She sounded almost delirious, as if under the spell of an anaesthetic.

'Jules, your address,' he said impatiently. 'I need it for the satnav. Where do you live?'

Thankfully, Jules slept for the majority of the journey back. This was a relief. It was also a relief that she didn't throw up again. In the dark, under the occasional flash of overhead lights, Sonny found himself looking at Jules' shapely tight-clad thighs from time to time. The hem of her short dress was ridden up. It surprised him he was looking. He wondered about this and at how vulnerable Jules was. Also, at what kind of a man he was. What sort of life he was leading. What sort of life other escorts led. What had they seen, done? What decisions had they made? In situations like this. Men like that – what was his name? The guy who had Sonny's work phone before him? Brett, Burt? The 'piece of work', as Stacey had described him. The photos she had deleted.

He shuddered to think what a man like that would have done in a situation like this.

By the time Sonny got home, it was gone one o'clock. Way past the allotted time of his booking. And way past his bedtime. He plonked himself straight into bed exhausted, not even touching a drink; the trials of the day had left him drained and bereft of any desire to do anything at all. But still, sleep wouldn't take him. It rarely did straightaway. Lying there awake in the dark, he questioned if he could go through that again, even with the money on offer. It was mentally and physically exhausting. This made him worry again about the Susan trip, and was he cut out for this? The long gigs anyway.

# CHAPTER 14

The next morning Sonny felt better, fresher. He didn't have a hangover for a start. And now that he had rested, the night before already becoming a memory, he could distance himself from it and put things in perspective. Put the money in perspective. The effort vs reward so to speak. The satisfaction that he had netted over six-hundred quid for a day's work – two weeks' of his normal wages for one day! Six-hundred quid…What could he do with it? Save it. There was more coming. Much more with the Susan trip. Watch his bank balance swell for once. When was the last time that happened? Years and years ago.

He needn't have worried about the Susan trip. She was her amiable, likeable, albeit eccentric self. And after the last two fiascos (and spending time with someone like Jules), it was a breath of fresh air, almost like seeing an old friend. They travelled to Liverpool on a train – first class, no less. Sonny had never travelled first class on a train, couldn't even remember the last time he'd been on a train. And he'd never been to the city of Liverpool either. They had comfy, spacious seats, facing each other, and were waited on hand and foot. They had buck's fizz with their breakfast, followed by a bottle of prosecco, olives and other titbits during the course of the journey. Susan was in her element, and so, to some extent, was Sonny. It didn't feel like work, put it that way. He was starting to think she was a bad influence on him, a partner in crime. 'How come we're doing the train anyway?' Sonny asked after they had settled in. 'As opposed to Ian, I mean?'

'Why wouldn't we?' Susan said, glass in hand. 'I love it. I always get excited going on a train, makes me feel like a little girl again. Besides, it gets a bit messy trying to wine and dine on the back seat of a car!' They both laughed. 'Seriously, Ian gets twitchy at the mess and tells me off. He's very particular about the Jag, especially the upholstery, takes great pride in it. It's his weekend off anyway, bless him, he gets one a month...'

Sonny pondered about this for a moment as he stared out of the window at the landscape rushing by. It really *was* a different world some people lived in. 'How long have you had him for?' he said.

'I presume you're talking about Ian? You make him sound like a cat!' Sonny nearly spat his fizz out. She really tickled him sometimes, the things she came out with. Susan smiled, apparently pleased at her little joke and its effect. 'Hmm... let me see... some years now. My husband employed him originally, ex-husband I should say, still pretty much pays for him in fact.'

'Really? So he's not – you're husband's not...'

'Dead? No. Divorced, have been five years, but not dead – more's the pity... Probably still chasing every bit of young skirt in the capital. No, I shouldn't say that, the *dead* thing. He did right by me financially, still does, just couldn't keep it in his trousers, that's all. Unless it was with me! When a woman gets on in years, starts to fill out, starts to spread. A few grey hairs here, a few wrinkles there... we become *otiose*. Redundant. Superfluous to requirements. Physically anyway...' This subject appeared to have hit a nerve with Susan, something that still rankled. Sonny felt he had inadvertently opened up a can of worms and regretted bringing the subject up. Especially so early on in the day. He gave a sympathetic smile.

'Well, I'm sorry it didn't work out for you guys. More fool him, I say.'

'Ah, you're too kind, bless you. Anyway – enough of this serious claptrap. We're here to have fun, aren't we? Here's to a weekend in Liverpool?!' She raised her glass. 'Top me up!'

Liverpool was a whirlwind for Sonny. And, on reflection, one of the best, horizon-broadening, cultural experiences he had ever had. From embarking at Lime Street station and immediately seeing St. George's Hall opposite – merely a taste of things to come in terms of the plethora of historic buildings on show – right through to the unique hotel they stayed at. Susan had chosen the Titanic. A relatively new hostelry, housed in one of Liverpool's most historic and iconic buildings, the Northern warehouse at Stanley Dock. The rooms were of a jaw-dropping size – in keeping with the hotel's namesake and theme. Plush and tastefully furnished, and with unique views of the dock area. Sonny had never experienced anything like it.

In terms of sight-seeing and culture, they fitted in as much as they could. The cathedral. The museums. The Albert Docks. A ferry across the Mersey. The Beatles stuff. Retail therapy for Susan at The Cavern Quarter boutiques. The eateries on Lark Lane. But the unanimous highlight for both of them was a visit to the Walker Art Gallery, home to one of the best collections of Pre-Raphaelite art in the world. Sonny didn't take a massive interest in art, but had become a big fan of the Pre-Raphaelite Brotherhood after watching a TV drama series called *Desperate Romantics*. A tale of debauchery, alcohol and mayhem, set against the backdrop of 19th century industrial London, along with the creation of some simply stunning and iconic paintings, such as Millais' *Ophelia* and Rossetti's *Proserpine*.

Sonny loved the unmistakable style of the Pre-Raphaelite paintings and movement, but was merely a passing observer compared to Susan. She was a font of knowledge on the subject, and the Walker art gallery was the main draw for choosing Liverpool as their weekend away, the jewel in its crown. Susan loved that they had another thing in common and enjoyed educating Sonny further on the subject, showing off her knowledge. Sonny was happy to let her do so. It was fascinating.

And then it was over. There had been no awkwardness, no throwing-up, no aching hours of time-dragging; it went too quickly if anything. No misunderstandings as to where they stood with each other. No awkwardness with the rooms or sleeping arrangements. No drunken, kamikaze passes, doomed to failure, on Susan's behalf. Just kisses on the cheeks and a big hug when they parted back in the East Midlands. A mutual sense of gratitude and residual glow at what a nice time they'd both had.

It was dark when Sonny arrived home. He parked his car on the street out front where, space permitting, he always did – it could get busy with the newsagent's customers at peak times. Being Sunday evening, however, the shop was closed. His thoughts immediately turned to Buddy and if he'd survived OK. Sonny had asked Mary, an elderly neighbour of his, to feed the cat whilst he was away. Mary was sweet, if a bit scatty. Ninety if she was a day. Well-meaning, but sometimes over-friendly in an old-fashioned way. Always wanting to chat, always popping round with random jams and toxic wine – more like Molotov cocktails – she had made, or homegrown tomatoes.

Sonny shouldered his overnight bag, locked his car, and commenced the tedious walk to his back door; he didn't have a front one. His thoughts returned to Susan and what a fab time they'd had. What a fab time *he'd* had. If this kept up, he was going to start feeling guilty at charging her. Talking of which, his bank account was another grand to the good, even after the deductions. Surely it couldn't carry on like this? Earning this sort of money on top of his day job. He really would be able to jack it in at this rate. What an unexpected turn his life had taken...

Rounding the front corner of his house, Sonny then noticed something amiss. Something that took him totally by surprise. The small lane that led up to the rear yard was stained blue with police lights; they were emanating from a panda car parked further up the lane, blocking it. The sight of it made his stomach drop. Police again. But what the hell had gone on? Save for his immediate neighbours – whose rented house was attached to his, both within one large, divided house – there were only two other properties on the lane, both bungalows, one of them being Mary's; he sincerely hoped nothing had happened to her.

As Sonny approached the car, the driver's side door shot open, startling him, and a police officer sprung out. Blinded by the police lights, Sonny hadn't noticed him lurking in the car. 'Stop right there!' the officer said, holding his palm up. 'Please state your name and your business here.' Bit OTT, Sonny thought.

'My name is Sonny Garfunkel and I live here. What's going on?'

'Live where? What's your address?'

'There, at–'

'Wait!' The officer stopped him and pulled out a pad and paper. 'OK, go on,' he said. 'Full name and address please.' Sonny repeated his name and gave him his address. 'So, if I'm correct, you live at that property there' – he pointed with his pen to Sonny's property – '4a.'

'Yes.'

'Which backs onto Number 4?'

'*Yes*.'

'Is there access to Number 4 through your house?'

'No. Why? What's gone on?' he asked again.

'None at all?' Just then there was a clattering sound, carried on the night air across the yard, and the officer spun round. 'What was that?'

'The cat flap,' Sonny said. He recognised the sound.

As if on cue, with a mewl and a scrabbling, Buddy appeared at the top of the gate post.

'Jesus!' said the officer.

Why was he so jumpy? Sonny thought. 'Hey, boy,' he said, approaching Buddy. It was good to see him.

'Wait! Don't go any further!' the officer said.

'I'm only going to stroke my cat! I've been away and he's probably missed me.' And it did seem like Buddy had missed him for once, rubbing his cheeks against Sonny's hand as he reached up to him. 'Hey boy.'

'Don't go any nearer the gate, please, not until we've established a few facts first,' the officer said. It was then that Sonny noticed the police tape for the first time, blocking the gate.

'Wait. Hold on,' said Sonny. Things had suddenly got more serious. 'That's the only way into my house. It's shared access. It's not Mary, is it? The old lady? Nothing's happened to Mary, has it?'

'I'm not currently at liberty to say. Come and join me in the car please and we'll take some more details.'

Sonny reluctantly followed the officer – who, as it turned out, was only a community support officer (which explained a few things) – to his car. It made Sonny feel as if he'd done something wrong, getting in it. As if he was being formally questioned. What would Mary think? If she was still alive that was...

After answering numerous questions, mainly as to his whereabouts over the last twenty-four hours or so, along with his connection to the couple next-door – how well he knew them, any recent dealings with them etc. – Sonny was finally granted permission to enter his house. Not without the officer radioing a senior for permission for this first, or without him having to accompany him. The officer had still given little or nothing away during their discourse as to what had gone on. But, reading between the lines, it was apparent that it involved the couple next door. Something had gone on over the weekend, something serious by the sound of it. Something in their house. Therefore, Sonny was keen to spot anything with his own eyes as they pushed the latch on the gate and entered the back yard.

To his surprise, the lights were on all over the neighbours' house. 'Straight ahead please,' the officer said. This instantly made Sonny look to his right, where there was more police tape blocking the rear path to the neighbours' back door. As he walked past their kitchen window to his own back door, he couldn't help but have a nosey through the slatted blinds into their kitchen. Due to the kitchen light being on and to Sonny's shock, he could see that their kitchen was in disarray; the table was overturned and furniture and smashed items were strewn about. 'Keep going,' the officer said, giving Sonny a firm hand in the back.

'Alright, alright,' Sonny said. The over-zealous, jumped-up officer was starting to wind him up. He could almost feel him breathing down his neck as he fumbled for his back door key. 'You're standing in the light, mate. I can't see a thing.'

Finally, they were inside. Buddy shot inside with them, mewling for food and sniffing his empty bowls. Sonny placed his bag down on the kitchen floor. 'Right, I need to feed the cat and I need a piss. You babysitting me all night or what?'

'No. I just need to get confirmation with my own

eyes that there is no access to next-door from within this property – I've been given orders – then I'll leave you in peace. Can you show me round the entire property please?' Sonny sighed; this was literally all he needed after returning home after a draining weekend. He showed the officer round. Satisfied and true to his word, the officer then made to leave. 'It goes without saying, do not think about visiting next-door or having a nosey – it's a crime scene and we are waiting for the forensics to show up tomorrow morning. You will be committing a crime yourself if you do. If you've got anything further you want to add, or you remember anything you feel might be important–'

'I wasn't here, like I said.'

'I know. So you say. But in general... I'll be outside until twenty-one-hundred hours, where I will then be relieved by a fellow officer.'

'So, you guys are gonna be here all night?'

'Correct.'

'Well, can you at least turn your lights off then please?'

# CHAPTER 15

After (another) sleepless night – all he needed was something else to keep him awake – Sonny rose earlier than usual. His mind had been turning over all night as to what had gone on next-door. The mind boggled. Forensics… that sounded serious – like 'dead body' serious. That was what he had been thinking about most specifically, that there might be a dead body lying there next door. It gave him the creeps. And if so, whose? Had the neighbours got into a drunken, drug-fuelled fight and one of them stabbed the other? They may have been an odd couple, but they'd always seemed pretty close. Sonny had never heard any fights or arguing as such; the only disturbances were their rowdy parties.

Sonny opened the blind of his upstairs landing window and peered out into a misty morning. As expected, the police car was still there, but with a different officer in it. It was still strange seeing the car though. Serious. Adding light to the scene, however, and making Sonny smile, was Mary in her dressing gown at the open window of the car, bending the officer's ear by the looks of it. As he chatted to her, he was dunking a biscuit into a mug of tea or coffee, made and provided by Mary no doubt. That would be typical of her. At least the sight of her confirmed she was still alive and not mixed up with that business next door. He needed to thank her for feeding the cat. She was probably keen herself to know what had gone on. But she'd be better off asking Kerry, who ran the newsagent's, rather than the officer; she was the font of all local gossip – saw being a medium for giving and receiving it as a solemn duty. And that's exactly what Sonny intended to do before work. Ask her.

'It's alright, I saved you a copy!' Kerry said upon Sonny entering the shop.

'Ey?'

'The *Mail*. You didn't come in Saturday, so I saved you a copy. I know how you love your crossword! It's in the back room, I'll just grab it.' Before he could stop her, she was off.

'Ah, bless you!' Sonny said. He religiously got the *Daily Mail* for the crossword from Kerry every Saturday morning without fail. Obviously, this weekend he had been away. Not that this had stopped him doing the crossword. He'd bought the paper in Liverpool, and despite Susan initially turning her nose up at it, they had done the crossword together during the course of the weekend. It had been fun, and the first time Sonny had fully completed it in a while. He didn't have the heart to tell Kerry he had already bought it.

Sonny scanned the shop for something to buy as an excuse. He'd only come in here to 'pump' Kerry. A tin of cat food, that would do. Wincingly expensive, but hopefully worth the price for some info. Kerry returned with the paper and slapped it on her counter. Ah, he was going to have to pay for that too... Kerry punched the price of the cat food into her old-fashioned till with a brown, nicotine-stained finger. She actually looked like a cigarette; pale, thin as a rake, but with a patchy, orange fake tan face. Forty-going on-seventy. Smoked far too much, always hanging around on the corner outside, having a chuff. 'Ninety-five pence please, darl, you can 'ave the paper.'

'Ah, no, I couldn't do that.'

'You can! I would've got rid of it anyway with all the other surplus.'

'Ah, well as long as you're sure.'

'Quite sure.'

'Here, keep the change.' Sonny handed over a quid.

'Thank you. I'll stick it in the charity box.' Here goes then, Sonny thought. He had never before blatantly asked Kerry outright for gossip, it was normally doled out whether you liked it or not. Taking advantage of the shop still being empty other than him, he said, 'Kerry, do you know anything about what's gone on next-door? I came back last night from being away for the night, Saturday, and there was a police officer guarding access to Number 4. Was very cagey and jumpy. Couldn't get anything out of him other than that they were waiting for forensics.'

'Forensics?' Kerry said, her ears visibly pricking up. 'Sounds serious.' Her tone of voice had changed, become more of a whisper, as it was wont to do when engaging in juicy gossip.

'Yeah, that's what I thought.'

'Well, here's the thing...' She leant forwards on the counter. 'Saturday afternoon, from about fiveish, the street started to slowly fill up with cars. Think them lot next-door were 'avin' one of their dos – but a bigger one than normal. You should've seen some of the shower turnin' up and goin' in there.' She rolled her eyes and tutted. 'Anyway, by the time I closed up at six, there were cars lining both sides of the street and you could 'ear the music thumpin' through the walls of the back room. I thought of you, actually, but then figured you were away as you didn't come in for yer paper and yer car wasn't there all day. Hoped for your sake you were anyway.' She didn't miss a trick, Sonny thought. 'Well, I locked up and left about sixish, thinkin', those bloody cars better all be gone by tomorrow mornin' otherwise I would not 'ave been 'appy! You couldn't get anywhere near the shop. And some of my regulars are elderly and decrepit, like to park outside the front door. Sunday mornings are the busiest time for papers. Anyway... thankfully, come Sunday morning, the cars had all gone. Disappeared. All accept that black car of 'is next-door – the bloke one out the two – but he often parks out front, especially when they're using their garage – think their drive's a bit tight for two cars.'

'How do you even know that?' Sonny couldn't help but ask, smiling.

'Oh, I often see 'em when I'm putting my rubbish in the skips out back. Messing about with that motorbike and that. Rum pair. Anyway... so, that was that – or so I thought...' She nodded conspiratorially, as if there was more to come. There was. 'Come Sunday lunchtime, about twelvish, I was 'avin a fag on the corner and I noticed a police car down there for the first time, like you say. Then at some point one of me regulars came in and said there was two of them down there. Everyone was talkin' about it, but nobody knew what 'ad gone on. Nobody saw anybody comin' or goin' or being taken away, like, so it's a bit of a mystery. I was wonderin' if you knew anything actually.'

'No. Only what I've told you. And I haven't seen either of them since.'

'Hmm... forensics though, you say. Well, something queer's gone on. Pardon the expression.'

In the days and weeks following, it soon became apparent that the Elton John neighbour from next-door – Sonny didn't know his name – had disappeared. Sonny hadn't seen him since before that weekend of the party and then the police showing up. On paper, this didn't bode well for Elton, Sonny thought. Especially since his car hadn't moved once from out front either. But if he was the one that had sinisterly 'bought it', the partner he had left behind certainly wasn't showing it. Lesley-Anne was carrying on as normal, even having other male acquaintances round. Clearly, in the police's eyes at least, she couldn't have been involved.

One day there was another shoe-box-sized Amazon parcel on Sonny's doorstep, addressed to number 4. Still intrigued and knowing Lesley-Anne was in, Sonny took it round. Normally, he would leave their parcels on their doorstep, but that day he knocked on the door instead. A man with long hair and a scouse accent opened the door, surprising Sonny. The smell of weed was prevalent. 'Alright, mate,' the man said.

'Hi. Sorry to bother you,' Sonny said. 'I've got a parcel here for Lesley-Anne, was delivered to mine by mistake.'

'Ah, no worries, I'll take it.'

'Oh, is she not in?' Sonny said, unwilling to hand the parcel over so readily. He tried to peer past the man, into the interior of the property.

'Who, Lesley? Yeah, she's in. Lesley!'

Lesley-Anne quickly appeared from the smoky fug-gloom of the kitchen to stand behind the long-haired man. Sonny didn't see her up close very often, so it was always a bit of a shock. She was a walking mass of contradictions. Physically, she was tall and wide with manly features, hands like spades, as she took the parcel from Sonny. She sounded like a man too, saying, 'Hello, love. You alright? Ah, bless you, I've been waiting for that,' in a deep voice. But, contrastingly, she was dressed like a woman, in a floral house dress – like Dolph Lundgren in drag – as she flicked her blonde hair to the side in an almost flirtatious, feminine way.

'No worries at all,' said Sonny. 'How you doing?' A feeler question, accompanied by what he thought was a sympathetic smile, hoping for an inkling, a titbit of information in regards to what had gone on. And, again, he tried to see into the property, but it was now nigh-on impossible with Lesley-Anne's vastness filling the doorway.'

'Yeah, good, thanks. You?'

'Yeah, not bad,' said Sonny. There was an awkward pause. This wasn't going anywhere fast. 'Sonny, by the way.'

'Ah, pleased to meet you properly, Sonny,' said

Lesley-Anne. 'I'm Lesley-Anne. This is Rob.' It was crazy that they had been living next-door to each other for the best part of six months, but had never had a proper conversation or introduced themselves.

'How you doing, Rob,' Sonny said.

'Sound, mate.' Rob shook his hand. There was another awkward pause.

Sonny was dying to ask questions, but didn't know how to without sounding like he was prying – which he was. 'Well, I'll leave you guys to it then,' he said.

'Yeah, nice one mate. Sound,' said Rob.

'Thanks for the parcel,' said Lesley Anne.

Sonny walked away and they closed the door. He was still none-the-wiser as to what had gone on, how poor Elton had met his demise. Even more baffled in fact. They were acting as if nothing had happened; meanwhile, it looked as if Elton had been replaced by another man. What did they do? Bump him off? He would have to report his findings to Kerry.

Spring rolled on and Elton's car remained where it was; it had developed one flat tyre and was accumulating dust, leaves and birdshit. Sonny was kept consistently busy with his escort work. Stacey had taken to WhatsApp video calling him some evenings, as she knew he worked during the day, to discuss bookings and client details, rather than standard emails. As a result, Sonny probably spoke to Stacey rather than any other female, including his work colleagues. He enjoyed their chats and seeing her face, whilst sitting on his sofa with a beer of an evening. He'd even told her about the whole neighbours'

murder-mystery thing. She was intrigued and made him promise to keep her updated.

Sonny started keeping a record, a hand-written account book, of his bookings and how much he earned from them. On average he was netting – *netting* – around six-hundred and fifty quid a week. Crazy money to him.

Sometimes he enjoyed the dates, especially if it involved something stimulating or different that he hadn't experienced before. Sometimes he even secretly looked at his bookings as potential mates for himself. His fantasy scenario being that he meets the *single* woman of his dreams, has a string of half a dozen dates with her – which she would be paying for of course – then they both fall in love; at which point she would cease being his client and they would live happily ever after.

More often than not, however, he didn't particularly enjoy the dates – especially the standard, restaurant-meal ones. These were becoming a chore. His clients' thirst for them was insatiable. The perennial, go-to favourite. God, he'd seen some restaurants... Chains, brands, Indians, Italians, pubs, little independent eateries... Increasingly, he would find his mind and eyes wandering during these dates. Studying the waitresses rather than his client, trying to gauge which one he would most like to sleep with. He felt awful for this. The other major downside of regularly eating out was all the excess calories being consumed. It was becoming a genuine struggle to burn them off. He'd already had to undo his belt a notch. He was seriously considering cutting back his hours at the deli – if they would let him that was, one less day a week for example – to join a gym. Historically, paying for a gym had always been out of the question for Sonny; he'd never had the means and was far too frugal. He saw gyms as an unnecessary expense when you had your own weights, a bench and some willpower.

Along with his expanding waistline, it was becoming harder and harder to hide his new, secret life from his kids – not only wanting to verbally share his recent turn of good fortune with them, but also the money itself. He wanted to spend it on them. Spoil them in a way he hadn't been able to since they were little.

'How come we're eating out? You won the lottery or something, Dad?' Olly, his son, said. The four of them were in a local pub, tucking into a Sunday lunch with all the trimmings. A rare treat.

Sonny laughed. 'No, I wish.'

'What's with us eating out then? We never eat out. Unless it's a special occasion – and then it's Wetherspoons!'

'Suspicious,' said Bea.

'Highly suspicious,' said Charlotte.

Sonny burst out laughing again. He found himself doing that more and more often of late.

'There he goes. Laughing again as well,' Olly said. 'Dad never laughs. Suspicious...'

'What are you lot like?' Sonny said, still grinning. His kids cracked him up. 'There's nothing suspicious going on at all.'

'I reckon he's got a new girlfriend,' said Bea. 'A rich one.'

'Is that so?' said Sonny, enjoying the banter and sitting back in his chair. He'd had a few pints of real ale.

'Yeah, that's why your beard's gone all fancy and trimmed.'

'And he's putting on weight. She must be a feeder,' said Charlotte. They all sniggered.

'Erm, excuse me!' Sonny said. 'No need to get personal. Anyway... if you must know, I have had an unexpected and considerable tax rebate that's all. Taken the pressure off a bit. Talking of which, I've got a proposition to put to you all... How do you fancy a few days away during the Easter hols? A little seaside break?' They all groaned in unison. 'What? It'll be fun. I was thinking Weymouth. It's lovely down there, the beach and that.'

'I'll be working during the Easter hols,' said Bea. 'Those driving lessons don't pay for themselves.'

'Yeah, so will I,' said Charlotte. 'Need to save for my car insurance.'

'Don't be silly. You've plenty of time for that yet. And to book it off. You haven't even got a test date.' It was hard to get them to do or commit to anything.

'Yeah, if you've got money to spend on a holiday, can't you just put it towards our insurance instead?' said Bea.

'Cheeky sod! No. I've already helped you out with that. Besides, I want to do something special with you all. Spend some proper time with you. Create memories.' Olly made a pretend retching sound. Then there was silence. 'So, Weymouth it is then. I'll get back to you with some dates so you can book it off.'

In comparison to his kids, Sonny's father didn't notice any change in Sonny's appearance or lifestyle – he was too self-absorbed – other than noticing Sonny had less time to spend with him. A source of irritation to him: 'You're always too busy! I could rot and die here for all you cared!' The old man's latest scheme was to try and purchase extra Parkinson's medication off the internet, as, according to him, his current dosage was nowhere near enough. This was a recurrent theme, an obsession with his meds and trying to wangle more out of the doctors. He was adamant he was going to send an email complaining to Michael. J. Fox, seeing if he would help him. This made Sonny laugh; his father was incapable of sending an email to anyone. He felt his father was becoming even more rambling, more detached from reality. Despite this, they still managed to have the odd game of chess, with Sonny forcing another couple of draws; annoyingly, however, he was still unable to snatch that ever-elusive victory from the old bugger.

In keeping with company policy, Sonny's dates with Susan inevitably and sadly came to an end. They had reached their maximum of six. The fact that Susan knew well in advance that this was going to happen didn't make it any easier for her. Sonny, too, had grown fond of Susan and started to look at her as a friend. There was no pressure with her. Everything they did was easy and relaxed, even if it was simply having a game of cards or watching a movie. Their similar personalities and likes somehow allowed them to dovetail together seamlessly. Sonny often found himself thinking how it was a shame that he didn't fancy her. But he didn't. He was very sure of that. Perhaps that was another reason it was so easy.

For their last date, as if trying to make the most of it, Susan booked him in for a whole, fun-packed day in

Nottingham. The itinerary was as follows… A matinee performance of *The Mousetrap* at the Theatre Royal. Followed by crazy golf. Followed by late-afternoon cocktails at the Alchemist and then dinner at World Service, Nottingham's fanciest restaurant. Crazy golf! Typically, eccentrically, Susan, Sonny thought when he read it. Even Stacey had remarked how she was getting envious of their dates: 'They sound like so much fun!'

This was all well and good, but it didn't sit right at all with Sonny that Susan would have to foot the bill for all this indulgence, especially when paying for his time as well. Lord knows, she had sent enough money his way over the last couple of months. And if he could have done anything about that aspect of it, he would have, but there was Stacey's living to consider too, her percentage of his bookings… The one thing he *could* change was his own voluntary input. So, unbeknownst to Susan, or Stacey, in the run-up to the date, Sonny planned and organised to cook a special meal for her at her place in the evening, rather than the restaurant. Providing he was still standing, of course, after an afternoon of cocktails. It would be his way of giving something back, of saying thank you to Susan. And a proper goodbye.

He was going to spring it on her as a surprise and had covertly arranged with Ian for him to pick them up. Sonny felt he knew Susan well enough now to be confident she would prefer this anyway, being at home on their last night, rather than in a formal restaurant. They could stick some 50's tunes on, maybe watch a film as well.

The day was a hoot and went according to plan. Susan was thrilled at Sonny's surprise, and having him, her own personal chef, in her kitchen, cooking. She cried when he told her. They ended up watching *A Streetcar Named Desire*, a favourite of both of theirs and in keeping with the 50s vibe. 'Now there was a man in his prime,' said Susan, enthusing about Brando. 'Both artistically and aesthetically. Look at him... Look at him, Sonny.'

'I am looking at him!' Sonny laughed. 'He's amazing.'

'It's funny isn't it,' said Susan. 'How an actor – or actress – can remain immortal due to being captured on film. They never age, never get old. Preserved for all eternity within your TV set.'

'I like that,' Sonny said. 'Preserved for all eternity within your TV set – I'd never thought of it like that.'

Susan cried a hell of a lot more when it was time to part at some ridiculous hour of the morning. Both of them steaming drunk. 'I can't believe I'm not going to see you again,' she sobbed.

'You will,' he said. 'Somehow, somewhere.'

'Don't say that if you don't mean it, it's too cruel. I know I'm just a client to you.'

'You're not just a client. You're more than that. You're a good friend.' He put his hand on her face tenderly.

She took his hand and kissed it. 'A good friend. That makes me sad and happy at the same time.'

Sonny felt a bit flat in the days after saying goodbye to Susan. He had formed his own personal attachment in a way. Purely platonic of course. But an attachment nevertheless. A connection. He could see why they didn't allow dates to go on indefinitely. Parting was too hard. He hadn't got away with keeping the cooking the meal secret from Stacey either. Susan had spilled the beans apparently in an emotional email to Stacey, gushing with how wonderful Sonny was. '*That was naughty of you, but very sweet*,' Stacey said in a WhatsApp message to him. '*You're a sweet man*.' She followed the message with a kiss.

# CHAPTER 16

And then the Weymouth trip came round. The Garfunkels couldn't have been luckier with the weather. The Easter holidays coincided with a prolonged spell of hot, dry, sunny days. Sonny was beyond excited setting off with the kids in the car, eagerly looking forward to spending some quality time with them. Marred only slightly by the almighty fuss his father had kicked up at him going away. It made Sonny feel guilty, possibly his father's intention. But Sonny wouldn't have dreamed of inviting him along. It would have stressed him out and ruined the whole thing. Totally defeated the object. Sonny needed a break from him, as much as anything else. He would have made it all about him, monopolised everything. There wasn't any room for him in the car for a start, let alone his walking frame, wheelchair and paraphernalia. Pressure cushion, urine bottle, medication... He would just have to survive on his own for a few days. Sonny was already dreading the phone calls he was going to get from him. He'd half a mind to block him whilst he was away.

As was tradition, Olly was in charge of the music for the journey. Sonny was happy to let him. The kids had a good, eclectic taste and Olly was usually indulgent and sympathetic to everyone's individual favourites, a crowd-pleasing DJ. They were soon singing along together – Sonny loved these moments; they reminded him of the old days when the kids were young – and thoughts of his father soon dissipated.

After three hours or so travelling, prior to hitting the coast, they passed through the country lanes of rural Dorset. A fact hammered home by a couple of bizarre wild-life related incidents in close succession. First, they had to swerve round a gruesome bit of roadkill, a small deer, possibly a muntjac, lying in the road. It looked as though it had been there for a while; it's crimson stomach, hollowed out, exposed and drying in the sun. Two carrion crows were perched atop it, ripping off strips, as if it was choice, venison jerky. 'Eew!' The girls screamed. Then, merely five minutes later, a suicidal pigeon thudded sickeningly into the car in front of them, exploding in a confetti of feathers. They all screamed this time as they sped through them, the feathers surrounding the car. 'Jesus! Welcome to the countryside, folks!' said Sonny.

And then they arrived at their destination. The seaside resort of Weymouth. Sonny had picked out a reasonably-priced hotel. A traditional, grand, Victorian one, slap-bang, front and centre of the town high street, facing the sea. He had been sold by the views from the rooms on the website; huge bay windows that afforded almost a panoramic vista of the beach. Even the kids were impressed upon checking in. 'Woah! Check out the view!' They all stood there, open-mouthed. It looked like a seaside postcard out there. The sky a bubble-gum ice cream blue. Mr. Whippy clouds. White-gold sand. The beach busy with colour and people, stretching off into the distance in both directions, as far as the eye could see. Like hundreds and thousands on a cake.

With towels and sun cream, the family hit the beach. The sand was hot underfoot. The sea-breeze was warm. Almost tropical. It was perfect. They alternated between sunbathing, then cooling off in the sea. Sonny and Olly drank cold bottles of beer. The fluffy clouds lazed like icebergs across the bluetiful sky. The girls watched the tanned boys, playing cricket and volleyball. The boys watched the girls tan. Oh, to be young, thought Sonny, involuntarily sucking in his torso. One particular lad close-by to them, must have been late-teens, looked for all the world like a young Roger Federer. Wavy dark hair. Ray-Bans. Peach-coloured swim shorts, perfectly offsetting his olive-skin. Annoyingly cool. Probably rich. It didn't take long for the girls to notice him and start giggling. 'He smiled at me,' said Bea, as he walked past them.

'No he didn't, he was smiling at me,' said Charlotte.

'No, he wasn't. He was smiling at me!' said Bea.

'Slut,' said Charlotte.

'Skank,' said Bea.

'Alright you two, knock it off,' said Sonny.

'It was neither of you anyway. He was smiling at me,' said Olly, droll as ever. Sonny laughed.

'We'll see, if he walks past again,' said Charlotte.

'Well, you won't have to wait too long, I'll bet,' said Sonny. 'Reckon that's the third time he's walked past already.'

'Yeah. Clearly fancies *me*,' said Bea. 'Bet he asks for my Snap.'

'Snap? We didn't bring any snap,' said Sonny.

Olly spat his beer out, laughing. 'Oh my... She means Snapchat. Her Snapchat name.'

'Oh, is that still going?' said Sonny. 'Thought it would have died a death by now, all that gimmicky photo disappearing stuff.'

'Nope. Bigger than ever,' said Bea. 'Probs use it more than anything. For messaging and connecting with people.'

After a good couple of hours or so, true to form, Sonny started to turn pink. He needed some respite from the sun. And some food. He got his phone out and googled the Wetherspoons in town. Old habits die hard. Plus, he didn't want to appear too flashy with money. The kids would smell a rat again. 'Right, who's ready for some grub?'

'Me,' said Olly, saying it as a beer-belch.

'Oh, do we have to,' moaned Bea. 'I'm not ready to go yet.'

'Doesn't want to miss Loverboy if he walks past again,' said Olly.

'Er, yep,' said Bea. 'And your point is?'

'Come back again after we've eaten if you want,' said Sonny. 'Doesn't look like the sun's going anywhere in a hurry. Or Loverboy for that matter.'

'No, I'll be all bloated from eating.'

'Well, keep your top on then.'

'Then I won't be able to tan, defeats the object.'

Sonny groaned. Why did everything with teenagers take prolonged negotiations?

'We'll come, but we're having a drink,' said Charlotte.

'Well, course you're having a drink,' said Sonny.

'An alcoholic one.'

'You're not old enough, you won't get served.'

'We will, we've got fake IDs.'

'You haven't.' The girls sniggered. 'You have! Since when?'

'Since this guy at college started making them for everyone. Twenty quid a pop.'

'I can't believe this. Did you know they'd got fake IDs?' he said to Olly. 'I'm shocked.'

'Don't bring me into this!' Olly said, holding up his hands.

'Don't be such a prude, Dad,' said Charlotte. 'Don't tell me you never drank in a pub underage when you were younger, *'Back in the day'* – during the war or whenever it was.'

'Cheeky sod. And, yes, I did. But I didn't have a fake ID. Didn't need one come to think of it, they just served you. Even in your school uniform.'

The Wetherspoons in town was huge – and heaving. But the food and proper pints of beer were most welcome. They ordered on the app. Sonny was a nervous wreck when the drinks got brought over, a vodka and orange for Bea and pint of fruit cider for Charlotte. He had tried to talk them into ordering their drinks themselves, separately at the bar, so he didn't have to be involved. But they argued how, one, it was heaving at the bar and, two, that would only draw more attention to them. He'd resignedly acknowledged they were right. Confirmed by the fact that, blessedly, the girls didn't even get asked for ID when the drinks finally arrived; the poor kid that served them didn't look any older than they were. He had a panicked rabbit-in-the-headlights look on his face from how rushed off his feet he was. He dumped the drinks and scarpered, not batting an eyelid at who they were for or how old they were. 'See,' said Charlotte. 'You just need to chill, Dad. Be cool.'

'Yeah, Daddy Cool,' Bea said. The girls both sniggered and clinked their glasses together triumphantly. Sonny shook his head.

As usual, Sonny's pint went straight through him and he had to go for a pee. Feeling a little more relaxed now with the drinking situation and enjoying a beer buzz, along with being away with the kids, Sonny told them to order another round. 'Order on the app, I'm nipping to the loo.' He left his card and his phone.

'He *is* feeling flush,' Sonny heard Olly say as he set off.

The toilets turned out to be quite a trek upstairs. 'Food still not here?' Sonny said when he returned.

'Nope,' they all said.

Sonny settled back down. 'You ordered the drinks?'

'Yep,' Olly said. Then there was a strange silence. The kids looked sheepish, collectively furtive.

'What?' Sonny said. 'What's going on?' He looked at his phone. 'You haven't been going through my phone, have you?' He immediately picked it up, his mind panicking at what might be on there.

'Er, no. Gross!' said Bea. 'We don't want to know what you get up to.'

'You need a new phone by the way, I don't know how you can see anything on that thing,' said Charlotte.

'Yeah, I know. Costs money though.' He habitually pressed his phone open to check for any notifications. The screen lit up and there it was. A new booking request email from Stacey. Shit, he thought. He could feel his face immediately flushing. He glanced up at the kids to see if he had got away with it, hoping it might have only just come through. They were all looking at him, sipping their drinks, a couple of them with raised eyebrows, as if waiting to see what he did next. Clearly, they'd seen it, must have come through whilst they were ordering. Talk about timing. He blushed further. This happened quite often with the kids, they could embarrass him easily, make him feel uncomfortable. Wasn't that meant to be the other way round? Parents embarrassing teenagers? But what had they seen exactly? He cleared his throat, stalling, desperately trying to think of a story. An explanation.

'So, who's Stacey, and what's 'Plus One' then, Dad?' said Bea, never one to hold back. She took another slurp of her drink through her straw, looking as though she was enjoying this. The others shifted expectantly on their stools.

'Ah, that. Ah, it's just a bloody scam thing.' He waved his hand dismissively. 'Annoying. I was on the dating sites the other day, you know, just having a nosey–'

'Thought you'd given up on them?' said Olly.

'I have. I mean, I had. Just thought I'd have a little look.'

'See if there's any fresh meat out there, eh?' said Charlotte. They all laughed.

'Something like that. Anyway... you know how you get those ads on there?'

'Nope,' said Olly.

'Yeah, you know, tailored ads and that. Annoying pop-ups.'

'Not on *Tinder* you don't.'

'Well, I don't go on *Tinder*.'

'What do you go on, Silver Surfers. com?' They all laughed again.

'Yeah, I'm not that old... anyway, I inadvertently pressed on one by mistake, an ad, and it took me to this agency thing, which now keep bombarding me with spam; they've somehow got my details.' He was starting to think how far-fetched this was sounding.

'What sort of agency?'

'I dunno. Some sort of escort agency or something, I guess.'

'You inadvertently, just by accident, signed up for an escort agency?'

'Yes, I'm telling you!'

'You that desperate you've taken to using prostitutes now, Dad?' They really were enjoying this.

'Stacey, eh? Sounds like a prostitute's name. What's her speciality? Whips and bondage?'

Just then, the harassed-looking young waiter appeared with their food. 'Fish and chips? Who's having the fish and chips?' he said.

'That's mine thanks,' said Sonny.

'Burger with cheese?'

'That's mine,' said Olly.

It was a much-welcome and convenient distraction. The kids became pre-occupied with their food, Bea prodding hers and moaning about it as usual. Then the routine trek around the building in search of condiments and sauce sachets. Sonny breathed a mental sigh of relief. Close shave, but it looked as though he had gotten away with it. Lesson learned; he shouldn't leave his phone with his kids.

# CHAPTER 17

Post-meal and the agency email thankfully forgotten about, the girls were keen to get back to the beach. The combination of travelling, too much sun and drinking during the day, however, had done for Sonny. He couldn't stop yawning, could barely keep his eyes open. He chastised himself for peaking too early, indulging too much in his excitement of being away. He was no longer twenty years old. 'We keeping you awake, Dad?' said Olly.

'Sorry, it's the drinking during the day – gets me every time.'

'Why don't you have an afternoon nap?' said Bea. 'Isn't that what old people do?'

'Yeah, like a siesta – you are on holiday after all,' said Charlotte. A nap sounded good, very good. Crisp, cool hotel bed sheets...

'But what about you guys? What about the beach?' Sonny said. He hated leaving them, felt bad for it. They'd come away to be together; at least, he had.

'Oh, we'll be fine. Don't worry about us.' They sounded almost pleased about the idea.

'Poor old dad cramping your style, eh?'

'No...'

'Liar,' said Olly, yawning himself. 'I might join you actually, Dad. Quick nap back at the hotel. All that travelling's worn me out.'

'But what about the girls? Who'll look after them?' said Sonny.

'For Christ's sake, Dad! We're not eight-years-old! We don't need babysitting!'

'You're still babies to me. And you're in a strange town. There's some strange men out there.' He was purposely winding them up now. And it was working.

'Yeah, you for a start,' Bea said. 'The beach is literally twenty yards across a main road from the hotel. You'll be able to see us out the bloody window.'

'Ah, that's a good point actually. I'll be able to watch you. Keep an eye on you.'

'Now you're just sounding creepy.'

'Dad's a nonce,' said Olly.

'What's a nonce?' said Sonny.

'A paedo,' said Charlotte.

'Nice,' said Sonny.

'Right, I'm going. This is actually starting to make me feel like a child now.' Bea got dramatically up from the table.

'Woah! Wait for us then,' said Sonny. 'We'll drop you off on the way.'

Back in his hotel room, the first thing Sonny did was look out of the window to locate the girls. He couldn't spot them at first. It would be typical of them to go and sit further down the beach, out of 'eyeshot' to spite him, he thought. But then they wouldn't be able to keep their own eyes on Loverboy. Or do their best to attract him. But, no, there they were, setting their towels back up, bless them. And there was Loverboy, still cavorting in the sand with his mates. Feeling the effects of the daytime beers, Sonny smiled to himself, thinking about the conversation earlier. About him watching them. Keeping an eye on them. He ought to rap loudly on the window and wave to them to wind them up further. They'd never forgive him if he did. Probably wouldn't be able to hear him anyway...

A zephyr of sanguinity wafted over Sonny as he stood there watching the girls and the beach, the waves gently shampooing the rocks. A feeling of contentment and relaxation he hadn't known for a while. He put it down to being away. Spending quality time with the kids.

Sonny turned away from the window, yawned and surveyed the hotel room. It was a nice room. Spacious. He congratulated himself on how well he'd chosen. A fleeting, chastening, thought of wishing he had a partner to share it with crossed his mind. To crawl into bed with, under the sheets. Those days seemed long gone. He spotted his suitcase. Hadn't even unpacked yet. 'So, shower or bed,' he said out loud. He really couldn't be bothered to shower, but equally didn't want to get sand in his bed after the beach; there was nothing worse, and he was already feeling a little sore, his neck and the tops of his arms. 'Shower it is then.'

When Sonny woke, he felt disorientated. Where was he and why was it still light? Then he remembered. How long had he been asleep for? The thought and situation left him a little breathless. He grabbed his phone. To his amazement, he'd slept for three solid hours. He never slept during the day. And rarely slept so fitfully. Probably catching up. His thoughts then turned quickly to the girls. He shot up out of bed to look out of the window. The beach had dramatically thinned out, the sun was going down, and the girls and their towels were nowhere to be seen. He had a momentary panic, not knowing where they were. Whilst also feeling irresponsible. Loverboy had gone too. And his mates. What if the girls had foolishly decided to go off with them somewhere?

He grabbed his phone again to see if they'd messaged, saying they were back. They hadn't. He quickly sent a WhatsApp on their group chat, asking if they were back. Please don't take too long to reply, he thought. He'd have to go and knock on their door if they did. What if they were asleep though? Tired out after the beach. He'd wake them up. But how would he know where they were if he didn't?

Suddenly, his phone pinged with a message. He opened it up. It was Olly responding: '*Heard the girls come back about six* (his room was next-door to theirs) *so you can stop panicking. Reckon they're asleep though.*' Sonny breathed a sigh of relief. Panicking? Who was panicking? He thanked Olly. Bless him. It was good to know they were back, safe and sound. He then noticed the email notification on his phone from Stacey. In all the drama of keeping it hidden and then being so tired, he had forgotten all about it. That wasn't like him; he enjoyed hearing from Stacey. He opened up the email.

*Hey Sonny, hope you are having a good break with your kids (smiley face). Don't worry about responding to this until you get back. Just a standard booking request come through. Evening meal, the usual... Saturday night, peak companionship. Check out the date and confirm and I'll get it booked in. Don't worry till you're back though. Enjoy your break, Stacey. x*

Sonny noticed she put kisses on his emails now too. He wondered if she did that with all her escorts once she'd built up a rapport with them. Probably did. He was going to miss their little WhatsApp vid chats whilst he was away. He enjoyed those. The thought of another standard meal booking left him feeling a bit flat as well. He longed for something more exciting. Something different. Which was crazy. He should just appreciate the money.

That evening they dined at a pizza joint. A unanimous choice. Sonny had high hopes for the evening, wanting to make the most of it. Typical, boyish 'first night of a holiday' syndrome. Maybe a bar crawl of the town, then a late-night game of cards back in his room. But by the time the girls had got showered and ready after their late-afternoon nap – anyone would think they were heading out to the Oscars, not a night on the strip in humble Weymouth – it was getting on for 8:30.

By this stage, Sonny and Olly had sunk another couple of beers in the hotel bar, whilst watching a football match. Add to this a couple of bottles of wine shared with the meal and Sonny's tiredness began to overwhelm him again. He couldn't shake it. The girls, who'd had a couple of glasses themselves by now, were then pushing for a bar crawl of their own, to get to know the town – more in the hopes of bumping into Loverboy and his mates, no doubt, thought Sonny (they had ended up chatting to them earlier apparently). But despite how much he hated being the bad guy, especially as he didn't see the girls often enough, he just couldn't sanction it; not on the first night, not without them knowing the town better; and certainly not without Olly, who'd expressed little interest in being their chaperone for the night, whilst they chased and chatted to boys. Who could blame him?

Sonny tried to sweeten the blow with the suggestion of a visit to a cocktail bar for one round of cocktails, a nightcap, before they headed back. This, the kids reluctantly agreed to, costing Sonny a small fortune in the process. Once again, the girls didn't even get ID'd. What was it with Weymouth? Then they headed back to the hotel, by this stage, all of them more than a little tipsy. Sonny half-heartedly suggested a game of cards, but even he had gone beyond it. 'We're not staying up playing boring cards, Dad,' said Bea. 'Come on, Charlotte. Bed.' She took her fractionally younger sibling's hand, as a mother would with a child. Olly didn't get a say, which was often the case.

'Hey, wait,' said Sonny. 'Kiss.' The girls groaned.

'Come on.' Sonny gathered them both to him, hugging and kissing them goodnight. 'You can go out on your own tomorrow night,' he said, trying to appease them. 'Get your bearings a bit during the day first. Love you both. Goodnight.' He pushed them away.

'Love you too, Dad.'

'Your turn,' he said, holding his arms out to Olly for a hug. Something he rarely did.

'Really?' said Olly awkwardly. 'You're drunk.'

'No, I'm not. Night, Son. Love you.' He gave him a hug.

'Yeah, you are. Night.'

Despite the increasingly overwhelming tiredness Sonny had felt as the day had worn on, true to form, he struggled to sleep. It was always the way. He blamed the afternoon nap. But at some point he must have dozed off, for he had a vivid, unsettling dream. It was a black and white dream, or grey at least. Set in a grey, post-apocalyptic world. Like one of those pandemic or disaster movies, where displaced people roamed the streets. In this case, the streets were mainly full of children. And it was Weymouth, or a version of. Sonny was walking on one side of the thoroughfare. Whilst packs of children, orphan-like urchins in rags, walked on the other side of the road in the opposite direction. In the dream Sonny was in distress, searching for his lost children, amongst the crowds. He hadn't seen them for days. And then, to his elation, he spotted them, the girls anyway, but not Olly. The girls were younger versions of themselves, barely five or six years old. They were in a gang or group of other older children. Ragamuffins. Sonny called out to the girls and ran across the road to them in desperation. But on seeing him, Bea immediately hid Charlotte away from him, wrapping her in a great, grey overcoat of a taller, older girl. 'No, Dad, You can't see her!' Bea said. 'You can't look at her!'

'Why? Why can't I? What's wrong with her?'

He forcefully pulled open the coat. There, inside, was

a shocking, emaciated version of Charlotte. Starved. Big, hollow eyes. Sunken-in cheeks. Like those awful archive photos of poor Auschwitz captives. An ice-cold sob caught in Sonny's throat. 'I told you not to, Dad!' Bea wailed. And then she ran off into the crowds.

'No!' Sonny screamed, terrified of losing her again and chasing after her.

As he pursued her, just about keeping sight of her, Bea had become even younger still, possibly three or four years old. Her clothes had changed too. She was wearing an old-fashioned coat – a 40's wartime children's coat – along with white bobby socks and shiny black school shoes that stood out against the grey. Bea really didn't want to be caught. And the more Sonny called after her and chased her, the more determined she was to lose him. Eventually, she reached a series of intersecting roads, busy with cars, and with one last look behind her at her father, she made to dash out into the traffic. Sonny skidded to a halt. Terrified of losing her, but even more terrified that she was going to get run over if he continued to chase her. He tried to scream, 'Bea! Stop!' But no sound would come out. His throat wouldn't make the words. He felt desperately helpless. Powerless, with no control.

And then he woke, up. Still trying to call out. Sweating and terrified. He was in his hotel room. It was just a dream. Or rather a nightmare. A horrifyingly real nightmare. One that as Sonny lay there panting in the dark, he couldn't help but see the symbolism of. What the fuck? He needed a pee. He got up and padded over the soft carpet to the bathroom. He urinated, still shaken up by the dream. Needing a distraction, he then walked over to the huge window of the bedroom, curious as to what a seafront looked like in the dead of night. He pulled back the thin curtains and peered out, looking in both directions. Save for the intermittent glow of the lampposts on the promenade, he was surprised at how dark it was out there. You couldn't even see the sea. Just a vast, infinite darkness. All the houses built into the cliff-faces of the bay had disappeared entirely. As if a huge dam had burst somewhere nearby, filling the town with black water and extinguishing all the lights.

It's a small world, or so the saying goes... And if Sonny thought he couldn't possibly have another situation where his secret life might be exposed whilst away with the kids, he was very much mistaken. It was the last day of their mini-break. They were in one of the many tourist shops, the ones that sold inflatables, tat and nik-naks – the girls were looking for some souvenirs to take home for their mum and mates. Sonny was stood with Olly, lazily spinning one of the sunglasses stands round, both of them trying on various pairs and checking them out in the mirrors on the stands. A vaguely-familiar, female voice immediately behind Sonny then caught his attention. What was most familiar about the voice was its annoyingness. It was grating. A reminder of something he'd tried to forget. And then as the person let out a laugh, the penny dropped and Sonny's heart began to race, thumping a desperate beat.

Fortunately still wearing an impenetrable mirror-blue pair of shades, Sonny turned the sunglasses stand again on its axle slightly so that he could see behind him where the voice was coming from. To confirm his suspicions. The image reflected back was a little blurry, but the person was unmistakable. It was Jules. The annoying, disaster-of-a-date woman with the big mouth who had thrown up into the tulips. What on earth were the chances of her being in Weymouth, in the very same shop, at exactly the same time as him?

Again, fortunately for Sonny, in holiday mode now, he was wearing a short-sleeved, bordering on garish, Hawaiian shirt– he'd bought it to embarrass the kids – chino shorts and flip-flops. A far cry from the attire he'd been sporting that night on their date. But still, she was right behind him. He could even smell her perfume. Another familiar, sickly association. He couldn't let her see him. How would he explain it to the kids if she recognised him? Started asking him awkward questions about being an escort? Which was highly likely. Tact wasn't exactly her strong suit. He had to get out of there. But how did he do so without speaking? What if she recognised his voice too?

Slowly, he slipped the sunglasses he was wearing off and placed them back on the stand. Quickly, and in as loud-a-voice as he dared, Sonny said to Olly, 'Shit. Got to dash to the loo mate, meet us over there when you're done, the beach ones.' And without waiting for a reply, he scurried out of the shop, via the nearest exit.

'Oh. OK,' he heard Olly say to his departing back.

About five minutes later the kids sauntered over to meet him, clutching bags. 'Sorry about that,' Sonny said. 'Bit of a dodgy stomach this morning...'

'Lovely,' said Bea.

'Gross,' said Charlotte.

But he'd gotten away with it. Another close shave, but once again he had survived. And close shaves aside, the holiday had been a success. The weather had held out and, more importantly, Sonny had achieved what he wanted, some much-needed bonding time with his kids. To make memories with them. To feel part of their everyday lives again. To get to know them better as the young adults they were all-too-quickly turning into. He was proud of them.

Setting off home, a shared buoyant mood filled the car, along with a perceptible sense of everyone feeling closer to each other. To Sonny's delight, the kids all agreed they should do stuff like that more often. Mini-breaks away together. The girls had even come away with the added bonus of two new male acquaintances – Loverboy and one of his mates. They had hung out during the holiday and exchanged 'Snaps' apparently. Turned out Loverboy preferred Charlotte to Bea in the end. Bea didn't care, as she preferred Loverboy's mate to him anyway. On the way back, they were busy tapping away on their phones and enthusing about how they were going to drive down to Weymouth to visit the boys the second they passed their tests.

# CHAPTER 18

The immediate days following the holiday were tough for Sonny. It was like coming down from a high. After the euphoria of spending quality time with his kids, he missed them even more initially and felt a bit glum. A little lonelier. Not only that, the break had been a welcome respite from the demands of his father. Despite one phone call from the care home saying his father had had one of his 'tumbles', 'nothing to worry about', Sonny hadn't heard from his father at all whilst being away. A small miracle. Visiting him at the care home was another bump back down to earth, a reality check; and also, a bit of a shock. His father always looked cross, it was the nature of his face, but he looked positively fuming and very sorry for himself, sitting in his chair in his room, when Sonny arrived. His neck more stooped than ever.

He wouldn't look at Sonny at first, still sulking and pissed off with him for going away and leaving him – 'At the mercy of these bastards! The place has gone to the dogs!' He looked a state, his hair unkempt and overlong, white stubble on his gaunt cheeks; he was looking noticeably thinner in general, which was a worry. He was skin and bone as it was. He said he'd lost his appetite. Probably on hunger strike out of protest, Sonny thought. But if it was true, again, it was a worry; his father had always managed to maintain a healthy appetite, despite the plethora of pills he was on to keep him functioning.

In comparison to the rest of him, Sonny noticed his father's ankles and lower-legs were looking a little swollen, making his trousers a little tight. On top of that, underneath his trousers, it looked as though he was wearing incontinence pants too. That was a first, and another shock. Things seemed to have rapidly gone downhill in the four days Sonny had been away. It was a lot for him to come back and deal with – the stress and responsibility of it all.

Sonny voiced his concerns to a carer the second one appeared to check on him. 'We're keeping an eye on the legs,' she said. 'It's fluid build-up. He won't get up out of his chair. We keep telling him. He needs to put his feet up more–'

'*I can't get up out of my bloody chair!*' his father exploded, hearing correctly for once. 'I've got no movement! There's nothing left in the tank. No juice! They're not bringing me my pills on time. They're always late! It's that new nurse. He's totally useless – and a bully.'

Sonny looked at the carer. 'This is Dan, the new meds nurse. Him and your father have had a few run-ins. Didn't get off to the best start with Dan, did we John?'

'He's a bully. Tries to manhandle me, force me to move when I can't bloody move.'

'*Is* he getting his meds on time?' Sonny asked quietly, covering his mouth with his hand.

'Yes.'

'And what about these things?' Sonny gently tweaked his father's newly-bulked out trousers, near his hip.

His father slapped his hand away. 'Get off me!' He looked ashamed, staring straight ahead.

'Again, he's not getting out of his chair on time, he's had a few accidents recently. Some of them messy ones, if you get my drift.'

His father reddened further. 'I press the buzzer and you don't come!'

'Now, that's not true, John. We always–'

'It is bloody true! I press it over and over again. You're all out the back, smoking. I can smell it on you.'

Sonny didn't know who to believe. From what he had observed himself at the home, he was kind of siding with his father in this instance. 'Well, either his Parkinson's has rapidly gone downhill, or he isn't getting the meds on time, because this is a new thing,' he said. 'The accidents.'

'I can assure you he's getting his meds on time.'

'Well, just keep an eye on it please. Thank you. And make sure he's eating.' This was as close as Sonny got to confrontation; he hated it.

Sonny and his father had a game of chess before Sonny left, an attempt to calm the old man down. It worked. To Sonny's surprise, his father played mercilessly and with a steely determination that had been somewhat lacking of late. None of the recent dithering and lapses in concentration for Sonny to take advantage of. It was like the old days and Sonny didn't stand a chance.

Probably his father's way of exacting control again. Of dishing out a form of punishment to Sonny for leaving him for a few days.

An unexpected distraction then saved Sonny from his post-break malaise and stresses. He was sitting on the sofa at home one Saturday morning, doing the crossword, when a familiar sound he hadn't heard for a while out the back disturbed him. The pop and growl of a sputtering motorbike on the neighbours' drive. It wasn't until Sonny heard the motorbike that he realised he hadn't heard it since that weekend of the incident next-door – the incident that up till now there had been no resolution to. The 'murder-mystery' as him and Stacey now referred to it as. She still asked him if there had been any developments from time to time.

Curiosity piqued, Sonny clambered up on his knees on the sofa to peer out the back. As he did so, frustratingly, the sound of the motorbike died. The yard was empty and the gate was still closed. The garage door, however, that Sonny could just see the top of over the backyard fence, was fully open. Again, it struck Sonny that he hadn't seen that open in a while. As a couple, the neighbours had always been in and out of the garage. Maybe he hadn't seen them in there lately as he was at home a lot less now? Or maybe the motorbike just hadn't been used since the incident? Either way, Sonny couldn't help himself; he wanted to know where that motorbike currently was, and who had been riding it.

Feeling like a dreadful Nosey Parker, he slipped on his shoes, picked up the kitchen pedal bin liner that needed emptying anyway, and ventured outside. The dustbins were located, butted up, against the exterior fence of the yard, so he would have to walk out onto the drive and past the garage. As casually as he could under the circumstances, Sonny pushed open the gate. Lesley-Anne's car was on the drive, but no motorbike. To his left, out of the corner of his eye, Sonny could see the open garage. Most of it in dark shadow due to the door. Sonny turned right towards the bins. As he opened the bin lid and deposited his rubbish, he turned to peer into the garage again. To try and get a better look.

There, against the left-hand wall, illuminated by what little of the morning sun was penetrating the interior of the garage, was the motorbike. That explained that then. But who'd been riding it? Realising he was standing there gawping, still holding the bin lid open, Sonny closed it and slowly headed back towards the garage. As he neared it, he could hear the tick of the motorbike's engine as it cooled and settled. Could imagine the heat coming off it. Suddenly the skid of footsteps on a dusty garage floor made him jump. A figure loomed out of the shadows, and then a voice, 'Alright mate?'

'Jesus Christ!' said Sonny. His heart hopped like a wet frog in his chest. 'You scared me to death!' It was Elton – or whatever his name was – the presumed-deceased. His hair was no longer died blue, just very grey. He looked grey in general, his pallor. Thinner, too. A broken man. It was a shock. Like seeing a ghost. A ghost in bike leathers.

'Sorry mate, didn't mean to startle yer. Just collecting some last few bits.'

'No, no... I'm sorry. Just wasn't expecting anyone. I mean, I heard the motorbike...' He wasn't making much sense. Guilt probably written all over his face.

'Yeah, she's still going, noisy old thing. 'ad 'er fifteen years or more.' They both looked at the motorbike.

'So, the car out front...' Sonny couldn't help but say. 'That *is* yours too, right?'

'Ah. No, that's Poppers'. Or was. God rest his soul. I was just insured on it. Kept it running for him, like. Lost his licence, see.'

'Poppers?'

'Yeah. An old pal. Loved his liquid gold. Passed away at my leaving bash. OD'ed, the silly sod. Dreadful business. You must have heard? Didn't she tell yer?'

'No. No, I hadn't heard anything' – he refrained from saying, 'no one had' – 'I did wonder about the car, though... Well, I'm sorry to hear that.'

'Yeah. Ta. He was more 'er pal than mine, they went way back; that's why it didn't seem right still using 'is motor when we, you know, split, like...'

'Ah, yes. Of course. Well, I'm sorry to hear about that, too. You know, you guys...'

'Ah, these things 'appen. Things run their course...' He looked and sounded sad.

'Well, good luck then,' Sonny said. 'Hope you get sorted.'

'Yeah, cheers mate. You too. She in?'

'Who, Lesley-Anne?'

'Yeah.'

'I've no idea. Sorry.' Wonder if he knows there's a new guy living with her, Sonny thought.

'Ah. No worries.'

Sonny headed back through the gate and closed it behind him. So, that finally clears that up then, he thought. He couldn't wait to tell Stacey. And Kerry.

# CHAPTER 19

Sonny had been in the male escort game for three months. It seemed a lot longer. In that time he had made over seven-thousand pounds net and garnered ten five-star ratings. The significance of which being it meant Sonny's rate automatically went up. Something he had totally forgotten about. Stacey informed him of the fact in one of her CONGRATULATIONS emails. Guess it worked both ways, Sonny figured. Meant she earnt more too. Seven grand net though in three months was unbelievable. This was on top of his deli salary, of course, which, the job itself, was getting harder and harder to keep motivated for. But still he couldn't quite take that leap of giving it up. What if the escort work suddenly dried up? What if he just couldn't hack it anymore? It wasn't as though he enjoyed it. Entertaining women was exhausting. And that was the normal ones...

At least half of them wanted more than just companionship – even though that was all they had booked for. At the cheaper rate of course. He was starting to become more immune, less shocked and outraged, at the things that went on. The things that got offered and suggested to him. Always with the lure of some extra cash. Sometimes a crazy amount. 'There's nowt as queer as folk,' as the saying goes... He'd been asked to spank someone. Tie someone up. Do a full body massage. Do a striptease. Tell someone off. Be told off. Engage in various roleplays – the most extreme of which being to pretend to be a burglar, break into a lady's house and pretend to rape her whilst she feigned being asleep! Oh, and not forgetting the lady who turned out to actually be a man who wanted Sonny to defecate on him/her. That one was the creepiest of all.

But Sonny could hold his head up high, knowing he hadn't succumbed to a single offer, despite the amount of money that had been thrown his way. Ditto with if he had found a client mildly attractive – which had only happened once or twice anyway. He somehow seemed to be able to stick to his principles. To not cross that line. He didn't think he would ever be able to look his kids in the eye again if he did.

And then there was the money itself. The majority of which was sitting, accumulating, in his linked savings account. He was starting to think it was his ticket out of rented accommodation. A deposit for a house down the line. Finally getting back on the property ladder before he got any older. Something that his kids could benefit from. To give them a head start in life. He'd never been frivolous, so it wasn't hard to save. He was enjoying seeing the money grow, and that was his greatest motivation to continue.

Mid-June, a booking request came through that piqued Sonny's interest more than usual. It was in a week's time, 21st. June. The longest day, no less. But midweek. What was interesting about it was that it was for a walk. He'd never been booked for a walk before. Four hours, social companionship. Four hours was a long walk, thought Sonny. Still, he was partial to a country walk. Especially at the current time of year. Didn't get to do it enough these days. No one to walk with. There was no fun in walking on your own. He'd used to walk a lot with his ex, and then the kids, but even they'd kind of lost interest in it, always pulled a face when he suggested it. Could do with the exercise too, beat sitting in a restaurant, stuffing his face. The booking was for a Ms. S. Town. Stacey had sent the standard, accompanying, '*Let me know if you're available and I'll get it booked in. x*' message, nothing more. Probably as it was a lower-end booking. Not much financial return in it for her. Sonny didn't need to give this one much thought. He quickly checked his diary, then confirmed straightaway. He was already looking forward to it – being paid two-hundred and fifty quid for what was hopefully a pleasant, country stroll! Easy money.

The evening of the booking arrived. And what a glorious evening it was. Blue skies. Throbbing sun, dripping honey. Bursting hedgerows. Nature dressed in her finest livery of emerald and gold. More than fitting for the Summer Solstice. The meet-up location was an unexpected bonus too. Just on the outskirts of Bingham. Sonny knew it well. He could even walk to it. There was a network of country paths, just the other side of the railway track. The lady must be relatively local to know of them.

Five-forty-five and Sonny set off. They were due to meet at six pm, confirmed by a quick text and reply on the work phone. For the first time in a while, he hadn't known what to wear on a date. The usual shirt, smart trousers and shoes were the opposite of walking attire. In the end, he'd opted for jeans, a polo shirt, shades and some deck shoes. Comfortable, but smart-casual. He hoped he wouldn't be visibly perspiring by the time he got there. He chewed gum as he walked, feeling the usual nervous energy in anticipation of meeting a new client. He tried to enjoy the scenery.

After ten minutes or so, Sonny crossed over the railway track and hit the network of paths. They had arranged to meet at a sort of crossroads of dirt tracks that had a signpost pointing four ways, signalling where you wanted to walk to and how far it was. A few minutes early, Sonny got there first. He scanned the tracks in all directions, no sign of anyone yet. Just high hedgerows, cornfields and undulating paths, baked tan by the sun. You could see the whole outline of Bingham town from where he was, including, most noticeably, the church and its spire.

It struck Sonny as he waited, how rural their meet-up point was, how isolated. And, therefore, how trusting on the part of the client. Especially considering she was a new one. That was the beauty of the reviews, he figured. They built trust. Talking of which, he removed his shades; shades could be impenetrable, a bit intimidating. Eyes told a lot. He went to tuck his sunglasses into the button part of his polo shirt, so that they hung down, like models do in catalogues. Then he changed his mind, not him, too corny – what was he on, a yacht?

Minutes passed. Sonny kept checking his work phone for any new messages. There weren't any. What if he didn't get any signal out there in the middle of nowhere? He kept scanning the paths, not knowing which way his client would be coming from. Surely it could only be one of two of them, the Bingham town one he had come down, or the one that led to the main road and the new build estate? The other two went on for miles into pure countryside. How weird would it be if his client lived in Bingham itself? That would be another first for him. Oh God, what if she knew him?! From the deli or something?!

With these thoughts crossing his mind, he finally noticed another human being in the distance down one of the tracks, the one that led to the main road out of town. Or at least the hair and top of the head of another human being. More promising still, the head and hair looked as though it belonged to a female, hopefully his client. It was hard to see any more at that stage due to the winding nature of the paths. As the woman neared, he kept getting tantalising glimpses of her head and shoulders, but she was still too far away for her face to be seen properly. The hair was a chestnut brown. She too was wearing shades.

The nearer the lady got, the more the hairstyle started to look familiar to Sonny. Very familiar. Bobbed hair and a fringe. The lady rounded a corner and was finally on a straight path towards him, less than ten metres away. Sonny could see her properly for the first time. All of her. Dressed in a white, sleeveless blouse and khaki knee-length shorts. The body-shape looked familiar too; everything did except the clothing. Five metres away now. It couldn't be... What the fuck? Sonny thought.

'Oh my God, Stacey. What the *fuck* are you doing here? Pardon my French,' Sonny said.

'Oh, charming,' Stacey said as she reached him. 'Is that how you greet all your clients?'

Sonny laughed out loud and bent to put his hands on his knees, genuinely poleaxed. It was such a bizarre and unexpected situation. Stacey was his 'boss' in the office who presided behind a desk, a voice on an email or message, or at most a face on a video call. Not a paying client that he met for a date, especially not in the middle of the countryside. Just seeing her in normal clothes was bizarre in itself. 'But I mean, genuinely, what the hell?' he said, standing back up. He was struggling for words.

'Call it mystery shopping,' Stacey said, removing her shades. 'Quality control. An agency boss has to check out who she has on her books from time to time. You know, to ensure company standards are maintained and all that.' The words were full of bravado, maybe even prepared in advance, but Sonny could see Stacey was blushing, more than a little nervous. That was a new thing. He'd never seen her nervous before. She looked nice in her casual clothes, pretty. Her eyes were a lovely green. Her bare shoulders were lightly freckled.

'Wait, so I'm not getting paid for this?' Sonny said, finding his tongue and trying his best to keep the banter up. He too felt suddenly nervous. His stomach was doing strange things.

'You already have been. Check your bank account – or are you making so much money these days you don't have to anymore? I'll have to up my cut...'

Sonny laughed again. 'So you *are* paying for this? That's insane! I am so confused...'

'Are you going to keep talking about money, or are you going to take me for a walk? If so, I might have to give you a bad review. It's bad form to discuss the money on a date remember?'

'Point taken,' said Sonny, trying to recompose himself. 'So… do you want to go for a walk then, seeing as you're here?'

'Yes, I want to go for a walk!' Stacey laughed. 'That's what I paid for.'

'Ok, let's walk then. Erm. Which way do you want to go?' He pointed to the sign.

'Which way is it to the pub?'

'That way, Car Colston,' Sonny said, pointing straight ahead.

'Then that's the way we're going then.'

'After you,' Sonny said. And they set off.

They walked in silence for a bit. Sonny felt tongue-tied, under pressure. It was such a strange scenario. It really did feel as though he was being judged and reviewed; but then on the other hand, it felt more like an actual date – a private, rather than professional one – not like one of his normal gigs. Hence, his head was all over the place. 'Are you normally this quiet on a booking?' Stacey said, breaking the silence. 'If so, I don't know what all the fuss is about. All these glowing reviews and ladies gushing over you. I'm a little disappointed, I must say. You're meant to be entertaining me.'

'Woah, give me a chance!' said Sonny. 'And to answer your question, no, I'm not normally this quiet. I'm still trying to get my head round this. You've got to understand, I was expecting just another gig, you know, routine – and then you show up.'

'Sorry.'

'No. It's a pleasant surprise. A very pleasant surprise. I'm just not sure what this is yet.'

'Just treat it like a normal gig. Talk to me, get to know me...'

'OK... well, it's no good asking you what you do for a living, as I already know. So... what else can I ask you, Ms. *Town*. Is that really your surname by the way, or was it a secret pseudonym?'

'No, it's my surname.'

'Really? What, Town?'

'Yes, Town. Why?'

'Dunno. It's just quite unusual, that's all. Never come across it. Like, take me to Stacey Town!'

'Let's see how this evening goes first,' Stacey laughed. 'You're not ready for Stacey Town yet.'

They carried on walking, crossing a small wooden bridge and navigating the edge of a field, tall with grass. It really was a beautiful summer's evening. And a beautiful walk. Pure countryside. Close up, the hedgerows and fields were bespeckled with wildflowers, a whole spectrum of colours. There were butterflies everywhere, hovering and flitting about in the sunshine. A brace of tortoiseshells directly in front of them appeared to be engaged in an intense mating dance or ritual. Swooping and spiralling in an aerial ballet, dive-bombing like two Spitfires. Then, out of nowhere, another one gate-crashed the party. Then another and another, till there were five of them, a whole squadron. Chasing each other and darting about, faster than the eye could keep up with. Sonny and Stacey both stopped to watch them in wonder. 'My dad'd love that,' Sonny said. 'He loves his butterflies. Such a shame he can't access places like this anymore.'

'Yeah, that's sad, bless him. How's he doing?' She always asked after him.

'Not the greatest, to be honest. Gone downhill a bit. He's off his food and losing weight. But his legs are starting to swell up a bit as well, his ankles and shins.'

'Oh God. That is almost identical to my mum,' Stacey said. 'Both those things. The not-eating and fluid build-up from being sedentary. You want to keep an eye on that, they can develop nasty sores. Mum did.'

'Really'

'Yeah, got infected. She was useless when it came to her meds – unlike your dad – just sort of gave up and gave in. Stopped moving. Stopped trying. But it was the not eating that got her in the end. Sorry, I'm not meaning to worry you.'

'No, not at all. I'm sorry to hear it. Your mum.'

'Yeah, it was a relief in the end, sounds awful I know, but there's no cure for it is there? They're never going to get any better... Oop, there they go!' The butterflies had performed their curtain call and were currently waltzing off over a hedge. Sonny and Stacey watched them go, then resumed walking.

'So, you like the countryside then?' Sonny said, keen to move on to a more cheerful subject. 'Walking and that.'

'Oh, I love it. I happen to think there are few things more appealing in life than a compact, luscious clump of woods.'

Sonny laughed. She really *did* like the countryside. But it was nice getting a taste of her true personality.

Hearing her thoughts. 'Oh, I think a cold, frothing pint of beer comes close.'

It was Stacey's turn to laugh. 'Well, good job we're heading to a pub then, isn't it?'

'It is. Did you know this walk by the way? The area and that? The pub?'

'Nope. That's why I was a little late. Was further from the main road than I expected.

Just looked for a local walk with a pub en route, and it sounded nice. Plus, I knew you lived in Bingham of course.'

'You did?'

'Yeah. From your personal details. I've been doing my research too... That's a lie actually, I know all of my escorts' addresses...' Sonny had forgotten for a short while about that dynamic between them. That that was what had brought them there. It had been nice forgetting that for a short while.

'Of course you do. So, do you spring these 'quality control checks' often on your escorts then?' He said it tongue-in-cheek.

'No, not really.'

'Have you *ever* done one before?'

'Nope. How much further's this pub then? I'm getting thirsty.' Stacey quickened her pace. Sonny followed her, smiling.

# CHAPTER 20

They reached the pub. It was in the middle of nowhere, but somehow still packed. No wonder; there was an extensive beer garden with lots of benches, affording panoramic views of the surrounding countryside. The British loved nothing more than a cold pint in a pub beer garden on a summer's evening. Sonny pointed to a spare bench, still full of empty glasses. 'Do you want to grab that table and I'll go and get the drinks?' he said.

'Oh, do you normally pay for the drinks on your bookings then?'

'Nope. What you having?' Sonny said.

Soon they were both seated with cold pints of lager. Or lager tops to be precise. They were both thirsty. 'Cheers,' they both said, clinking their glasses. Sonny took a long gulp. It tasted heavenly. It was nice to be sitting opposite Stacey, to be able to look at her properly. The sun was reflecting on those green eyes of hers. They really were something. He'd never noticed them in the relative gloom of the office, behind that fringe. Stacey caught him looking and he blushed and looked away.

She did too. They both sipped their beers for a moment in silence, looking anywhere but at each other. The car park had lots of classic cars in it. Chitty Chitty Bang Bang type cars. Must have been a thing. Sonny cleared his throat. 'So... sorry for bringing this up again, but you didn't really pay me for this, did you? You were joking?'

'No, it's already in your bank, as per the usual protocol. And at the new rate – timed that one well, didn't I?'

'You've got to be kidding, I don't want it – not unless it really is a work thing, a quality control check. I'm still not sure...'

'I just fancied a walk that's all.'

'If you fancied a walk, all you had to do was ask. You didn't have to book me as an escort! Isn't that unethical by the way?' he said. 'Booking a date with one of your escorts? You know, a conflict of interest, or against company policy or something? I'm sure I read something to that effect in the contract.'

'Ah... you're thinking of escorts not being permitted to be in a relationship with a *client*. I'm not a client, and as far as I'm aware, we're not in a relationship.'

'Well, technically,' said Sonny, aware he was sounding like Rikipedia, 'You have just booked – and paid for me – apparently, so, doesn't that *make* you a client?' He let it hang and they both laughed. 'Seriously though, this *is* kind of ridiculous, all you had to do was ask...'

'What can I say? I'm shy. I thought you might say no. I'm no good with rejection.' She sunk her head to sip her pint. Her fringe protecting her again.

'Shy? You're one of the most confident, remarkable

women I've ever met. The way you run your business and that – a successful business – and all by yourself by all accounts.'

'Yeah, but it's a front. A front for the business. I'm a mess in my private life.'

'I don't believe it.'

'It's true. This was a big thing for me, believe me.'

'But I had no idea. I mean, no idea you were even interested.'

'Who said I am? Let's see how tonight goes. I haven't reviewed you yet.' The bravado back. 'Anyway, enough about me, tell me about your 'other life' as a chef. I'm dying to hear all about it.'

'Oh God, no. That is so boring, honestly. I get asked about that all the time.'

'Erm. Whose date is this here? I'm paying for this privilege. You need to entertain me.'

Sonny groaned theatrically. She was hard to resist. 'OK, but I need another beer first if we are going to do this.'

'Wow, that one didn't last long,' she said, noticing his near-empty glass.

Welcome to Sonny Town, thought Sonny . 'It's beer weather. Some days are made for drinking! Same again?' he said, getting up.

'Oh. Just a half for me, I'm driving. And I'll get these,' she said, reaching for her pocket. 'It's my round.'

'I think you've already paid enough,' he said.

'Right, what do you want to know then?' said Sonny.

'I don't know, what's it like being a chef, I guess.

Give me an insight into your world. Your career.' Stacey sloshed her fresh half-pint into what was left of her previous drink.

'Erm... OK... cornflour is the messiest substance known to man – it goes everywhere.'

Stacey laughed and rolled her eyes. 'Come on. I think you can do better than that.'

'OK... tinned tuna is the devil's food. It should be banned.'

'Oh, I love tuna mayo! Especially with pasta.'

'Ugh, yuk. It's like cat food.' Stacey laughed again.

'Anyway, that's not really what I'm after – your likes and dislikes. Tell me about cheffing, tell me about your *career!*' It was Sonny's turn to roll his eyes.

'Well, firstly, cheffing can be very boring. Increasingly so in this day and age, all the red tape and that, the paperwork. The food allergies... Drives you mad. And secondly, that would take forever!'

'Well, humour me. Give me a quick summary.' Sonny reluctantly did. She was impressed.

'So, you've kind of come full-circle with it really, it's more about the hours now than anything? Which I don't blame you for, I guess.'

'Yeah, my days of 'chasing stars' are long gone.'

'So, did you cook for anyone famous back in the day then? You must have done.'

'Not really. Few other top chefs. Couple of footballers. Couple of TV presenters. Rosemary Connelly was a regular once upon a time – she liked her vegetables steamed...'

'Rosemary Connelly? I don't think I've heard of her.'

'She does diet cookbooks. Or did. The Rosemary Connelly Diet?'

'Nope.'

'Oh. Never mind…'

'You've never been on the telly then? One of these *MasterChef: The Professionals* or anything?'

'No, not really my thing. The limelight and all that. Having said that, I did win a competition back in the day.'

'Really? What was that?'

'Wait for it… I am *officially* the fastest potato peeler in the UK. Maybe in the world, in fact.' He took a long sip of his pint.

'Give over. You're having me on,' she laughed.

'No, straight up. I won a national competition. Went through the heats and everything. The finals were at Rempstone Steam Rally in 2008. I was on *East Midlands Today* – my five minutes of fame.'

She laughed again. 'Sounds like some country bumpkin thing. What else did they have? Pie eating competitions? Gurning?'

'Probably,' Sonny laughed. 'But the potato peeling was deadly serious. I was up against a chippy from the fens in the final – a seasoned pro – went by the name of 'Mick the Spud'.'

She burst out laughing again. 'Mick the Spud! Shut up.'

'Seriously. He was the favourite, a southpaw, had the tip of one of his thumbs missing from taking it clean off with a peeler. Had never been beaten apparently – I practically had to flee the site with my trophy afterwards, hounded by travellers.'

'Oh my. You're making it sound like a boxing contest. I still don't know whether to believe you. How do they know you're the fastest then? How did they gauge it?'

'You really want to know?'

'Of course. I'm all ears...' Stacey took a sip of drink and leant forward on her hands.

Sonny took another sip of his drink and sat up straighter. He hadn't talked about this in years. And he was secretly quite proud of it – his claim to fame. 'Well, it was a sweltering July day. I'd just scraped through the semi-final earlier that day – mainly on technique – like with the heats. Everyone has their own technique; you see some right cack-handed ones, lefties, righties, underarm, some use long strokes, some a short, quick, jabbing motion.' He demonstrated with an imaginary potato and peeler. 'Some are wet peelers, some are dry. I prefer a long, wet stroke whilst rotating, get a good rhythm going, then finish the top and bottom quickly.' He was about to demonstrate again, when Stacey snorted laughter.

'Sorry,' she said. 'I shouldn't laugh, but now you're just making it sound dirty. My puerile mind. Sorry.'

Sonny laughed himself. 'That wasn't my intention, I promise.' He took another sip of his drink. 'Where was I?... Ah, yes, anyway... like I say, I got through to the final, and – to answer your original question, I was getting carried away – they time you with a stopwatch. Each guy – not being sexist, never saw a girl doing it – gets their own table, side by side with your unopened sack on it.'

'Dirty again,' she said.

'Standard sack,' said Sonny, ignoring her. '25 kilos.'

'Impressive.' She sniggered. 'Sorry.'

'You also get a litre of water for dipping or splashing, a knife for opening, not peeling, and a bin for your peeled spuds.'

'Hold on. 'Dipping or splashing'?'

'Yeah. For splashing your potatoes with. You get one minute, only when they say so, to open up and prepare your sack. Some people, like myself, choose to 'splash' or wet their potatoes with the water. Like this.' He demonstrated dipping his hand in water and flinging it liberally like a baker sprinkles flour. 'Others just re-arrange their spuds and keep them dry. Never got it myself. I use about two thirds of the water, get them good and wet, you get a cleaner, sharper peel, and the remainder for dipping – cleaning the peeler – they get caked up with soil, it blunts them and hampers you.'

'This really does sound like serious stuff,' she said.

'Oh, there's more... So, I open up my sack, and there it is, a bag of beautiful red Desirees – big, clean, uniform size... the *dream sack...*'

She nearly spat her drink out with laughter.

'What?' Sonny laughed. 'That's what we call it, a 'dream sack.'. You don't want small or knobbly potatoes, they slow you down. A sack of small spuds can cost you up to a third to twice as long. Especially if they're heavily soiled. Seriously. And they're dangerous – that's how you end up taking your fingernails, or even tips, off – like Mick the Spud. Had a few injuries myself, I've seen guys caked in blood...'

'Jesus,' she said, suddenly looking serious. 'That's crazy. Why do they take it so seriously?'

'Dunno. It's a 'man thing', I guess. Competition. Wanting to be the best. Most peelers are representing a workplace as well, chippies or pubs or whatever, so there's pride at stake as well.'

'Gosh.'

'Yeah. Anyway. I get this dream sack – don't laugh –

and I'm thinking, 'this is it', I've got 'im. I felt good, you know, something inside, a confidence, a destiny thing. My heart started thumping like mad. I could feel it. I didn't dare look at him, or his sack – I never do – it ruins the concentration. I just had to concentrate on mine and my technique. The whistle blew, and that was it, I was away, and went into the zone. There were loads of people there watching, egging us on, cheering, a huge crowd, all surrounding us in a circle, but I blotted them all out. Some of Mick the Spud's lot were getting out of hand apparently, pissed from the cider tent, swearing and carrying on, throwing their drinks about, trying to put me off even. But I didn't even know they existed. Like I say, I was in the zone. And I didn't stop till everyone of those red spuds was peeled clean and white. And when that last one got chucked in the bin and the klaxon went off, that was when I stood up from being hunched over, looked up, and actually heard and saw the crowd for the first time. They were going ballistic! I couldn't understand why. The guy was holding my hand in the air – like a boxer! And that's when I saw the time…' Sonny looked up for the first time in a while. At Stacey. He'd been in the zone again. Living the moment.

'What?' she said, surprisingly taking his hand, as if she could glean the end of the story through it.

'I'd broken 20 minutes. Smashed it. 19 minutes and 41 seconds to be precise – a sub-20-minute sack; no one had ever done it before – like the 4-minute mile – or certainly ever recorded it.'

'You're joking?'

'No.'

'Wow. I'm amazed. And impressed. So, are you like in the *Guinness Book of Records* then?'

'Sadly, no,' Sonny said. 'You need officials there – Guinness officials – for things like that. Besides, there isn't even a category for it, I looked! And I've googled it since, I still do from time to time, but can never find anything official, anywhere in the world. So, I still like to think of myself as the unofficial 'fastest potato peeler in the world' – until someone or something tells me otherwise!'

'Well, you are – in my eyes anyway – how marvellous. Well, here's to you! What a fantastic story and achievement.' She let go of his hand and held her glass up to his. 'Cheers.'

'Thank you,' said Sonny. 'Cheers.' They clinked glasses. Then he sat back, still feeling a bit of an adrenaline rush from reliving that day. He took a sip of drink, a faraway look in his eye. 'Yeah, they used to call me the 'rumbler' after that, that was my nickname.'

'The rumbler?'

'Yeah, it's a machine that peels potatoes for you. You get them in commercial kitchens – and chippies. To save you time, *supposedly*. Talking of chips… do you want to know what my party trick is?' Drinking the two pints quickly had gone to his head. He was trying to impress now. On a roll.

'Go on,' Stacey said. 'I'm intrigued.'

'I can stir chips round in a hot fryer with my hands.'

Stacey gasped and screwed up her face. 'You can't? I don't believe you!'

'I can. Honestly.'

'How? I know chefs are meant to have asbestos hands and that, but that's ridiculous. Just the thought of it makes me ill.'

'It is a bit of a trick, I admit. But not for the faint-hearted – or fainthanded! When we blanch our chips – which means, you know, par-cook them in advance – it cools the temperature of the fryer slightly, temporarily, and you can then move them round with your hand. But you have to be quick. And you have to keep dipping in and out.'

'OK. Stop talking now,' Stacey said, shuddering theatrically at the thought of it.

'Sorry,' Sonny said. 'Yeah, it's not one to try at home. You have to have built up a lot of resistance in your hands...'

'I said 'stop talking'...'

The sun was setting as they headed back. A fiery, incandescent disc, low in a burnt-orange sky. The air was warm. Fragrant. They were both feeling the effects of the beer. Sonny more than Stacey; he'd had three pints to her pint and a half.'So, how about you? You enjoy walking, the countryside, the *great outdoors*...' Stacey said, returning to their earlier conversation.

'Yeah, I do,' said Sonny. 'Just don't get chance to do it enough these days. Or have someone to do it with.' He hoped that didn't come across as self-pitying.

'Yeah, I know what you mean. Life's busy. Too busy. But when you do, you always feel better for it, don't you? Clears your mind. Soothes your soul. Especially on a night like this, when the light's like this. Isn't it a lovely light?'

'It is. Stunning.'

'I mean, we go from our screens to work – more

screens in my case – then back to our homes and screens without looking around us or venturing outside. When we have all this around us' – she gestured with her arms out wide – 'woods and fields and stars and the sky and sunsets...'

'I love a good sunset,' Sonny said. 'But I like a good silhouette even better.' Stacey laughed. 'I do. I want a haunted house to live in – not really haunted, just one that looks like one, like one off those cartoons like *Scooby Doo* – with bats flying above it, all silhouetted against a killer sunset, or maybe a huge, creamy moon.'

'I reckon you're a dreamer,' Stacey said. 'Like me. I'm a dreamer – my mum always said so,'

'Maybe,' Sonny said. 'I want one of those fake bookcases in my haunted house too, the swivel ones with a secret passageway behind it, again like out of *Scooby Doo*. Oh, and maybe one of those spooky knight's suit of armour things, standing in the foyer.'

'*Interesting*... Planning on living alone then?'

Sonny laughed. 'Maybe. Hopefully not... I need to save enough money first anyway. Joking aside though, I would love to live a simpler life too, a slower one... but with a sprinkling of magic in it, like the ones out of our childhood books.'

'Yep, definitely a dreamer,' Stacey said.

'Well, it's like you said – about going from our screens to work and vice versa. I totally get that. The weeks fly by, and then before you know it, the years do too. Far too quickly, without us experiencing or achieving anything extraordinary. Or stopping to look around us. We spend our lives, head down, just working to survive and chasing our own tails. Wishing you could fast-forward the clock at work to the end of the day. Or wishing the weekend would hurry up and arrive. Or for the end of the month to arrive, so you can get paid. But every time you wish for those things, you're just wishing your life away. Wishing yourself closer to death. I mean, what's the point in that?'

'Hmm... not just a dreamer. A deep thinker too.'

Eventually they reached the signpost and the crossroads. The sun all but slipped behind the horizon now, taking the warmth with it, but still staining the sky pink and orange. 'Well, guess this is us then,' Sonny said.

'Yep.' Stacey wrapped her arms around herself. Sonny wanted to hug her, to warm her, but didn't dare. He studied her face in the fading light, pressing his mind's eye against the glass of hers to see in, desperate to read her thoughts, to see how he had fared. 'What time is it anyway?' She pulled her phone out to check it. 'Nearly ten and still light.'

'Crazy,' Sonny said. 'I'll be having to charge you extra soon, you only paid for four hours.' He regretted saying it immediately, a crass attempt at a joke, proving a reminder of the outside world and bursting the bubble they'd been in.

'Oh, I've got a few minutes left yet,' Stacey said, and then she looked up at him, directly into his face from under that fringe. But shyly. She reached for his hands. 'I wonder what our silhouettes look like right now.' And then to Sonny's surprise she pulled him to her to kiss him. Searchingly. Passionately. It felt wonderful to Sonny and his emotions soared. It had been too long, too long since he had felt something like that. Who was this woman? *What* was she? He wanted to know. To know everything about her. All this communicated in a kiss. And then it was over. Sonny felt a little stunned.

'Sorry,' Stacey said. Shy again. 'I didn't mean to overstep the mark.'

'It's OK,' Sonny said. 'But I might have to charge you for physical intimacy.'

'That's OK,' Stacey said. 'I get thirty percent.'

# CHAPTER 21

An hour after being back home, Sonny was still buzzing. He was on the sofa, getting stuck into the wine – a celebration drink! He'd been sitting there, debating whether to message Stacey or not, to thank her for the date. Was it too soon? Too desperate? He didn't know how long it would take her to get home. He'd never asked her where she lived. He'd not asked her a lot of things. What her home situation was… If she had kids… How long she had been single for. Presuming she *was* single! All they'd talked about it seemed was the countryside and his bloody cheffing career. He regretted this now. There was so much he wanted to know. The date had gone too quickly, far too quickly, like when summer comes to an end and you haven't made the most of it.

What if he left it and then she didn't message him? This would make him feel shit. It felt as if they had made a connection. And quickly. And then that unexpected kiss… *Wow!* 'Relax,' he said. 'She'll message.' It was her who had asked him on a date after all.

That reminded him, he still hadn't checked his bank account; it would be ludicrous if she really had paid him for the time they had just spent together. He picked up his phone to check, when suddenly his other phone, the work one, buzzed with a message. That was strange. He picked it up to check it out. The screen told him that the message was from PLUS ONE – that was the only contact stored in there. Oh, that and Susan. Susan... bless her, Sonny thought. Wonder how she was doing now? She had respectfully kept her distance; and he had moved on surprisingly quickly, but he still thought of her from time to time...

The text message read: '*Hi Sonny. Stacey from Plus One. Just checking how the gig went tonight with the new client. All good I hope?*' Sonny smiled to himself. She was cheeky, he'd give her that, a playful sense of humour. Before he could reply, his real phone pinged with a message: '*Hey you. Back home safe and sound. Thank you for the walk (smiley face). Just writing your review. Glass of wine on the go (winky face emoji). x*'. Sonny laughed out loud... he didn't know which message to respond to first – or which Stacey!

He went with the 'work' one, he could have some fun with that. It appealed to his sense of humour. '*Hi Stacey.*' he typed. '*Booking went OK thank you. Client seemed OK. One of the more normal ones, I guess... Kind of overstepped the mark a bit towards the end, but then I am getting used to this stuff now (shrugging emoji). Sonny*'. He pressed send and put the phone down, smiling and pleased with himself. He picked his other phone up to reply to the other message when it suddenly rang in his hand. It was Stacey on standard voice call, rather than WhatsApp video call. 'Hello,' he answered. 'Sorry. I was just going to reply to you. I got distracted by some work stuff.'

'Ah. Clearly more important than me then,' she said.

'Yeah. I've got a demanding boss. Sorry.'

Stacey cracked up laughing. So did Sonny. They both let out sighs and then there was a momentary silence. 'Sorry,' Stacey said. 'Just thought I'd call – it's quicker than typing – as fun as the messaging is! You in the middle of something? I'm not disturbing you?'

'Nope. Not at all. Just sitting here. Me, myself and the cat. And a glass of wine. You having one too?'

'Yeah. Pretty standard these days, a glass of wine before bed.'

'Surely not your bedtime yet?'

'Pretty much. Past it, in fact.'

'What time is it?'

'Getting on for eleven.'

'Shit. How did that happen?' Sonny looked out the window. It was finally dark. The long day had been deceptive. He'd actually been sitting there in the dark. He closed the blind and turned on the table lamp next to him.

'Well, we didn't finish our walk till gone ten.'

'This is true.'

They talked for another hour, both pouring another glass of wine. Conversation came easy. Topics came easy. Likes, dislikes. His father, her mum. His mum – how she had passed too – he'd never brought this up with Stacey; his father's condition always monopolised those conversations. Kids – she had one, a son, away at Sheffield uni. She was divorced. They talked about anything other than what *this* was. Or where it was going. They also didn't talk about the escort agency. That one could wait till the cold light of day. It was a complicated and strange scenario. It was too early to say what 'this' was anyway. Just roll with it, seemed to be the joint ethos.

Midnight came too soon, and they said a soft and sweet goodnight. Sonny hung up the phone and sat with it cradled in his hand, his face half in shadow from the lamp. He felt dazed and soppy and dreamy. Teenagerish. It had been a long time since he had felt that way. Buddy's voice popped into his head, singing, 'Words of Love', '*Darling, I love you...*'

As Sonny rolled into bed, he was still thinking about Stacey when something occurred to him. The dating sites, and was she on them? He'd certainly never come across her. Not that he could remember anyway. Feeling a little underhand to be doing so, he couldn't resist having a look. After ten minutes of searching in vain, it wasn't until Sonny broadened his age-range search – upwards, older than himself – that Stacey finally popped up. On *Bumble*. That was why he had never come across her. The age thing. He'd vainly – and foolishly in hindsight – only ever searched for women younger than him. Stacey was forty. A year older than himself. She didn't look it. Or act like it.

It made his heart pound seeing her. One with excitement, and two, as he still felt as if he was doing something wrong, checking her out this way. 'Looking for someone to get lost in,' her headline read. This tugged at his heartstrings. It sounded so sincere somehow, genuine and serious, not corny. It made him want to 'snap her up', before she found someone else to get lost in – *get lost in me!* She had a handful of photographs, which he eagerly checked out. It was so strange seeing her. An uninvited peek into her life. A countryside shot by a river. How Stacey! Another laughing with friends. Another dressed as a bridesmaid or maid of honour, a glass of fizz in her hand, her hair longer and heavily curled in ringlets.

He had a fleeting urge to message her, to reach out, through the dating site and surprise her. A joke. To carry on the banter – contacting her as if he were a stranger. But then he thought that might come across as a bit weird – why was he suddenly looking for her on a dating website? Why was he even on there, considering they'd just had a date themselves and made a connection? What if she thought he was still looking for other women, hedging his bets?! This final thought was enough to make him immediately close his phone down. It was about to run out of battery anyway.

# CHAPTER 22

The days following were a little strange to say the least. As if something had been created or acknowledged that Sonny and Stacey didn't quite now know how to proceed with. Or put back in the bottle. As a way of dealing with it, they kept everything light-hearted and jokey, carrying on the banter. Sonny asked how come his review and rating of their date hadn't appeared on his profile yet. Stacey said that, joking aside, it was probably in bad form – and possibly illegal – for a boss of an escort agency to review and rate her own escorts. Shame, thought Sonny.

It was especially strange when Stacey sent the first genuine booking request since their date through. Thankfully, the gig couldn't have been more strait-laced and professional – a plus-one for a local, wealthy business owner at a charity event – a bigwigs networking event by the sound of it. '*Better pull out the tux!*' Stacey had joked on the email. Business as usual, then, Sonny thought. '*Is this actually for a bona fide client? One never can tell these days...*' he had included in his reply.

But it did set him to pondering. How many escorts were in a relationship of their own? Especially the ones that did 'intimacy' and God knows what else? It seemed like a single-guy's line of work and way of living. And that had all been well and good when Sonny had started, it had suited him perfectly. Not that him and Stacey were actually in a relationship yet. It made him wonder how she felt about it, sending the bookings through now. Could she detach herself from it? Had her ex been part of the agency, or an escort himself? So many questions Sonny wanted to ask her. And at their next date, the following Friday night, he did.

In line with wanting to pay Stacey back for (foolishly) paying him to go on a date, the best way Sonny knew how, as always, was by cooking a meal. He couldn't face another restaurant. Not with Stacey. This meant Stacey coming to his house of course, the thought of which filled him with trepidation. It was so humble and, well, *rented*. 'Single man' written all over it. He imagined her to probably live in some big, swish house; she must make a fare old whack from the agency. But Sonny had to get over this quickly. He gave his house the biggest clean it had had since he moved in.

'*I'm here*. x' Stacey had WhatsApped him at arrival time.

Sonny wiped his hands on his striped apron in his steamy kitchen; the extraction was so pathetic, he had to open the window and back door when he cooked. '*Where?*' he replied.

'*In my car out front.*'

'*Why are you texting me?*'

'*Don't know. I'm scared. Lesley-Anne might get me.*'

Sonny sent sideways laughing faces. '*Walk down the lane and I'll meet you at the back gate.*'

'Welcome to my humble abode,' Sonny said, greeting Stacey with a kiss. She smelt amazing and was clutching a bottle of white wine.

'Ah, we're matching!' she said. Sonny looked Stacey up and down. They were both wearing black tops and blue jeans. Him a T-shirt, her a blouse. On her feet were dainty flip-flops with little jewels on them. Her toenails were painted burgundy.

'So we are! Ah, you shouldn't have,' Sonny said, acknowledging the wine. 'Tonight is my treat.'

'I can't ever visit houses without bringing a bottle or cake or something, it's a thing of mine. Mmm, God, it smells divine in here,' she said, crossing the threshold. 'I am so excited for this. To be cooked for by a proper chef.'

Sonny turned the music he'd been listening to down; he couldn't cook without music. 'Don't get too excited, it's only risotto.' He was playing it down. He'd gone to great lengths to impress, even preparing a trio of desserts for pudding, incorporating homemade ice cream. He still had his own machine from making ice cream with the kids when they were younger. They used to love it. Peanut butter being their favourite flavour.

'Only risotto!' she said. 'I wouldn't know where to start.'

Sonny poured Stacey a glass of wine. He'd already had a glass or two himself whilst cooking. Stacey sat at the kitchen table, watching him cook. He was very aware of it. The back door was still open. 'So, is that where it happened?' she whispered, pointing next door.

'Oh, God. Yes! That's where they live. It was in the kitchen I reckon.'

'Uggh,' she shuddered. 'You make it sound like Cluedo! With the lead pipe?'

'More likely a syringe,' Sonny said. 'Given the circumstances.'

'Yeah. Quite! It is strange though, you know when you've pictured somewhere in your head, and then it turns out to be nothing like it.'

'Really? You've pictured it?'

'Yeah. And your place.'

'Really? Well, don't say a word...'

'Ah, it's sweet. Homely.'

'Oh my. That was simply the best meal I have ever eaten in my life. Thank you,' Stacey said post-dinner.

'Don't be silly,' Sonny blushed.

'I'm not. That dessert was to die for – and the risotto. The flavours and seasonings... How am I ever meant to eat normal food again? Can you move in and be my personal chef?'

'Depends how much you're paying. I earn a pretty decent wage on another sideline I've got going. Talking of which... You've asked me about my career, now it's my turn.' Stacey groaned. 'No, see – I had to go through it, it's boring when it's about yourself, isn't it?'

It turned out that Stacey had set the agency up with money from her divorce. A divorce she had done very well out of. Therefore, her ex-husband had had no part of it. This was somehow a relief to Sonny. She'd wanted to throw herself into something apparently. She'd got the idea from hiring the services of an escort herself not long after the divorce – a strictly professional, companionship booking, she was quick to add – and was blown away by how much money they charge. She'd researched it, developed the idea and set it up, being very sure from the outset that she wanted to provide a platonic, companion-based service. 'Not that things don't still go on,' she said, rolling her eyes. 'A separate transaction between two adults in the privacy of their home is entirely up to them. I, or we, the agency, have no part in it – financially or otherwise. It's illegal for a start – to sell sex. But Plus One will never advocate or promote or offer that type of thing. As I say, it doesn't mean that things don't still go on... Social companionship with 'intimacy' can unfortunately be a gateway to it. That's why...' she stopped suddenly, as if changing her mind over what she was about to say.

'Why what?'

'No nothing.' She was blushing, fiddling with her fringe, that surprising shy version of her that sometimes unexpectedly popped out.

'Tell me...' Sonny took her hand across the table and squeezed it gently. It was the first time they had touched all evening, intimately, like that anyway. It felt good.

'No, I feel silly.' She squeezed his hand back.

'Tell me.'

'Well, I'm just glad that you never gave in to that.'

'What, the intimacy stuff?'

'Yeah.'

'Ah. I'm flattered.'

'You should be. I mean, it wouldn't have mattered at first, I didn't know you from Adam. But the more I *did* get to know you, the more I hoped you wouldn't change your mind and that it would happen. Like I said, I respected you for that. Still do. You are literally the only one on our books that doesn't do it.'

'Really?' Sonny was shocked.

'Yeah. Straight up. You have no idea how many enquiries I've had for you for that, phone calls and emails. A small fortune's worth – for me and for you!'

'You're joking.'

'No. I mean, I told you about them at first – you know I did – but when you were adamant you were never going to do that, that was good enough for me; so, I just screened them on your behalf from then on. Took great pleasure in it, in fact. 'Nope. Nope. Nope. Sorry, he's not interested in that.'

'I had no idea.' They went quiet then, as if both of them were trying to understand what this admission signified. Sonny sat back and took a long glug of wine. 'So, does this mean…' It was his turn to falter, to trip on his words.

'Mean what?'

He was shy to say it. So, he let the wine do the talking. 'That your heart is mine, Ms. Town.'

'Yes. I suppose it does.' His stomach did a little dance, and he leant across to kiss her. She tasted of wine. The kiss was electric, like before. He ran a hand through her hair. Someone to get lost in, he thought. He wanted that too. Just then, Sonny's phone on the table rang, making them both jump.

'Shit!' said Sonny.They both laughed, embarrassed at how carried away they'd got. 'Fuck, it's the care home. Sorry, I've got to take this. Hold that thought! Hello,'

Sonny said in a serious voice. Stacey watched Sonny talk, whilst trying to listen. 'No, no problem... OK... Is he OK?... Do you need me to come up? You're sure... I can pop up... OK, as long as you're sure... OK, thanks for letting me know. Let me know if anything changes. Tell him I'll be up to see him in the morning. Thanks. Bye for now.' He hung up the phone.

'Everything OK?' Stacey asked, concerned, taking his hand again.

'Yeah. No real drama. Just Dad's had another fall that's all.'

'Oh no. Is he alright?'

'Yeah. That's two in as many weeks though.'

'Could be low blood pressure? Has it been checked recently?'

'Not sure. Think his brain just gets ahead of his body. Tries to shuffle-run when his feet are still asleep – was probably trying to dash to the loo! Stupid sod. But he's banged his cheek or eye socket apparently this time. Had to get the paramedics out. But they've checked him out and he's fine. Just bruised.'

'Aaw, bless him.'

'Bless him. You've never met him. The man's a monster! Bane of my life. Makes Hitler look like David Attenborough!' Stacey burst out laughing.

'Well, maybe I *should* meet him.'

'Ooh, bit early for that isn't it? Meeting the in-laws! We've only just become an 'item' – that did just happen by the way? Can we just confirm that? Before we rudely got interrupted.'

'Yes, yes I think that did just happen,' Stacey laughed and blushed.

'Phew,' said Sonny. 'Be typical of my dad to ruin everything for me, as usual. Besides, if you did meet him, it might scare you off – thinking that that's what's waiting down the line for you in old age.'

'Now who's getting carried away?' Stacey took a slurp of wine.

'He does look like me, or rather, I look like him, I'm ashamed to say...'

'Really? Now I really do want to meet him. You sure you don't want to go up there now? To check he's OK? We can if you want. I don't mind at all.'

'God, no! It's the last thing I want to do right now, deal with him. They said he's fine – and he's been checked out. I'm going to see him in the morning anyway.'

'They are looking after him up there, aren't they? You know, some of the things you've told me... about his legs and that, and the not eating. You have to keep on at them. I found that with Mum.'

'Oh, was she in a home then too?'

'Yeah. And I regret it now. Always will. Wished we'd tried the live-in care approach first. But I was just so busy at the time, setting up the business and that. A kid... It was the easiest option – despite the costs, the most *convenient* – to hand it over...' She looked sad. Sonny didn't like that.

'Ah, well don't beat yourself up over it, like you say, you were busy setting up a business. Hindsight's a wonderful thing.'

'Yeah, I guess.'

'I know my dad would struggle with live-in care; he can't get on with anyone for more than five minutes! But I do wonder about them up at the home, especially lately.

They're always short-staffed. At least they phoned the paramedics about his head, and informed me, I guess.'

'Yeah, but that's just protocol. They have to do that by law. It's procedure. I remember it with Mum.'

'Well, I dunno…'

'I'm free tomorrow if you're going up? Whip them into shape!'

# CHAPTER 23

Sonny and Stacey pulled up at the care home in Stacey's car. A plush Mazda with all the gimmicks. She'd picked him up. 'Here we are then,' Sonny said. It felt strange being there with Stacey, or anyone else for that matter – a trip he had done so many times, and always alone.

'Looks alright from the outside,' Stacey said. 'Nice grounds.'

'Yeah. Not that Dad's barely seen them.'

'Really?'

'Yeah. I've never known them take him outside once in the whole time he's been here.'

'That's disgusting,' Stacey said. 'Really makes my blood boil. What are they paid for?'

'I know. Tell me about it. Costs him twelve-hundred quid a week to stay here.'

'Doesn't surprise me. About standard these days...'

'You ready then?'

'Gosh, I feel a bit nervous now I'm here at the thought of it, of meeting him.'

'Don't be. He *is* going to wonder who the hell you are though! It's gonna take some explaining – and then he won't be able to hear anyway.'

They got out of the car and rounded the corner to the reception door. True to form, there was a gaggle of staff outside, sitting at their 'smokers' table'. Less of them than normal, though. And a couple of faces Sonny didn't know. That had been happening more and more lately; less regulars, more agency staff. Sonny said 'hello'. ''Ere, I'll buzz you in,' one of the regulars said. 'Saves me getting up again.'

'Ah, thanks,' said Sonny.

'No problem.' She buzzed them in, then went back outside.

'That really boils my piss too,' Stacey said.

'Boils your piss!' Sonny laughed.

'Sorry,' Stacey said. 'It's the Essex in me. Pisses me off. Them lot sitting outside the front doors, smoking like that. But, more to the point, who's looking after the residents when half the staff are outside?'

'Tell me about it.' They entered the foyer. Immediately in front of them was the usual congregation of residents, asleep or lounging on the sofas. The chaotic sounds hit them both straightaway too, the incessant beeping of the call alarms going off, the wailing of distressed residents, either nomadically roaming the corridors, shuffling, or from their rooms. Sonny was used to it, had almost become immune to it, but Stacey wasn't.

'Jesus,' she said. 'Is this a dementia home? You didn't say it was a dementia home?'

'It's not, not specifically anyway, it's mixed.'

'Well, I can guarantee you all of these poor souls have

got dementia, look at them! It should be segregated. Separate buildings even. Your dad hasn't got dementia, has he?'

'No. *Demented* yes, but dementia, no.' Stacey didn't laugh at Sonny's joke. 'Here we are, the one with the stairgate.'

'Woah. A stairgate. What's that all about?'

'It's to stop the other residents getting in. They wander into his room otherwise, get in his bed even.'

'Sonny, that is not right. That's why they shouldn't be mixed. How does your dad get out? Those things are a devil to open.'

'He can't. Not without help. He doesn't want to anyway, he gets mobbed. Who could blame him?' Stacey's lips had thinned, and she had a look on her face that, up till now, Sonny hadn't seen. Oops, he thought. He knocked on the doorframe and peered in. His father was sitting in his usual spot, in his chair in the corner. His head was sunk forward. Looked as if he was dozing. Sonny opened the stairgate. 'Hi, Dad, it's me!' They walked into the room. 'Sorry about the smell,' he said to Stacey, feeling embarrassed.

'Gosh. Open a window, Sonny, it's roasting in here,' Stacey said.

'Yeah, it is a bit warm. Oh, just shut that behind you,' he said, indicating the stairgate. 'They'll be in in seconds otherwise.' Stacey clicked the gate closed as Sonny opened a window. The breeze was a relief. 'Dad, it's me, Sonny. We've got a visitor.' His father stirred and tried to lift his neck up, but it was a struggle. As if it was too heavy; he didn't have the strength. But it was enough to see that one of his eyes was bruised and swollen. It didn't look good. Black eyes never did, especially on an old person. He opened his eyes, looking dazed and very sorry for himself. 'Shit, Dad, look at your eye.' Sonny crouched down, to try and get in his field of vision.

'What are you doing here?' the old man said. 'Why didn't you tell me you were coming?'

'I told the carers to. And I tried to call you this morning. Twice. But you didn't answer. And I left a voicemail.'

'Bollocks.'

'Dad, before you start kicking off, we've got a visitor, look–'

'Thirsty.' He pointed with a shaky, crooked finger to the plastic jug of squash on his portable table.

'You want some squash?'

'Yes!' Sonny poured him some squash. The old man took it from him with trembling hands and sucked it greedily through a straw.

'You're welcome,' Sonny said. Stacey sat down gently on the bed and they both watched him drink. His lips looked dry.

'He's dehydrated,' Stacey said. Sonny's father grunted and shoved the cup back to Sonny.

Sonny placed it back on the table. 'Dad, look, this is Stacey. A friend of mine,' he said.

'Huh?' The old man turned to Stacey, registering her for the first time. He looked surprised, then held out his hand for a shake. 'Hello,' he said.

Stacey shook his hand. 'Hello, John. I'm Stacey,' she said loudly.

'Tracey?'

'No, *Stacey*,' she laughed.

'Stacey.'

'Yes. Stacey.'

'Why didn't you tell me you were bringing someone with you?' he turned to Sonny and scowled. Then he tried to brush his hair down with his hand, to tidy it up.

'I did, Dad. On the voicemail.' His father humphed.

'I would have put on a fresh shirt if I knew we'd got company.' He brushed at the drool stains on the one he was wearing with his hand.

'How are you doing today, John? I hear you've had a fall,' Stacey said. 'Your eye looks sore.'

'Are you a nurse?' he said, turning back to Stacey.

'No. No, I'm not a nurse,' Stacey laughed. 'I'm a friend of Sonny's.'

'No. You're too pretty for a nurse. And slim.'

'For God's sake, Dad!' Sonny said, blushing. His father had always been an old flirt. Straight in there. But at least it was cheering him up.

'I said your eye looks sore,' Stacey said. Then, surprising them both, she lifted his chin up gently to see it better. 'Hmm... Just bruised fortunately. At least it's not cracked the skin. You have been in the wars, haven't you, bless you?' She stroked his hair briefly, before sitting back on the bed. The old man was loving the attention, Sonny could see it on his face.

'Had a bit of a tumble, that's all. I have these dizzy spells,' he said. 'Get a bit lightheaded. But they have to make such a meal of it here, call the bloody ambulance. I told 'em I'm not going back into hospital!'

'Blood pressure,' Stacey nodded to Sonny. Then to his father: 'When did you last have your blood pressure checked?'

'My compressor checked?'

'No, your blood pressure. Blood pressure!' she said, demonstrating on his arm.

'Oh, the ambulance crew did it. The guy with the clumpy feet.'

'And what did they say?'

'I've no idea.'

Sonny sighed in frustration. 'Told you, he's a nightmare.'

'Shush you, let's have a look at these legs as well, shall we.' She knelt down in front of Sonny's father to examine them. Sonny was amazed and fascinated at seeing this side of Stacey, a tender, nursing side. Not that it surprised him.

'Hmm, yep, they're just like Mum's. And that one is starting to crack and weep, look. They need looking at by a GP, before they become infected.'

'Are you sure you're not a nurse?' Sonny's father said. Stacey laughed again and stood back up. She surveyed the room. As she did so, one of the residents appeared at the doorway and started rattling the stairgate, trying to get in. A vacant expression on his face. It happened all the time.

'Sorry, this is not your room,' Stacey said, going over to him.

'Is the bus here?' the man asked.

'No, no bus here. Sorry. This is not your room. Goodbye.' She waved and gently closed the door on him, then turned back round. Sonny's father made an approving noise. 'And what are those doing in here?' she said, pointing to a huge stack of incontinence pants, piled against a wall. There were dozens and dozens of them.

'I've no idea,' Sonny said. 'I've never seen them before.'

'Well, they can't just dump things in here. That's about two boxes worth! It's not a storage room. And what is that smell?' She wandered over to the bathroom. Sonny braced himself. 'Oh God, phew!' She made a noise. 'Don't they ever flush this thing? And why is the toilet constantly running?' She flushed it.

'I must have told them about three times about that!' Sonny called.

'Right, I'm tidying this place up!' Stacey said.

Sonny and his father both looked at each other. 'What's she doing?' his father said.

'Having a bit of a tidy up, I think.'

'Oh. Good. Can you bring her here more often?'

After ten minutes or so of listening to Stacey rattle around in the bathroom, water running and sprays being sprayed, the door finally opened. 'Right, that's better,' she said, dispensing a pair of hygiene gloves into the pedal bin.

'Can we get a cup of tea now or what?' his father said. He seemed to have cheered up.

'Yeah, I haven't seen anyone to ask though, Dad.'

'I'll press the buzzer. Not that they'll come,' his father said.

'Wait!' Stacey said. 'Sorry, John.' She put her hand on his. 'Before you do, what time is it?' She turned to Sonny.

'Dunno,' Sonny said. He got his phone out to check. 'Twenty past ten, why?' And then the penny dropped. 'Meds.'

'Exactly,' Stacey said. 'Was he due them at ten?'

'Yeah. Every three hours. Seven, Ten, One etc.'

'That's what I thought. And we've been here, what,

233

twenty minutes or so, we got here just before ten, I remember. And he hasn't had them yet. Unless he had them before we arrived.'

'Dad, did you have your ten o'clock meds?'

'Beds?'

'Meds! Your ten o'clock meds. Have you had them?' His father looked confused. 'Dad, it's a simple question – did you have your ten o'clock meds before we arrived?'

'No. I'm still waiting for them.'

'Well, it's twenty past ten now.'

'I told you, they're bloody useless! This is what I have to put up with! That's why I can't move. That's why I've ended up with these bloody things on!'

'Alright, Dad. Calm down. It's not on though, is it?' He turned to Stacey.

'No, it's not on. I'm really not impressed by this place, Sonny. Mum's was nothing like this.'

'Can I press the buzzer now?' his father said.

'Yes, press the buzzer.'

A full five minutes later, a member of staff appeared at the stairgate, looking harassed. 'Yes? Can I help?'

'Yes, can we get a cup of tea, please. Three cups of tea actually. Sorry,' Sonny said.

The carer sighed and rolled her eyes. 'You'll have to bear with, we're a bit short-staffed.' She made to dash off.

'Wait!' Sonny said. 'And my dad hasn't had his ten o'clock meds yet. His Parkinson's meds. It's nearly half ten!'

'Oh. Oh, sorry about that.' She changed her tone of voice. 'Has Dan not been in?'

'No, no one has.'

'Right. Bear with!' And off she went.

Another five minutes later a male nurse Sonny hadn't seen before turned up. He let himself in. 'Here we go, John. Meds time.' He stood there sweating and breathing heavily whilst Sonny's father took his meds.

'Erm, sorry, but they're half an hour late,' Stacey said. 'More than half an hour. It's ten-thirty-five.'

'I'm sorry?' the man said, clearly annoyed at being questioned.

'You're over half an hour late with his meds. He's got Parkinson's.'

'I'm fully aware he's got Parkinson's, but we're short-staffed. It's the weekend.'

'That's not an excuse,' Stacey said. 'Those meds are time-specific. Even being five minutes late can cause havoc.'

'Rubbish. The guidelines give half an hour leeway each side.'

'Well, you're even outside that, aren't you?!'

'Only by five minutes.'

'That's thirty-five minutes late! Why are you arguing with me?'

'I'm not being spoken to like this.' The man made for the door, shaking his head. 'Who the hell are you, anyway?'

'I'm Stacey Town – and I'm going to be speaking to your manager about this.'

'You do that!' The man said, glaring at Stacey and slamming the stairgate shut.

'And about the fact that he's being neglected. Look at him! Dehydrated. Low blood pressure. Black eye. Swollen legs. Never taken outside. And you can't even give him his meds on time!'

The man stormed off, shaking his head again.

Then there was silence in the room. Stacey turned to face Sonny and his father. They were both looking at her in shock. For Sonny, the whole thing had escalated so quickly, he hadn't been able to get a word in edgeways. Talk about a force of nature, he thought. 'Sorry,' Stacey said. 'But he didn't even apologise for being so late, that's what put my back up.'

'No, that's alright,' Sonny said. 'He was out of order. Well out of order.'

'Told you he was a bully,' Sonny's father said.

Back in the car, from totally out of nowhere, Sonny broke down in tears. One sniffle turned into a sob, then it all came out. A build-up of pressure. Years of it. He was mortified – and shocked at himself. 'I am so sorry,' he said, covering his face with his hands.

'Oh gosh, no, you poor, silly man, come here,' Stacey said, pulling him to her. 'Come here.' He succumbed, leaning to rest his head in the crook of her neck and sob.

'I am so embarrassed,' he said, but unable to stop. 'I never cry. Ever.'

'Shush. Don't be silly. Everybody cries once in a while.' She stroked his hair. It was warm and fragrant and comforting in the crook of her neck.

'I just feel like I've let him down. Took my eye off the ball. Look at the state of him.'

'Gosh no, don't be silly. You do everything for him. You, alone. It's them that's let him down.'

'There just isn't the time to deal with all of his problems. It's like a losing battle. I can't be with him constantly. It's like this constant, overwhelming pressure.'

'I know. I've been there myself, but at least I had siblings to help bear the brunt. You not got any yourself? No brothers or sisters?'

'No.' It was always easier to say "no" than to explain. He was too young to remember it anyway.

'An only child, eh? Well, that's not much use then. But that's what the care home are for, they are paid to look after him. Full-time. You've got a full-time job yourself. Two jobs! And your kids. And look at what you still do for him. He'd be lost without you.' Sonny was starting to calm down, listening to her words of reassurance.

'I've just been so alone with it all. I think that's what's got to me, what happened in there. You fighting his corner too. Someone to share the burden with. I've got so I can't see the wood for the trees, that I can't cope. I've been trying to juggle everything. And then he's never satisfied or grateful. All he does is give me grief and shout at me!' Sonny laughed at this, despite himself.

'Bless you,' Stacey said, stroking his hair again.

It felt nice, but Sonny sat back up, extricating himself from her fragrant embrace, still mortified at showing so much vulnerability so early on in their relationship. 'Sorry,' he said again. 'I don't know where that came from. I literally never cry. I'm famous for it! You'll think I'm some sort of wet lettuce.'

'Well, your face is a little damp...' They both laughed. Sonny wiped his eyes. 'Seriously though, you're not alone, not anymore.' She put her hand on his. Sonny looked at her. 'I'm gonna draft you an email, to send to the management. A formal complaint – if that's OK with you of course.' Sonny nodded, but was unsure. He hated kicking up a fuss. 'What's going on in there isn't right, Sonny. They're meant to be caring for him – and being paid for it – but they're actually neglecting him. You hear about this stuff on the news. Like with that stairgate, he's like a prisoner they're just shoving a plate of food at from time to time, slipping it under the door to keep him alive, regardless of whether he eats it or not. Same with his meds. That lack of regard. They have to be given on time.'

'I know they do.'

'It's inhumane otherwise, he can't move. Can't function. The knock-on effect being the fluid retention, the swollen legs – which he needs to see a GP about. Not to mention the falls. There's no human interaction... He's not venturing outside, or even outside his room. He shouldn't even *be* in a place like that, it's a dementia home, another thing we're gonna complain about...' It sounded awful to Sonny when she put it the way she had. It did sound neglectful. He hadn't taken his father out lately on his scooter himself either, he'd been too busy. He felt bad about this. 'Have you ever considered, you know, trying the home care approach, maybe even living with him to keep the costs down?'

'Oh God, no. We'd end up murdering each other, living under the same roof. Or I would him at least, he wouldn't have the strength.' Stacey laughed.

'Not even if it was an annexe or something? Or separated slightly? Maybe you could keep him behind your secret bookcase – in a secret room!' Sonny laughed. It was a funny thought.

'Yeah, I wanted a haunted house, but not haunted by him! Nah... I don't know... how would we even afford it for a start?'

'Didn't you say he'd got savings? Do it as a joint venture, he pays the deposit and you pay the mortgage? Gets him out of there and you back on the property ladder. Even if it was just for a couple of years, or till it got too much – for both of you.'

'But what about us?' He looked at her earnestly. 'Living together… I'm joking,' he said, seeing the look on her face. He patted her leg.

'Yeah, *definitely* too soon to be thinking about that. We've only just met.'

She was right, Sonny thought. More was the pity.

# CHAPTER 24

True to her word, Stacey drafted a letter to the care home, making a formal complaint. She emailed it to Sonny and he sent it to the manager of the care home. The letter was impressive, professionally done, but quite damning. Strongly worded, and demanding a quick response. Sonny still felt uneasy about sending it; it wasn't the kind of thing he normally did. But Stacey seemed to know what she was doing, so he went with it. Trusting her.

The whole incident, and subsequent conversation in the car, had given Sonny much food for thought. It seemed to him as though things with his father, in regards to his care and where he was at, had reached some kind of a head. Almost, a crisis point. Things couldn't carry on the way they were. Stacey was right, he thought, his father *was* being neglected – and paying an obscene amount of money for the privilege.

But it wasn't just his father's situation that seemed at a bit of a crossroads. Stacey's words had stuck in Sonny's head; and for the first time he was seriously mulling over, contemplating, the prospect of maybe living with his father for a bit. Looking into getting a house even. He knew he would never be able to do any of the 'caring' as such, the nitty gritty – his father could pay home carers for that and still save himself a fortune – but he could certainly keep an eye on him better, oversee things more. Making sure his father had a proper meal in the evening for example, and being there overnight. Or if he had a fall... Take more control of his meds... maybe set up some of those dosette box things for him etc.

And then there was Sonny's work situation to consider, to throw into the mix: did he jack in the job at the deli and concentrate solely on the escort work? Lord knows he was earning enough money from it. Quitting the deli would free up a whole new world of available booking hours for him. Why would he earn barely above minimum wage when he could earn hundreds of pounds an hour? It was a no-brainer. And with him and Stacey now in a relationship, a 'partnership', maybe this could form some sort of working partnership too; she could push and promote the hell out of him. Preferential treatment. That was a point – Sonny wondered if the other escorts would ever get wind that he and 'the boss' were in a relationship. He couldn't ever imagine Stacey wanting them to. And how would they ever find out? It wasn't as if he ever met or came across any of the other escorts. They were all one-man bands really, working for themselves. Stacey just booked them and took a commission.

Was he getting ahead of himself thinking about all this, though? Dangerous to put all his eggs in one basket. What if he and Stacey fell out? Where would that leave his agency work? You don't think about these things when Cupid surreptitiously strikes; the heart wants what it wants, follows its own path. He still couldn't believe that it had happened, that he was in a relationship. It had crept up on him, happened so quickly, but also somehow so naturally. He hadn't even really been looking of late. Too busy what with everything going on. Another thing that he hadn't told the kids. He really ought to, about Stacey at least...

The week went on. Stacey and Sonny couldn't wait till the weekend to have a proper evening together again. Literally – they were like a pair of lovestruck kids – so, Stacey invited Sonny over to hers midweek. She did it in a cheeky faux-formal email, almost like a booking again, requesting his company for an evening of food, wine and companionship – with a strong possibility of 'intimacy' (winky face emoji). Sonny formally accepted the invitation; he loved this stuff and couldn't wait.

Stacey's house was an envy-inducing and impressive four-bedroom detached job. Nice gardens. Her Mazda on the drive. Stacey opened the door to him, looking flustered but stunning in a figure-hugging cream dress. 'Do you know how much pressure I am feeling, cooking for a chef? I should have organised a bloody takeaway!'

'Oh God, don't be silly,' Sonny said, giving her a big hug and kiss. She smelt amazing as always. 'As long as there is plenty of wine, who cares about the food? A bowl of crisps would have done! Talking of wine, I followed your lead. Here. A bottle of Viognier, no less.'

'Ooh, Viognier. Lovely,' she said, examining the bottle.

'Yeah, first time I haven't bought a bottle of wine from Aldi in years! And these are for you, my dear.'

He also passed her a small bunch of flowers. Lilies. He remembered them from her office.

'Aaw, you shouldn't have. I love lilies. Thank you.' She took the flowers from him and gave him another kiss.

'Careful, you don't want to get the pollen on your dress.'

'God, yes. Anyway... do, come in...'

Sonny followed Stacey inside, into a nice, spacious hallway with a galleried landing. 'Shoes on or off?' Sonny said.

'Oh, keep 'em on. I do.' Sonny was glad. He liked shoe-on houses.

'I'll just put these in some water, then I'll give you a quick tour – unless you want a glass of wine first – I'm already on my second. Follow me, anyway.' Sonny followed Stacey down a hallway. Enjoying doing so. Watching her walk in that dress, drawn to the shape of her. 'Anyway, what makes you think there's going to be plenty of wine? Bit presumptuous. Haven't you got to drive home later?' She said it in a jokey, leading manner. Or at least Sonny hoped she was joking.

He went with it. 'Well, there's always *Uber* should things get a little carried away. Besides, you did say 'an evening of wine..."

'I did say that actually, didn't I?' she laughed.

Both with a glass of wine in hand, Stacey gave Sonny a tour of the house. It was lovely, a different world to his own. It was strange seeing her bedroom, where she slept every night. Her ensuite bathroom – bigger than Sonny's normal bathroom – where she bathed and showered. Her toothbrush. And then seeing her son's room. A typical teenage boy's room. Sonny still couldn't imagine her somehow as a mother. But he felt privileged seeing it all, being there, having that insight into her life. Most surprising of all was a hot tub outside on the decking. Sonny's stomach churned a little at seeing it. 'You have brought your trunks, haven't you?' Stacey said. Sonny laughed nervously. He wasn't ready for that. He'd never been in a hot tub before, and told her so.

'You're joking! Oh God, I love it. Especially with a glass of wine on the go. Very relaxing at the end of a working day. Especially when the evenings start to cool and you're all warm and cosy under the water, enveloped in steam.' It did sound good, Sonny thought. 'Don't worry, one for another day,' she said, patting his arm. 'I don't think either of us are ready for that yet!'

The night went on. They ate. They drank. They listened to music. They talked. They discussed the living with his father situation further. Sonny's job situation. Stacey said that if he was seriously thinking about getting a mortgage *and* quitting his day-job, it was imperative he secured the mortgage first; he wouldn't get a mortgage on the strength of his escort earnings, regardless of the money he was pulling in; according to her, they wouldn't take any self-employment earnings into consideration until there was at least two years' worth of consistent figures. Sonny marvelled at how much Stacey knew. So worldly-wise compared to him; a businesswoman. It turned him on.

They also talked about the care home, and their next plan of attack. The home had sent a swift reply back, saying that they took any complaints very seriously and would be looking into the matters raised immediately. They would respond with their findings in due course.

'That's just a holding email,' said Stacey. 'A bit of a fob-off. We'll reply, demanding a timescale and a face-to-face meeting.'

Night fell. It was gone ten o'clock. They were both still at the kitchen table, talking and drinking. They hadn't used the lounge at all. Or washed any of the pots. 'So, you're still here then,' Stacey said, a little flirtatiously. They were both a little tipsy. Had at least a bottle of wine each.

'Yep,' Sonny said. 'But I'm not charging you at least, so you can relax.' Stacey laughed.

'No, but we've both got work in the morning.'

'You kicking me out?'

'I didn't say that.'

''Cause I can always call an Uber. Can probably have one here in ten minutes.'

'You could… Be a shame, though.'

'It would.' The atmosphere seemed to have changed, to be loaded. Charged with electricity. Stacey's voice had changed too, and the look on her face.

'Or… you could always stay the night…' Sonny's stomach whirled at the words. At the magic. At the possibilities. He'd wanted her to say it and she had. And then Stacey broke into laughter, shattering the charged atmosphere. She put her head in her hands. 'Oh, God. You don't know how hard it was to say that. My heart is thumping.' She was blushing. The other Stacey had popped out, the shy one. Like Jekyll and Hyde. 'Pheeew!' she said, fake-fanning herself and appearing to try and make light of it. Then there was silence again. And then Stacey looked at him. Their eyes met. 'Well, don't leave me hanging then!' she said.

'God, sorry!' Sonny said, taking her hand across the table. He'd forgotten to speak. So wrapped up in the whirl of emotions. 'I'd love to,' he said. 'As long as you're sure. As long as you're OK with it.'

'Nope. I'm not sure at all!' she laughed. 'I haven't felt these feelings in a long time, so I'm not sure at all what I'm meant to be doing or thinking.'

'Me neither,' Sonny said, and their eyes met again. Serious.

'We might have to share a toothbrush. And I sleep on the left.'

Sonny's stomach somersaulted again. At the thought of it. Of spending the night with a woman, sharing a bed. He fought to control it, to stay cool. 'Ah, it's OK, I brought my own.'

'You didn't?'

'I did. And an overnight bag.'

'You didn't?'

'Yep, it's in my car.'

'Now that *was* presumptuous. I don't know what to think. What kind of a girl do you take me for?'

'I know. I'm sorry.'

'So, you should be... not that I was secretly hoping you would or anything...' She sat back and drained the rest of her wine in one go. 'Come on then,' she said, getting up suddenly from the table. 'I guess I'd better show you upstairs...'

'Oh, OK.' Sonny drained the rest of his glass too. He stood up. 'Shall I go and get my bag?'

'No. I think your bag can wait a while.' She took his hand and led him upstairs.

It was dark in Stacey's bedroom. She drew the curtains and put on a bedside lamp. Then she pulled some nightwear out of a chest of drawers. Sonny watched her, fascinated but nervous. Then, to his surprise, she said in an authoritative voice, 'Alexa! Play my Ed Sheeran playlist,' and Sonny couldn't help but laugh.

Alexa immediately responded from somewhere, 'Playing Ed Sheeran playlist on Amazon music.'

Then Ed Sheeran came on. 'Drunk'. Quite apt, and Sonny liked that one.

'Alexa, volume four!' Stacey commanded, and Sonny burst out laughing again. 'What are you laughing at? You have to be firm with her, or she gets contrary and doesn't listen.'

Sonny was in stitches now.

'What?'

'Sorry, it's just funny, that's all. You talking to her in that voice. Unexpected.'

'Well, I'm glad it's amused you.' She was laughing herself now, and it had certainly broken the ice, which was good. 'Right, make yourself comfortable, get in or whatever' – she gestured to the bed – 'I'm just gonna use the bathroom...'

'Oh, could I quickly brush my teeth first?' Sonny said. 'I'll have to use your brush, though. Sorry.'

'Yes. Of course. Go for it.' Sonny disappeared and brushed his teeth.

When he returned, Stacey was sitting on the bed, clutching her nightie, singing along to the music. 'All good?' she said.

'Yeah, better, thanks.'

She stood up and they kissed. A lingering kiss. 'Be

back in a sec.' Their hands lingered too as she left. Sonny got undressed down to his boxers and got into bed. He felt self-conscious, lying in her bed, waiting, half naked. Nervous again. He told himself to relax, concentrated on the music, another song he liked and recognised, 'Lego House'. His girls liked Ed Sheeran, especially when they were younger, and had played him nonstop.

Stacey eventually returned and smiled sheepishly, looking a little shy and nervous herself. She scurried to her side of the bed in her silky, black nightie. She slipped into bed. 'Alexa, volume two, don't laugh,' she said.

Sonny tried not to. Then she turned out the light and snuggled into him, resting her cool hand on his chest. It felt wonderful. 'Ed Sheeran, interesting choice,' Sonny said, trying to keep things casual, to quell his nerves. He stroked her hair.

'He's my Barry White,' Stacey said. 'Very romantic. His old stuff anyway. I'm not a fan of his recent stuff.'

'No, me neither. You get to play him often then? To get you in the mood?' Sonny said.

'Oh, not really. Only when I'm alone...'

And then it was just them in the dark. They got lost in each other's bodies and the music. Stacey was right, it was romantic. The perfect soundtrack. Afterwards, both sated and full of wonder and relief, but still clinging onto each other, the song, 'One' came on. 'This is my favourite,' Stacey said. 'It's beautiful.' And it was. They listened in the dark, her head on his chest, their hands still restless, exploring. When it had finished, Stacey said, 'Alexa, quiet.' And then she kissed Sonny. 'Sonny, quiet,' she said, putting her finger on his lips, and Sonny laughed. She really was a character. 'Night, night.' She kissed him again.

'Night, night,' said Sonny. And then Stacey rolled over, offering her back to him, but pulling him with her by his hand. Sonny curled into her back, cuddling her, fitting the contour of her body. She didn't let go of his hand, clutching it to her warm chest. And as Sonny drifted off, spooning her like that, inhaling her scent, he couldn't remember the last time he had felt so content, so happy, so 'at one'. And again, for the first time in as long as he could remember, he slept straight through the night, not waking up once.

# CHAPTER 25

Sonny broke the news to his kids about Stacey over Sunday lunch – at the pub again. He explained that he had been given a long-overdue pay rise, so things weren't as tight as they used to be. Charlotte had passed her driving test too – much to the annoyance of her older sister – a source of banter and another good excuse for a celebratory meal. She had driven over in her car and given them a lift to the pub. It was such a strange experience for Sonny, seeing one of his girls drive first-hand. In charge of a vehicle. It didn't seem five minutes since they were tootling around in pedal cars. He still had the photos.

Coming clean about Stacey made Sonny feel slightly better about still keeping his other life under wraps from the kids. He felt he had to tell them about Stacey, they were in too deep already, and it didn't feel right, keeping it from them. Besides, having a girlfriend was nothing to feel ashamed about. He would genuinely love for them to meet her. Having said that, he still felt he had to tread carefully; it would be his first proper relationship – worth mentioning anyway – since he had split with their mum. A good three years ago now. There was still that lingering feeling of having deserted them somehow on Sonny's part. He didn't want them to feel he was setting up an entirely new life without them. Separate from them.

He needn't have worried. The kids, on the surface at least, took it in that nonchalant manner of theirs. As if nothing ruffled them. They claimed they already knew, surmised it had been going on for a while. Longer than it actually had. It was a relief for Sonny, nevertheless.

Sonny was at work – the deli. Mid-morning, he got a WhatsApp from Stacey. '*Hey hun, hope your day's going OK. You able to give me a quick call on your break? Nothing urgent, just a booking request that's all. Thanks. x*' Sonny liked being called 'hun' by Stacey. It was a while since he'd been someone's 'honey' – genuinely so anyway; he was all manner of things to women on his escort jobs. It was unusual for Stacey to ask him to call whilst at work, though. They normally texted on his break, whilst he munched his lunch. She also knew that he kept his other life secret from his work colleagues (as well as his kids), so she usually emailed about that stuff.

Sod's Law, it was an especially busy lunch. So, it wasn't until two-forty-five that things had died down enough for Sonny to leave Rickipedia to it. He rushed out the back with his lunchbox, cracked the lid open, and plonked himself down on the stairs to the flats. His usual spot. He'd got fifteen minutes; he immediately rang Stacey. Be typical if she was on another call herself, he thought. He'd been kind of thinking about it all day, why she'd asked him to call, kind of intrigued.

Stacey picked up almost straightaway. 'Hey you. How you doing? Busy day?'

'Hey. Yeah. Bit of a crazy one. Only just sat down. Good job there was two of us on.'

'Yeah, I figured that, bless you. Late lunch for you then.'

'Yeah. The rest of Bingham usually gets fed before me!'

'Aah. What you got?'

'Oh, the usual. My snap. Basic sandwich, crisps, yoghurt, banana, chocolate bar...'

Stacey laughed. 'Sounds like a kid's packed lunch.'

'Yeah, that's what they say here!' They both laughed, then it died away. There was a pause. 'Anyway, enough about my packed lunch... to what do I owe this honour, me getting to hear your voice whilst I'm at work? I'll have to keep my voice down by the way if we're discussing, you know, 'work stuff'.'

'Yeah. No, of course. Yeah, it was just a booking that had come through, that's all. A big one. A few weeks away yet. Weekend of Saturday 22nd.'

'OK...'

'Just wanted to check your availability and that, whether you want it. It's... it's for two nights.'

'The whole weekend?'

'Yeah. With travel. London.'

'Gosh, that's a first. Two nights!'

'Yeah, would carry over to the Monday morning, you see, so would affect your other job, figured you would have to book it off or something. Plus, I know you like to see your kids on Sundays.' It was sweet how she listened, Sonny thought, how she remembered things, the little details.

'Hmm… that is a dilemma,' Sonny said. 'Bet it's big bucks, though.'

'Yeah. Biggest one yet for you. By far. Especially with the new rate. Haven't worked it out exactly, but you'd be looking in the region of two and a half grand total costs for the client.'

'Jeez. That really is a dilemma,' said Sonny. 'Be a shame to turn it down – for me and for you.'

'Yeah, I suppose…'

'You OK?' She suddenly sounded a little flat, not her bubbly self.

'Yeah.'

'You sure?'

'Yeah… It's just… God, this is so hard to say! I've never had to deal with this before. I feel such an idiot!'

'What? Tell me. What's going on?'

'It's just, I dunno… the thought of it. You being away for two nights with another woman. God, this is crazy – I told you I was a wreck! I've let someone in and I'm not used to it.'

Not for the first time, Stacey's words made him want to melt. That he mattered to someone. That what he did, his actions, mattered to someone else – and that she was human. Vulnerable underneath. Like all of us. 'Oh God, bless you. That is so sweet. And unexpected. And of course, I'm only just digesting it – you've only just asked me – but it goes without saying, I wouldn't go, I wouldn't do it, not if you weren't comfortable with it.'

'But you shouldn't have to not go. This is your livelihood, my livelihood, and that's a huge sum of money to you. That's why I'm annoyed with myself, for even bringing it up, for letting it get to me, it's so unprofessional.'

'No. Not at all. It just means you're human.'

'You know what it was – that got to me the most, what set me off – initially, she asked for companionship with intimacy – and I know you wouldn't do anything! I know I can trust you. I really do – but it sowed the seed. I thought, here we go, another lonely woman, looking for a weekend of fun – at my expense! With my man! Tart!' Sonny laughed at this, and blushed; he loved being someone's 'man'. But his head was whirling with this new stuff to deal with. 'And I tried to put her off, suggesting she tried one of the other escorts, but she was adamant she wanted you. I didn't like that either. Clearly liked the look of you.'

'Well, like I said, I don't have to do it, not if you're not comfortable with it. There's more to life than money. This is a whole, new situation for both of us. Things to consider. Feelings. You know... I don't know how I would feel myself if the situation was reversed. If it was you clearing off for the weekend with another man, to entertain him and stroke his ego, especially one who had chosen you and clearly wanted a bit more...'

'Yeah, it's a way of looking at it. That makes me feel a bit better. Thank you. And for listening. For being understanding.'

'No problem. Balls in your court with this one.'

Later that afternoon, Sonny got a WhatsApp from Stacey. '*Right, I've calmed down and given myself a stern talking to. Time to put on your Big Girl's pants, Stacey! You run an escort agency, for Christ's sake. I have no problem with you going – other than the prospect of missing you. I'm pleased for you and want you to earn the money. Separate rooms of course! Shall I book you in? Oh, and PS... I might have done a bit of Facebook stalking and she's fat and ugly (monkey face emoji.) Love you. x*'

Sonny smiled. It was the first time she had said it. He messaged straight back. '*As long as you're sure. Love you too. x*' He now had a quandary as to what he would tell the kids about re-arranging a Sunday again. He'd told them he'd had to cover Rikipedia at work last time.

Later again that afternoon, just before finishing work, Sonny got a call from the care home. His father had barricaded himself in his room earlier. When they had eventually got in, he had warded off the staff with his walking frame for the best part of half an hour. They'd had to restrain him in the end. The thought of picturing this broke Sonny's heart. His father had been totally spent since apparently and was refusing to eat; he'd thrown his food plate at a carer. They wanted Sonny's permission to get a dementia test done, as they thought his father had got it. Therefore, he should be in the designated dementia wing of the home. This lit a fuse in Sonny. He was fuming. 'Designated wing?!' he said. 'The whole place is full of dementia patients! He hasn't got dementia, he's just a very angry and frustrated man – and understandably so; he's not even getting his meds on time! It plays havoc with him.' He headed straight up there to calm his father down and to try and talk him into eating.

It was so sad seeing him for Sonny. Damaged and defeated. Like one of his beloved butterflies trapped in a jar that had tried but failed to escape. He was trying to whittle a random piece of wood with one of his round-ended fruit knives. Sonny enquired with a senior carer if his father had seen the GP yet, as requested. He was told that Dr Benning was currently on leave and therefore not doing his usual weekly rounds of the home. His stand-in was only doing check-up calls over the phone, unless it was an emergency. Again, Sonny was fuming and exasperated. It was a ridiculous and frustrating situation. A fob-off. When did it become an emergency? When the old man keeled over and died?!

Afterwards, Sonny relayed what had happened to Stacey. She was fuming too. 'They're going to end up killing him through neglect. Do you want me to give you the name of that mortgage broker? See what your options are?' Sonny agreed. 'I'll give him a quick call myself first, a headsup that you are going to call. If anyone can sort it, he will – he's got all sorts of tricks – just make sure you've got all your info to hand when you call. Your income and outgoings etc. What kind of deposit you guys could potentially put down. And if it still isn't adding up, then maybe there are ways I can help out too.'

'Stacey, I couldn't possibly accept your financial help with something like that, or anything for that matter, we've only just started seeing each other.'

'I know, but the offer's there. It breaks my heart what is going on at that care home, and even if there's a way

I can help you to secure a mortgage – to get him out of there – I'm willing to help. I know first-hand how much money you are pulling in every month, it's just annoying you won't be able to use it as legitimate income just yet.'

'It's very kind, but really I couldn't.'

'Just make the call, Mr. Stubborn.'

Sonny did make the call. It was touch and go at first. But with a fair bit of wangling on the broker's part, using Sonny's escort work savings as part of a deposit, along with a hundred and twenty-five-grand contribution from his father – the higher the better – the whole thing was doable; Sonny could borrow enough to look for properties in the region of two-hundred grand. If his father would go along with the whole thing, that was...

That night Sonny and Stacey discussed the matter further and in-depth over wine at his house; weirdly (in Sonny's opinion), Stacey liked the cosiness of his house and enjoyed the cat being around. Stacey was thrilled that getting a mortgage was an option for Sonny. But there was still so much to think about and consider. Location for a start. Sonny was pretty adamant he wanted a three-bedroom place, as it gave them more options. Firstly, it meant his children would still be able to stay overnight if needed – not that they did very often anyway, nor for want of Sonny trying – but he would hate for them not to have that option, like at Christmas or special occasions for example.

But stretching their finances to a three-bedroom place would definitely mean looking out of area, a cheaper one to Bingham. This wasn't a problem in itself to Sonny. Maybe he could move nearer to the kids? Move nearer to Stacey? What was a little commute to work in the morning? And how long would he remain at the deli job anyway, given the way the escort work was going? But the thought of being back on the property ladder was an exciting one, a stimulating one, for Sonny. Providing he could put up with his father of course. And that's where that extra room would come into play again. More space, so they weren't under each other's feet; and if it did get too much down the line, or his father needed an increase in care – Parkinson's was a degenerative disease after all – it gave them the option of a live-in carer. Sonny could then stay at Stacey's as much as he pleased.

And then there were his father's meds to consider, of course – the 'regime' – Sonny would be responsible for these. A daunting prospect. But, again, Stacey said she would help with this. She'd done it for her mum for a time, setting up daily dosette boxes for her, before she moved into a home.

Of course, Sonny hadn't mentioned a word about any of this to his father yet, as he hadn't wanted to get his hopes up. Knowing his father, there was the possibility he might reject the idea out of sheer stubbornness anyway, despite the fact he had mooted the idea himself to Sonny on several occasions himself over the years.

# CHAPTER 26

But it was decided, in Sonny's mind at least. Thrashing out the finer details with Stacey, along with her numerous and much-appreciated promises of support, had swayed him. Allayed his fears. For better or for worse, he wanted to go for it. To take the leap. Sonny invited his father over that coming Saturday for lunch and a game of chess, and, more specifically, to broach the idea with him. It was something Sonny knew he didn't do enough, have his father over at his and entertain him there. But all he did was moan about how none of the chairs were comfortable enough, even with one of his pressure cushions, or that he was cold – the care home was like a furnace that the 'inmates' got acclimatised to. Sonny could see this as a potential source of conflict down the line; he was the opposite, used to the cold as he'd never been able to afford having his heating on.

It was a lovely warm, summer's day and Sonny set his small kitchen table up outside in the sunshine of the yard. He sometimes did this with the kids too. Being short of time as usual, he'd prepared a bought-in quiche, new potatoes and salad for lunch. Next to zero preparation or cooking time. He wanted to be able to concentrate on talking to his father, not being stuck at the stove. Sonny also knew it was something his father liked to eat. He wanted to get a decent meal inside of him sharpish.

Sonny's father had been unusually quiet since being picked up, subdued and thinner than ever. As if the previous day's protest and ordeal had really taken it out of him. As if the fight had gone out of him. He didn't even appear to have the energy to moan. He seemed more confused than ever too, struggling to understand the most basic of questions and instructions. As always, his lack of hearing didn't help, but it seemed to be getting harder. Communication was getting harder. Whereas someone who keeps dropping things is referred to as 'butter fingers', it was as if his father had 'butter brain'. Where his thoughts were no longer cohesive, he could no longer hold or contain them, they just kept slipping through.

Sonny put his father's plate in front of him and poured him a glass of cider. Whilst he distributed the rest of the bottle into his own glass, Sonny watched his father, willing him to start eating. The old man was staring at his plate, an all-too-familiar look of disappointed disdain on his face. He prodded at the quiche with his knife and humphed. Sonny felt the also-all-too-familiar anger, quick to rise in him.

'What, Dad? It's quiche, new potatoes and salad. You love quiche.'

'I get quiche every day at the home. That's all they ever give me, cold quiche.' He literally said this about everything Sonny ever cooked for him, fish and chips, lasagne, gammon, omelette... he got them all *every day* at the home apparently.

'Well, this quiche is warm. Broccoli, mature cheddar and bacon, your favourite. And those are not just any new potatoes, they're Jersey Royals, buttered Jersey Royals, bet you don't get them at the home.'

His father humphed again. 'Is it homemade?'

'What, the quiche? No, it's from Sainsbury's, I didn't want to spend hours in the kitch– look, never mind about the quiche, just eat it, will you – I've got something I want to discuss with you. Something important.'

'Something in Norfolk?'

'What? No' – his father was obsessed with moving back to Norfolk, his 'spiritual home' – 'Something important!'

'Oh.' His father looked disappointed again.

'Dad, will you just eat something please? Then we can talk, I need you to listen.' His father picked up his fork and begrudgingly speared a potato with it. It was too big to eat. So, he began to try and cut it in half with his fork. It was winding Sonny up, watching him. Like watching a child eat. Eventually, his father got the potato in half and with a shaky hand transferred it to his mouth.

'Thank you,' said Sonny. He let out a deep breath. Dealing with his father exhausted him. It made him instantly question what he was about to propose – he must be mad. He took a long slug of cider. 'Right, Dad, I've been doing some thinking, and I've got a proposal for you.'

'Huh?'

'A *proposal*. A suggestion, to get you out of that home...' Sonny could practically see the cogs whirring in his father's head, trying to hear and understand, his watery eyes oscillating from side to side. 'How would you feel about us getting a place together, a place of our own, to live in?'

'I'm sorry?' he said. 'I don't follow.' Sonny repeated the question, but louder. 'What, to live in together? Me and you?'

'Yes. A bungalow.'

'To buy?'

'Yes.'

His father looked deep in thought again. Then a scowl of suspicion crossed his face. 'I've asked you about that before. Several times. You said you'd never consider it.'

'I know, but–'

'Why the sudden change of tune? What are you up to? Who's going to pay for it?'

Sonny was dreading it going down this route, his father was so paranoid, especially about his money. 'I'm not *up to* anything, Dad. I just thought, what with things not going well at the home–'

'That's the understatement of the year! They're crooks! Steal your money, whilst imprisoning you. Take your meds off you and dish them out as and when they please–'

'I know, Dad, you don't need to tell me. We've made a formal complaint, that's why we want you out of there.'

'Well, you've never cared up till now! Let me hammer my savings week in week out whilst I rot away up there! You never take me out on the buggy. Never take me down the cutting. Butterfly season will be over before you know it!' His father broke into a coughing fit, his face reddening, his eyes watering.

'Calm down, Dad, you'll wear yourself out again. Here, have a drink of cider.' Sonny passed him his glass. His father took a drink, then fished around in his pockets for a handkerchief to wipe his eyes. 'I will take you down the cutting again, I've just been busy, that's all. Just calm down and stop being so angry. I'm trying to help you. Things have gotten bad up there at the home lately, very bad. And, admittedly, we – I – should have done something about it sooner. That's why I'm looking into alternatives now. I've looked into it properly, the financial side of things, and we could do it. A joint venture. You pay the deposit and I pay a mortgage every month. I'm earning better money now...'

'How much deposit?'

'A hundred-and-twenty-five-grand.'

'A hundred-and-twenty-five-grand?! You're mad! That's nearly half my savings!'

'It's how much it's gonna cost, Dad, the price of property these days.'

'What's your contribution in all this?'

'Around eighty-five. So, initially, sixty-fortyish in your favour. Plus, like I said, I pay the mortgage. The bills, we'll split fifty-fifty.'

'And what about care? Who's going to look after me, shower me, you?'

'God, no,' Sonny shuddered. 'I'll take over your meds and that and help out as I always do – cook some meals – but you'd have to pay carers for the nitty gritty.'

'More money!'

'Dad, it's going to be a quarter of what you're shelling out now. This is a good offer I'm putting across to you.'

'I still think you're up to something, getting me to sign up to a property, then hoping I pop my clogs no doubt.'

'Don't be ridiculous, I'm trying to get you out of that home, to make your life better.' His father humphed again, then took another sip of cider, calming down a little, as if considering. This was a positive sign at least.

'Where you thinking?' he said. 'Norfolk?'

Sonny couldn't help but laugh. The old man's persistence, his single-mindedness. 'No, not Norfolk. Forget bloody Norfolk. I can't move to Norfolk, my kids are round here, my job – and Stacey.'

'Racing?'

'Stacey! My girlfriend, Stacey' – it sounded strange saying it out loud, still new – 'The lady you met at the home, remember?'

'Ah, the nurse. The pretty one. She going to be living with us?'

Sonny laughed again. 'She's not a nurse, we cleared that up, remember. And, no, she's not going to be living with us.'

'Ah. That's a shame.'

'It is. So, does that mean you're considering it then?'

His father didn't answer, maybe he hadn't heard, he was sipping his cider, but Sonny took it as a yes. An initial victory. He took another sip of cider himself. 'Come on, eat up, and we'll have a game of chess.'

Lunch cleared away, most of his father's left untouched, Sonny set up the chess board. It was pleasant sitting outside. The sun was still shining and Sonny was onto a second bottle of cider. It was nice just not to be arguing with his father for once. He was looking forward to a game of chess. It had been a while.

The game began. Sonny was white – they took it in turns – so he went first. As usual, he didn't have any specific, opening sequence planned. He knew there were several, but he didn't know what they were. Sometimes he thought this threw his father, who was a traditional, methodical player, and liked an opponent to play that way. Sonny just started advancing his pawns, protecting each one as he went, and getting his knight and other major pieces out into play as soon as he could.

The game went on and the sun continued to throb overhead. But progress was painfully slow. More so than usual. His father was taking an age over every go, deliberating every move for minutes on end. As if his mind was buffering, like a computer or smart TV with a spinning circle of delay as it struggled to make connections, to figure out what he had to do. But physically too, it seemed too much of an effort to reach out and lift the wooden pieces.

Sonny put his father's lassitude down to the sun and the cider, and maybe the exertions of the previous day still, the lack of food. He even nodded off at one point and Sonny took the opportunity to message Stacey, to see how her day was going and let her know that early signs in regards to the potential move were positive.

Sonny, in contrast, felt alive, sharp and alert. Seeing his next chess moves clearly. Seeing the board clearly, any potential threats and openings well in advance. Therefore, it didn't take long till he began to dominate the game. He was two major pieces – one of them being the all-important queen – and a couple of pawns up. He'd been quietly working on something and truly believed it was about to pay off. Two more moves and he'd got him. He really thought he had this time, and an almost irrepressible thrill bubbled up inside Sonny. But then he'd felt that way before. Been absolutely certain and his father had somehow wriggled his way out of it or invoked some obscure technicality. 'Check,' Sonny said, diagonally advancing his queen to threaten his father's king. There was no response from his father. 'Dad, it's your move, you're in check.'

His father stirred; his head had been sunk onto his chest. 'Huh?'

'It's your move, you're in check.'

'What? When did that happen?' he said.

'Literally just now. You nodded off. Again. You need to concentrate.'

'Too much effort,' his father said.

'Come on. I don't want you fobbing me off when I beat you that it's a draw or some sort of null and void game due to some arcane 'sleep-clause'.

'Castle,' his father said drowsily, swapping his king and rook in positions with shaky fingers. 'Castling' was a legitimate move and go-to tactic of Sonny's father's, the only one where you could move two pieces simultaneously. But in this instance, it wasn't going to work. Not today. 'Ah, ah,' Sonny said, barely able to contain his glee. 'You can't castle whilst you're in check, remember? You taught me that.'

'Hmm,' his father said, perplexed. 'So I have. Schoolboy error...' Sonny waited, but his father didn't put the pieces back, his fingers still hovering above them. In the end, Sonny moved them back for him, his own fingers shaking slightly in excitement and anticipation. But his father looked as if he was going to nod off again.

Perhaps that was his tactic; he could see he was in deep trouble and was trying to protect himself, like an animal, playing dead. He currently only had one move available that wouldn't put him in check again, that was plain to see, but Sonny couldn't take his go for him. Sonny could also see his own next move. The end game. Checkmate. 'Dad, it's your move. You've got to move your king. You're in check still.' His leg tapped under the table nervously whilst he waited.

'Huh.' His father came back to life again, blinking, trying to rouse himself, trying to orientate himself.

'You've got to move your king.' Sonny pointed to it. Slowly, his father registered the situation. He reached out and moved his king to the only safe space, a sideways shift, one square, down the back row. He was now all-but-trapped, in front by one of his own pawns, and to his left by a knight of Sonny's, covering the adjacent square. Immediately Sonny countered with his next and telling move, a simple but deadly shift, one diagonal square of his bishop, putting his father in check again. But this time with nowhere to go, no available pieces to block with. He was done for. His fate sealed. 'And that, I believe,' said Sonny triumphantly, 'Is checkmate.' He stared at the pieces. Stared at the situation, double and triple-checking, still fearful of some way out for his father, a Houdini-like loophole or escape; it had happened too many times. But there wasn't one. It was checkmate. Sonny was sure it was. 'It is. It's checkmate. I got you. I finally got you! After all these years, I got you! Ha!' Sonny clenched his fist and let out a jubilant cry. Then he looked up at his father for a response or some sign of acknowledgement. How would he take this, his first, unprecedented defeat at the hands of his son? A nod of the head? A shake of the hand? But there was neither. His father had nodded off again, as if the game – and defeat – had taken everything out of him.

Sonny sat back in his chair, still unable to believe it. It had taken him the best part of thirty-five years of playing chess with his father to finally, genuinely, beat him. A momentous day. Still smiling, he drained what was left of his cider and got up from the table to go and get another bottle, a celebratory bottle. He also needed a pee. He took his phone with him so he could message Stacey on the way and inform her of his victory. She was fully aware of their ongoing chess battles and found it sweet and amusing.

With one last satisfied look at the chessboard, Sonny headed inside, consulting his phone. It was too bright to see it properly outside. Stacey had since responded to his previous message. '*Hey hun. Day is going OK, thanks. Busy! Can't wait to finish and see you (smiley face). What time you finished with your dad? Aaw, so pleased he seems up for the move. Will be so good for him. Love you. x*'

Sonny smiled, reading the message, and replied straightaway, informing her of his victory at chess and telling her he loved her too. He smiled again. Life was good. Life was so good. He went for a pee, still thinking how good life was. He pulled a fresh, chilled bottle of cider out of the fridge, still thinking how good life was. How and when had that happened? He'd been living a dun-coloured, drab existence. Now his future seemed as bright and wonder-inducing as a fresh tin of orange paint. He was sleeping properly again. He was earning good money, crazy money. He had Stacey, whom he was very much in love with, and that felt wonderful. Made him giddy. Their relationship had only just begun, they had the rest of the summer ahead of them, their whole lives ahead of them… Like Bowie said, 'Absolute Beginners'. He'd still like to see his kids a whole lot more, but they were thriving, driving, making their own way in life – a parent couldn't ask for more than that. And he was possibly on the verge of getting on the property ladder again – something that would ultimately benefit his kids down the line and that meant so much to him – and busting his father out of that awful care home situation in the process…

Sonny stood at the kitchen sink, cracked open his bottle and took a swig. Through the kitchen window he could see his father was still asleep in the sun. Really ought to wake him up, Sonny thought, he's going to get sunburnt. A flickering of movement then caught Sonny's attention. A small, dark butterfly had appeared from somewhere and was flitting over the chessboard, hopping from piece to piece. Butterflies often made their way into Sonny's back yard; there was a mature red valerian plant in a huge ceramic urn, left by a previous tenant, that attracted them. Buddy liked to rub himself up against the drooping flowers and sniff them too. But this particular butterfly seemed more interested in the chess board. Or maybe it was his father's cider glass that had attracted it, the remnants of sweet nectar within. Did butterflies like sweet things?

Intrigued as to what type of butterfly it was, Sonny moved to the kitchen doorway to see better. It was hard, as the small butterfly moved quickly, barely staying still for a second. Where is my dad when I need him? Sonny thought. To his amazement, the butterfly then alighted on his father's hand, still resting on the table. 'Dad!' Sonny hissed. 'Wake up!' But it was no use, he was out for the count. As stealthily as he could, Sonny emerged from the kitchen doorway and crept towards the table. Miraculously, the butterfly stayed still long enough for Sonny to see it better. It was a very dark brown, almost black, with an abundance of chequered white squares covering its wings, almost like a chessboard itself. Although not a butterfly Sonny had ever seen in real life, its distinctive markings were still somehow very familiar. Sonny's mouth went suddenly dry and his heart began to pound. He had seen that butterfly maybe half a dozen times on a welcome board at the entrance to the linear walk. It couldn't be, could it? The elusive grizzled skipper?

'Dad, wake up!' Sonny said again. It would be a travesty if he missed this. Sonny took another couple of steps forward, but his movement was enough to spook the flighty little butterfly, and it set off again. 'Damn,' said Sonny, following it with his eyes. 'Please don't go!' He moved towards the table and his father, whilst still following the butterfly's movement. To his immense relief, it didn't fly away, merely headed straight to the red valerian plant, where it flitted for a while, then settled again.

Sonny quickly put his hand on his father's shoulder to shake him awake. His neck was still in that stooped position and his thin, wispy white hair had already left his scalp pink from the sun. 'Dad, wake up!' Sonny said again. His head lolled as Sonny shook him. Although still distracted by the little, chequered butterfly that had now spread its wings again, warming itself in the sun, something then struck Sonny as not being right. Something in the movement of his father's head and neck. Sonny immediately moved his hand to his father's chest, to feel for movement, to feel for breathing. But there was none. A sudden sinking feeling hit Sonny, a feeling of dread. 'Dad?!' he said. Panicked, he placed two forefingers on his father's neck. His skin was warm, but he could feel no pulse. But Sonny was no doctor. Perhaps he was pressing in the wrong place. 'Dad, wake up!' He grabbed his father's wrist, putting his fingers there instead. Again, there was warmth, but no life. No pulse.

Then, from out of the cool and shadow of the kitchen, Buddy suddenly appeared. With a mewl, he made a beeline for the plant and the butterfly, attracted by the flicker of its movement. Buddy pounced, but the butterfly was too quick for the cat. Wasting no more time, it took flight and darted off over the fence and into a blue sky of possibilities.

## THE END

# ABOUT THE AUTHOR

Despite being a full-time chef, Adam Longden fulfilled a lifelong ambition when his debut fiction novel, *The Caterpillar Girl*, was published in October 2016. This was followed by its sequel, *Seaside Skeletons*, the third book in the series, *Asylum*, and two separate novellas; *Eva: A Grown-up Fairy Tale* and *The Meddling Ghosts*.

Adam has three children and resides in the East Midlands where his books are mainly set.

# OTHER BOOKS BY ADAM LONGDEN

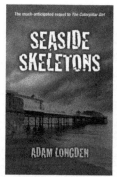

All available from Amazon